EMILIA FROM BEYOND

SHYRA N

PENGUIN BOOKS
An imprint of Penguin Random House

PENGUIN BOOKS

Penguin Books is an imprint of the Penguin Random House group of companies whose addresses can be found at global.penguinrandomhouse.com

Published by Penguin Random House SEA Pte Ltd
40 Penjuru Lane, #03-12, Block 2
Singapore 609216

Penguin Random House SEA

First published in Penguin Books by Penguin Random House SEA 2026

Dingbat designed by Freepik

10 9 8 7 6 5 4 3 2 1

ISBN 9789815351033

Typeset in Spectral by MAP Systems, Bengaluru, India

www.penguin.sg

For my mother—who gave me my first book and never let me doubt that one day, I would write my own

1

On the few occasions Emilia had envisioned her own death and pondered dying, she'd always imagined it as something elaborate and interesting. What Emilia had not envisioned was being stuck in the same mundane routine every day as though she were still alive.

The simple fact was that Emilia was dead.

She remembered the moment the black jeep with its tinted windows had slammed into her and sent her tumbling down the gravel road. She remembered staring blankly at the sky as her vision began to blur and breathing became inevitably painful. She remembered the sun's warmth against her skin as her mind began to drift, somewhat aware of the coming disaster and wishing she'd have another day to live.

But time was running out, and she was moving closer to death's embrace with each passing second. She remembered keeping her eyes open—forcing them to stay open—afraid and not quite ready, but unwilling to look away from her own demise.

Death, as does time, waited for no one. And despite her attempts at keeping herself rooted to life,

Emilia succumbed to her injuries not long after, her eyes dull as she stared unseeingly above.

The world went on around her as she lay unmoving on the road, her blood pooling and blossoming into a puddle of red that surrounded her like a gruesome halo. It would have been poetic, had it not been for its sheer morbidity.

Time passed, though its redundancy meant that its value was lost upon her. No one knew how long she laid there after her death, but help did arrive at some point, though it proved to be just as redundant as time itself.

Emilia had long been dead, and no help was ever going to change that one constant fact in this narrative.

Still, as her motionless body was carried atop a stretcher and wheeled to the emergency room, her subconscious mind was elsewhere, busy preparing her for what was to come.

And what, indeed, *was* to come next?

Whatever it was, it far exceeded any expectations she might have had.

Her frayed mind compared her current situation to a video game. In which she, as a character, had died and somewhere in the real world, someone had pressed the reset button to drag her back to minutes before the appearance of the 'Game Over' on screen.

It was a childish theory, but it seemed probable. Especially when she found herself lying on the road in the same position, wearing the same clothes, and staring at the same sky just before her life had ended abruptly.

Except, this time, she wasn't covered in blood.

Emilia blinked against the sun's harsh glare, the world around her slowly sharpening as if her senses were creaking back to life after a long dormancy. Her mind was rebooting, sluggishly coming alive after being frozen in death. Confusion swept over her, though the word barely scratched the surface of what she truly felt.

She sat up with much difficulty, groaning as her head throbbed in protest at the sudden movement. She closed her eyes, waiting a moment or two before opening them again and glancing around at her immediate surroundings.

Everything appeared to be stencilled with graphite on paper, like a sketch with no colour and no depth. She was somewhere else, a place that had been created to replicate the scene of her death. Wherever she was, for as far as her eyes could see, there was nothing.

There was only the gravel road beneath her and the sky above her, both spanning farther than she could fathom. And that was it.

Emilia frowned. Just as she decided to investigate matters on her own, a shadow fell over her, blocking her view. With their back to the sun, Emilia could not make head nor tail of the person standing before her.

'Hello,' the stranger said.

Emilia's frown deepened at the unexpected familiarity of his voice.

'Do you remember who you are?' he asked.

Emilia kept her silence for a few seconds, thinking it was an odd question to ask, though she whispered her name, nonetheless.

'Wonderful,' the boy said, and she could almost hear the smile in his voice.

'Right, then,' he continued. 'I was a little late on my way here, so you must be confused. But not to worry. I'll explain everything. First, let us get you off the ground, shall we?'

The boy reached forward and offered Emilia his hand. He nodded as a sign that it was okay for her to grab on to it. Reluctantly, she did, and he pulled her to her feet.

Emilia was just shy of the boy's height despite their apparent difference in age. She glanced at him surreptitiously and felt her throat constrict in shock. The boy grinned at her and tilted his head in amusement.

'What's wrong?' he asked.

She blinked, taking in his characteristically messy hair as it fell over his too-familiar rustic brown eyes. Eyes that were now filled with curiosity as they continued to stare at her. Emilia broke away from his intense gaze and glanced at the suit he was wearing. It was different, but maybe . . .

She grabbed his arms to keep him still as she peered intently at his face. The boy stared back and though his eyes showed no sign of recognition, Emilia's widened in disbelief at what she was seeing.

'Eldon,' she murmured but stopped the second she noticed the sympathetic smile on his face.

Slowly, he pried her fingers off his arms but instead of letting them fall limp by her sides, he held on to them tightly between his own.

'You're not Eldon,' she said, her voice barely above a whisper as she kept her gaze fixed on their cocooned hands. The lack of recognition in his eyes was proof that he wasn't there with her, that he was not real.

'I'm sorry, Emilia,' he said, and he really did sound apologetic. 'I was fashioned from a fraction of your subconscious, and this appearance was the one you find most comforting.'

'My subconscious?' she repeated. 'I don't understand. What is this place?'

'Emilia,' Eldon said, afraid she would lose herself to the frenzy before he had a chance to explain. 'What do you remember?'

She paused, before speaking with uncertainty, 'I . . . I died?'

'Yes,' Eldon confirmed, nodding. 'You died.'

'But . . . I don't appear to be dead. There's no blood.'

This time, Eldon shook his head.

'I will explain everything, but I need you to understand that you are no longer alive. The only reason you're here is because you're dead. You do understand that, don't you?'

His words bore an unspeakable weight upon her, and she nodded, unwilling to accept the truth but convinced of it.

Satisfied by her understanding of her current state, Eldon went on to explain that they were in a carbon copy of the world where the Living resided.

'An alternate universe?' Emilia asked.

'You could say that,' he said. 'We're in a space called the Void and though part of the afterlife, it's more or less like a waiting room.'

'What exactly am I waiting for?'

'The next phase,' Eldon said. 'Life after death.'

When Emilia said nothing except to stare at him in incredulity, he took it as a sign to continue.

'This is where you choose between two fates. If you wish to be reincarnated, you'll be sent to an alternate universe for the dead: the Spirit World. Or you can choose not to be reincarnated. Upon which, you'd be judged and sent somewhere else.'

Eldon continued to explain that once dead, the spirits of the deceased would wake in the Void, or 'the waiting room', as he called it. From there, a decision had to be made, and the next phase would begin.

'So,' he said. 'Have you made a decision?'

It wasn't a particularly difficult question and not one she had to consider. Her death had been too sudden and there was much she needed to prepare for the real Eldon before she could even think about leaving the world permanently.

'Reincarnation,' she said without hesitation.

As soon as the words were spoken, Emilia felt an unnatural wave of lethargy sweeping over her. She stumbled, arms reaching out for balance as she tried to keep herself steady. She felt Eldon's grip on her arm as he gently guided her to the ground, murmuring quiet words of comfort and assurance as though to soothe her.

'Will I see you again?' she asked, eyelids drooping. 'In the other world . . . Will you be there?'

'I'm afraid not, Emilia. I'm merely a projected figment of your thoughts and subconsciousness, existing solely on this plane. Once you awake, you will no longer be able to see me.'

A part of her had suspected as much, yet a small fraction that still held on to hope with a tight leash could not help but wish for the impossible. Her eyes fell shut, no longer able to withstand the overpowering fatigue.

2

When Emilia next awoke, she found herself staring at the ceiling of her apartment. Everything seemed eerily normal, which only served to accentuate the oddity of the entire situation. She bounded out of bed and stumbled through her apartment, increasingly confused. Everything had been left exactly the way she remembered. Had it not been for the inclusion of a leather-bound book placed at the centre of her coffee table, she would've cast off the events prior as the workings of her overactive imagination.

The book was one she'd never seen before and had the words 'SPIRIT MANUAL' embossed on its cover, set in uppercase letters with a silver finish. It was filled with pages of regulations that governed the Spirit World as well as the basics of its functionality. Reading the contents gave her a refresher of what Eldon's echo had already told her, along with some additional information about the reincarnation process he'd not yet relayed.

What Emilia had assumed would be a tedious and intricate task turned out to be uncharacteristically bland when she learned that the Spirit World survived on a point system. Several points were required to qualify for reincarnation, and everything after that could be used to retain memories of one's past life. The more points, the more memories one could retain.

Points were used in place of currency in the Spirit World, which in turn meant that spirits were required to work to get points. Though the Spirit World reflected the Living World, spirits required little to survive and as such, there wasn't much that needed to be done.

The two major companies responsible for offering work in the Spirit World were the Postal Service and the Agency. The former managed the conversion and delivery of messages and gifts to the deceased, while the latter regularly deployed spirits to haunt the Living. In both cases, points were accumulated based on the number of deliveries made or the number of people successfully haunted.

The Agency was the more popular of the two choices, offering better payment and a wider range of jobs within the company—particularly the role of a Scare Agent, the highest-paying position in the Spirit World.

Emilia's main goal aside from reincarnation was to recall as many of her memories as possible, especially those of Eldon. Her efforts would be meaningless if she was thrown back into the Living World with no knowledge of her brother. She needed her memories to remain intact if she wanted to ensure his life was in good order. And if being a Scare Agent would make certain she'd get there in as little time as possible, then it was a given that she'd apply for that very position.

However, Emilia would soon learn that there was a reason for everything, including why being a Scare Agent paid so well. When something appeared too good to be true, it often wasn't true. She should have figured that Scare Agents were richly compensated because of the extreme difficulties that came with the job.

Months had passed in the Spirit World, though time barely mattered when it existed as a concept that separated the two worlds. Emilia was currently sitting in her boss' office—ignoring the suffocating tension coiling in the room—her gaze fixed on the engraved nameplate on the table. Her mind wandered, and her thumb absently traced the mark etched into the inside of her left wrist, a habit she'd developed the day after the number had first appeared. It was a tally, a visible reminder of the points she'd accumulated since signing her contract with the Agency.

And it hadn't changed since then, the 0 almost mocking as it sat glaringly obvious against the pallor of her skin.

Driven by her determination, she'd readily accepted the role of an agent. But her progress, or lack thereof, had been an issue from the moment she was officially initiated. She'd gone through the necessary training and sat through all the workshops, but it wasn't long before she realized that she wasn't cut out for life as an agent.

She'd been given a sympathy pass the first month when she'd carded zero scares, learning from her superiors that not everyone was capable of being scary on cue. But as one month stretched into two and then three, nothing anyone said could save her from the inevitable truth: she was not good at her job.

'Do you know why I called you to my office today?' Arthur asked, the question urging her to finally tear her gaze away from his nameplate.

As the head of the Agency, Arthur had a stern countenance that seemed to befit his position and though he was polite enough to seem friendly at times, he wasn't the type to form close bonds with those under his charge. Emilia rarely had the opportunity to exchange words with him, and it was not something she cared for in the least. The man's entire disposition filled her with an unexplainable dread bordering on fear. The last time she'd been in his office, she was signing her employment contract, and now, she couldn't help but wonder if she might very well be on her way to signing her letter of termination instead.

'We're here to discuss the progress you have made during your time with us,' Arthur continued when it became clear she was too distracted to pay much attention.

'Are you firing me?' she blurted.

'No,' he said to her surprise.

'I'm not getting fired?'

'No,' Arthur said. 'But the possibility still stands. The thing is, Emilia, you haven't carded a single scare since you started working with us.'

'Oh,' she murmured, dejection causing her blooming hope to dissipate.

'I understand it can be difficult, but you've been here for months, and you've attended all the training we provide to aid our agents. Others have excelled far beyond comparison with the same training, and yet you remain stagnant.'

When Emilia said nothing, swallowing her shame at having her faults so easily exposed, he continued, 'If you find yourself continuously struggling, perhaps it is time you accepted you are not entirely suited for this job.'

His blunt declaration of her predicament landed like a heavy blow, forcing her to confront the harsh reality she'd been avoiding. She knew she wasn't cut out to be a Scare Agent, but hearing him say it still stung, chipping away at the fragile pride she clung to. She was trying her best, and it grated on her nerves that he made it sound as if she wasn't taking her role seriously.

'Why do you insist on being an agent?' he asked, his question catching her off guard.

It wasn't an uncommon question, one she'd even prepared for during the interview. But it had never been asked and now, months later, the model answer had been completely wiped from her mind. Instead, all that remained was the truth. And even that appeared somewhat lacking when set against her superior's cold gaze.

'I need the points,' she mumbled.

She had no idea what Arthur was expecting from her, but the answer appeared to have disappointed him.

'I know haunting the Living isn't exactly something one would take pride in. It is a sordid affair, but I reckon it would help your endeavours to have even a little bit of gratification in what you do. If it's merely points you're after, wouldn't it be better for you to collect them elsewhere, where points are guaranteed?'

'This is the fastest way—'

'You're wasting your time here,' Arthur said, cutting her off. 'The job pays well, yes, but there is no purpose in it if you can't even do the job. All I'm hearing from you are excuses. You and I both know time doesn't work the same here as it does in the Living World. You could spend forever here, and it would only be a few hours out there.'

His words felt like a slap to the face. She'd stopped scratching at the numbered tattoo, now gripping her wrist firmly to avoid looking at it as her mind lingered on the way his piercing words seemed to ring true to her. She'd told him her reasons, yet why did the flash of disappointment in his eyes disturb her in a way she could not seem to place?

Arthur allowed his statement to settle, watching the way her deliberation caused deep lines to appear between her brows. After a few seconds, he said, 'What are your intentions, Emilia? Will you stay with us, or should I begin to draft a letter of termination for you?'

'You can't make me leave,' she said, her hands shaking at the thought of being fired.

'No, I can't. But you're wasting time. Both yours and mine. You need the points, and I need someone capable of doing their job. If it is points you're after and you don't wish to leave the Agency, I can always get you reassigned.'

'Reassigned?' she repeated, somewhat horrified.

Arthur fixed her with the same cold, lifeless stare, and Emilia's urge to protest died on her lips. She had no real argument to counter his suggestion. He wasn't wrong. She was far from being a good agent. Her options were slim, and she knew it. The alternative was to leave the Agency altogether. But then what? Work for the Postal Service, scraping together a single point for every message delivered? The thought made her stomach twist. She didn't have the patience for that kind of work.

Her silence was enough of an answer for him as he reached for a folder and handed it to her.

'The research department could use some help,' he said.

Emilia took the folder from him and had to control the grimace that threatened to show itself as she flipped through the papers. It was a new contract, officially reassigning her as a researcher. It didn't pay as well as an agent, but it was still a lot better than the Postal Service.

'Give it some thought,' he said. 'Drop by the research department. Get a feel for it and see how things are done. You might be a better fit there than you were in your role as an agent.'

Emilia mumbled her thanks, the sting of her failure still fresh, as she faced the uncertainty of her future.

'Emilia,' Arthur called just before she left.

'Yes?'

'Being an agent is not all that it's cut out to be. The Agency runs on more than its agents. Researchers are just as important. You'll find your place soon enough if you give it a chance.'

She nodded, wishing she could feel as confident as he did about her place in the Agency.

3

Emilia stood just inside the entrance to the research department; the folder tucked under her arm as her gaze lingered on the office floor. She'd told herself that she would go back to her desk, review the contract, and decide from there. Yet somehow, she'd ended up here, taking Arthur's advice despite herself. She wouldn't admit it out loud, but curiosity had gotten the better of her, and she wanted to see how the researchers did their work.

Everyone she'd befriended during her orientation at the Agency had chosen to be an agent, everyone except one. Scanning the bustling room a second time, her eyes landed on a familiar mop of dyed pink hair: Sadie.

As though having felt her stare, Sadie looked up from her computer, immediately zeroing in on Emilia before a wide smile broke upon her face. The girl grinned, pushing her glasses up her nose with a fisted hand before waving enthusiastically and gesturing for Emilia to come over.

'Emilia! What a surprise!' Sadie exclaimed, pulling her in for a hug.

Sadie was a lot shorter than Emilia and a lot friendlier. They'd sat next to each other during the orientation and were now friends since anyone who sat near Sadie automatically became her friend, owing to her infectious smile and bubbly personality.

'What are you doing here?' Sadie asked. They had hardly seen each other since the orientation, both preoccupied with work.

'I came to see how you're doing,' Emilia said, her eyes sweeping over Sadie's desk, where her laptop was barely visible beneath the mountains of books and papers. 'And what you're doing,' she added.

Sadie followed her gaze.

'Oh, you know, usual researcher stuff,' she said, shrugging. 'Looking into this and that and everything in between.'

Emilia found herself staring blankly at the books and papers and folders, and all of a sudden, she felt overwhelmed by what she was seeing. Was this really the kind of work she wanted to be doing for the rest of her time at the Agency? She had known when she first started that she wanted to be an agent. How had her plans gotten derailed in such a way?

'Are you all right?' Sadie's voice pierced her thoughts and dragged her back from the depths of despair that her mind had deemed fit to torture her.

'I'm fine,' she said, giving her friend what she hoped was a reassuring smile. 'Actually, I came to ask you something.'

'Sure. What's up?'

'What's it like working as a researcher? Is it . . .' Emilia trailed off.

What exactly was she looking for? What would convince her to join the research department and leave her position as an agent? Did she want it to be exciting? Interesting? Challenging? But her stint as an agent had been none of those things because she hadn't actually been an agent.

'I don't think you'll like it here, honestly,' Sadie said as though she knew Emilia's real purpose for being there.

'What?'

'I doubt you'd enjoy being a researcher. It's mundane and tedious work. We take weeks, sometimes months, to put together a file for a prospective target. And even then, the chances of them getting vetoed never goes away.'

'Oh,' Emilia said, frowning.

'And we only get points for every file that passes the inspection and clocks a scare for the agents.'

'*Oh*,' Emilia said again. Because that sounded a lot worse than just having to spend weeks on a file.

She couldn't help but wonder why anyone would willingly choose to be a researcher. Though she hadn't voiced her curiosity, her thoughts must have been written all over her face because it prompted Sadie to say, 'I can't speak for the others, but I like the work I do here. I find it rather relaxing.'

'Now,' she continued. 'Will you tell me what you're really doing here, or do I have to guess?'

Emilia gave up trying to be coy and explained her current ordeal. Sadie listened, and by the end of it, she said, 'It's simple, really. All you have to do is to haunt someone.'

'Well, that's the thing. I *can't*.'

'Are you sure you don't want to try?' Sadie asked. 'If you're going to be a researcher, you might as well work the Postal Service.'

They shared a look at her callous comment and then shuddered. Neither could comprehend a worse fate. Working at the Postal Service was the very definition of being overworked and underpaid. They were perpetually short on Runners and the ones they did have on staff were worked to the bone, sometimes going a full day without rest. It was horrible.

Steering them back to the conversation at hand, Sadie said, 'Have you tried to scare anyone? Anyone at all?'

'A few,' Emilia mumbled. 'About a month or two after becoming an agent.'

'And?' Sadie urged.

'It didn't work out. The consecutive failures really did a number on me, and I didn't want to try any more, I guess.'

Sadie frowned, and the obvious disappointment made Emilia wince, reminding her of a similar look on Arthur's face from just moments ago. *Fine*, perhaps she could have tried a bit harder before giving up, but it was difficult. And as much as she needed the points,

Emilia wasn't exactly hardy enough to withstand repeated failures and still come out of it unaffected.

'Would you be open to trying again?'

'I don't think I'm allowed,' Emilia said, holding out the folder as a reminder that Arthur really wanted her to leave her position.

Sadie was undeterred as she shrugged nonchalantly.

'So?' she challenged. 'You're technically still an agent. Trying to secure a scare now would just be you doing what you're supposed to do: your job.'

'I don't know . . .'

Sadie looked fed up as she said, 'All I'm saying is that I happen to have a few files that have just passed inspection. I was about to drop them off to the agents but if you'd like to have a look and take your pick, I wouldn't object.'

The pointed way Sadie stared at her said it all: she wanted Emilia to choose a target and scare them. As if it were that simple.

Without a word, Sadie dropped a thick stack of files onto the cluttered desk, the papers landing with a heavy thud in the small patch of free space. She pulled out a chair and gestured for Emilia to sit.

'Here,' she said. 'These are all my recently approved targets. You can have first pick of the lot.'

Emilia had little choice on the matter as she plucked the first file off the stack, flipping through its contents, then looking through another and then more. Sadie had put together a good stack, filled with targets that had one thing in common: none of them had ever fallen victim to the Agency before.

Because they were newly approved targets, there were no notes written by previous agents on how to secure a successful scare. Being the first to clock in a scare would earn her the most possible points. That is, if she could do it. Sadie's research wasn't completely unhelpful. She'd done more than her fair share of work, going so far as to include their fears as part of her investigation. That was something Emilia could work with.

As she flipped through the last few files, a loose piece of paper fell out and floated to the floor by her feet. She reached for it, noticing that it was another target information sheet. It had the same bright red 'Approved' stamp on the front, but unlike the others, this one had a short note scrawled at the top in messy handwriting.

'Pending,' she read aloud.

'Oops,' Sadie said, plucking the paper from her fingers. 'This one's not for consideration. He must've gotten separated from his file.'

She reached for one of the files amid the many on her desk and slotted the information sheet at the very top, securing it in place.

'Why is that one pending?' Emilia asked, eyeing the thick file. 'Looks to me like you've already gotten the approval for it.'

'I have,' Sadie confirmed. 'I'm just not sure if I want to send him off to an agent as a target.'

'Is there something wrong with him?'

'He's weak,' Sadie said. 'Surprisingly so for someone so young.'

She flipped through his file and stopped at the section titled 'Health'. There were several charts and diagrams denoting various factors of his well-being, all of which were in red.

Anyone in the Living World could potentially be a target, and the Agency wasn't too strict about it as long as the basic criteria were met:

1. They could not be sick.
2. They could not be dying.
3. They could not be children under the age of thirteen.

The man in question didn't exactly look like the picture of health . . .

'But he's not sick,' Emilia said, finishing her thought aloud.

'He meets the criteria,' Sadie replied with a shrug. 'But I don't know . . . I don't feel good about him.'

Seeing the thoughtful look on Emilia's face, Sadie quickly interjected.

'Don't even think about it. I'm telling you this is not a good idea.'

'What? You're the one who wanted me to try being an agent,' Emilia said in her own defence. 'Besides, he meets the criteria and he's already gotten approval. For all intents and purposes, this man is a target.'

'He's weak, Emilia.'

'Which makes him susceptible to scares.'

Sadie sighed, 'When I said I wanted you to try, this is not what I meant.'

'You told me to pick one of your approved targets,' Emilia retorted.

Sadie stared at her for a few seconds before huffing in mild annoyance.

'Fine. But don't say I didn't warn you.'

4

After her conversation with Sadie, Emilia dropped by the department responsible for handling travel and maintaining the doorways between the two realms. She used the term 'department' loosely because the place was nothing more than a counter manned singlehandedly by a bored and nameless spirit who hardly ever spoke and whose background was a mystery to everyone. If anything, he looked more like a concierge at a hotel than a gatekeeper.

He sat hunched behind the counter, the wall behind him mounted with a timber key shelf. Emilia handed him the target's file. He took it from her, glanced over the information sheet and then reached for a slot on the shelf. He took the key from the pigeonhole and replaced it with the file before placing the key on the counter before her. Then he went back to his seat, and it was like their interaction had never happened.

Emilia studied the key. It was an ornate thing made of brass and was considerably weighty, an antique skeleton key. She'd done this a few times since becoming an agent, but it was still a thrill whenever she travelled to the Living World.

The keys from the gatekeeper were modelled after skeleton keys and could fit into any keyhole. It didn't matter what or where the doors were. Once the skeleton keys were fitted into the hole and the door opened, the destination on the other side would be the target's current location. It was convenient and a two-way method of travel. But it also doubled as a source of anxiety because losing the key would trap you in the Living World with no way of returning.

When she stumbled through the door into the Living World, Emilia found herself facing a long, dimly lit corridor. The silence was unsettling, broken only by the faint buzz of flickering lights overhead. Metal shutters lined both sides of the passage, and it took her a moment to realize that she was in some kind of storage facility.

She moved slowly, her footsteps echoing in the stillness. Her mind wandered, turning over the question of what the target could possibly be doing here. With no windows, and the flickering lights doing little to dispel the gloom, an uneasy feeling settled in her chest. The farther she walked, the more she wondered if coming here had been a mistake. The target's frail appearance suddenly seemed like a mask for something far more sinister, and she couldn't shake the nagging thought that maybe Sadie had been right.

She could still turn back, retreat through the door she'd entered and leave this place behind. But something kept her rooted. A strange pull of curiosity. She wanted to know more about the target she'd chosen. If she couldn't scare him, she, at the very least, wanted to see him and find out what he was doing in a place as rundown and suspicious as this storage facility.

Emilia hated thinking of the technicalities behind a haunting, finding it gruelling and bothersome, particularly because she hadn't quite found a method that suited her.

Every agent had a preferred method for scaring their targets. The longer a spirit had been dead, the more they were capable of doing. Some preferred moving objects; others opted for phantom sounds that floated through the house under the cover of the night; and there were also those who conjured spectral visions, making their targets see gruesome sights that would startle even those who prided themselves on having a heart of steel.

Emilia, being newly dead, could do nothing of the sort, making her job even more challenging. She hadn't been dead long enough to do half the things others were capable of. Even the most basic techniques tended to take a toll on her because she could never scare them within the week, and to stretch a haunting for any longer would drain her.

So it wasn't entirely her fault. From what she'd read in the Spirit Manual, everyone was born with different energy levels that fluctuated and changed over time depending on how well they cared for themselves. In death, their energy no longer shifted and remained as one's last ties to the Living World. This energy was also used to manipulate and interact with objects and it was this store of energy that agents often used in their hauntings.

Unfortunately for Emilia, when she'd first started at the Agency, Arthur had been straightforward with her energy assessment and had told her that she had worryingly little reserves of energy. She'd felt almost insulted by the look he'd given her. Because what kind of life must she have lived to care so little for herself that her body held almost no positive energy in death?

He'd warned her against being an agent, though he hadn't outright stopped her from trying. After all, the Agency had seen agents do well despite their energy levels and Emilia might still prevail. But of course, that was not the case at all. Emilia had too little energy to do anything and it was beyond upsetting.

As she moved farther down the corridor, she started hearing sounds. Footsteps, things being moved about, a muffled voice. She followed the sounds until she came upon the unit at the very end of the corridor, its shutter half-drawn with light spilling out from within.

She hovered outside, the voice louder now that she was nearer, and she could make out some of the words she was hearing. Something about a . . . murder?

This intrigued her, and she inched closer. She passed through the half-opened shutter with ease and slipped inside. It was much bigger than she'd expected. Or at least, it would have been, if it hadn't been so messy. The space was littered with papers and empty takeout containers. There was a table pushed against the far wall, mounted upon which was a cork board pinned with newspaper clippings and other printed material. Just beside the entrance was a sofa that was very obviously being used as a makeshift bed.

Hunching over the table, was a lone figure dressed from head to toe in black. He was the source of the muffled muttering she'd heard earlier. She watched as he shifted documents around. Emilia couldn't make out what he was doing from where she stood, nor could she see what he was anxiously scribbling on his notepad.

The unit had clearly been converted into a bunker and looked well lived in. Emilia figured it must have been very different when they first set it up. *What was so important that he would willingly go out of his way to do all this?* Emilia wondered.

But Emilia couldn't see a thing from where she stood. Her intention for coming here had been to satiate her curiosity about the target and maybe get a scare in if she could. But she found herself consumed by another matter altogether. Throwing all caution to the wind, she decided to inch nearer to him. She wanted to take a closer look at the articles pinned to the board, at the documents on the table, and especially at his notebook with the written thoughts that seemed so important to him.

She was just about to peer over his shoulder when he turned abruptly, causing her to stumble back in shock. She froze for a minute before she scoffed. She'd conveniently forgotten that she was a spirit, a ghost. He couldn't see her. What was she getting so jumpy for?

But when she lifted her gaze, the weirdest thing happened.

One moment, he appeared to be looking through her at the half-opened shutter behind her, and the next, she swore that he looked right at her.

Their eyes met. She was certain of it. And if she had reason to doubt herself, then the flicker of fear that crossed his face was enough to silence her uncertainties. For a second, which felt more like an eternity, neither of them moved. And then, she blinked.

'You . . .' she started to say but got no further.

The target jerked at the sound of her voice, tripping over his feet as he stumbled and fell with a heavy thud on the ground. He'd hit the back of his head against the edge of the table on his way down, the pain doing nothing to stop the horrified scream that left his lips. The sound grated against her ears, fuelled by his rampant panic and fear.

She staggered back as though repelled by the audible exclamation of his fears. But as suddenly as he'd let loose such a cry of terror, it was just as quickly cut off. The sound gurgled to a stop in his throat, his eyes rolling to the back of his head as his body slumped in a faint. She stared at him, stunned, the immediate silence ringing just as loudly in her ears.

He'd fallen unconscious.

She didn't move. The unexpected occurrence had surprised her just as much as it had surprised him. But it didn't take long for one other little detail to surface in her mind: He had seen her.

The target had seen her.

That thought alone was enough to get her moving. Emilia stumbled away from his unconscious form and ran through the shutters. She didn't think. She didn't want to think. All she wanted to do was get out of there. She ran, racing for the door at the end of the hallway. Her hands were shaking when she reached for the corded key around her neck. She couldn't fit the key into the lock because of how horribly she was trembling. It took her several tries before she could do it, and even then, it was only possible because she used her left hand to steady her right.

She turned the knob and pushed the door open. Bright lights blinded her when she stepped through the threshold, and when her vision cleared, she was back at the Agency.

Emilia ignored the way the Nameless Spirit was staring at her as she placed the key on the counter. She tried to appear casual and nonchalant, but she was still shaking, and the thunderous beating of her heart was making it difficult for her to display even a semblance of normalcy. She was breathing hard and trying to control her breath was only making her look silly with the way her nostrils were flaring with every inhale and exhale.

She gritted her teeth, resisting the urge to curse aloud. She was dead, and yet it was the small redundancies that were likely to turn suspicious eyes upon her. The irony of the situation would be laughable if she hadn't been so worked up over it.

The Nameless Spirit exchanged the key for the file, and she nodded her thanks, not quite trusting herself to speak just yet. She hugged it close to her chest and headed back to her department where she slipped numbly behind her desk. She tried to compose herself as best she could and was almost getting there before a new email alert made her jump out of her skin.

This time, Emilia really did let loose a flurry of curses under her breath as she clicked on the icon to silence the annoying pinging. To her disdain, however, she met with the last thing she wanted to see when she was still reeling from what had happened earlier.

There, written in bold uppercase letters on her computer screen, were the words: ***CONGRATULATIONS ON YOUR FIRST SCARE!***

She wasn't quite certain if the message was intended for her because she had done such a 'wonderful' job scaring the target or if it was because she had somehow managed to be the one getting scared shitless.

Either way, scaring the Living did not feel as scintillating as she had thought it would.

It all felt rather . . . *lacklustre*.

5

The congratulatory message flashed repeatedly on Emilia's screen, heightening the dread accumulating in the pit of her stomach. She felt physically ill and could not comprehend the reason behind it. She swallowed thickly and moved the cursor to delete the email.

She didn't want to think about what had happened at the storage facility. But her mind kept drifting to the target and the way their eyes had met. And then her mind would start reeling again because their eyes *couldn't* have met . . .

Emilia had never quite mastered the finesse of a skilled agent, limited as she was by a long list of restrictions. She could not manipulate electrical currents, move objects, or make herself intentionally visible to the Living. There was only *one* possible reason he could have seen her, and it was not a good reason at all.

Her thumb traced over her inner left wrist, scratching nervously at the inked number until she realized something was different. The 0 that had been there for months was now a 100. As though the email wasn't proof enough of her successful scare, she now had it inked upon her skin.

Emilia couldn't tear her eyes away from the tattoo, feeling a mix of fear and guilt consuming her. She had only meant to scare him, not make him aware of her presence. The unexpected outcome weighed heavily on her conscience, a nagging sense that something was wrong . . . *very* wrong.

Her attention shifted to the plain manila folder that Arthur had given her. She had carelessly tossed it onto her cluttered desk before heading to the Living World for her scare assignment and had conveniently forgotten all about it.

Emilia opened the folder and saw the contract inside, the one she had ignored earlier. This time, however, she couldn't bring herself to look away. Something about her first scare had left her feeling uneasy about this whole arrangement. She tried to focus on her other tasks, but thoughts of the storage unit and its contents flooded her mind.

The image of the man she had encountered had been burned into her memory, his wide eyes filled with fear as they locked eyes. But there was something else behind that fear . . . something akin to recognition.

But how could it have been recognition in his eyes when she had never seen him before?

Emilia shook her head to rid her mind of the ramblings that would not cease. She grabbed a pen and before she could change her mind, she signed her name on the dotted line at the end of the contract.

There, that settled things. She'd just confirmed her transfer to the research department. She didn't have to worry about scares again for the rest of her time at the Agency. It was ironic how she had once craved to be an agent, eager to make as many points from hauntings as was possible, yet now all she desired was to escape that role. She wondered if things would have been different had she chosen another target, but dwelling on the past seemed futile.

Emilia was just about to head over to Arthur's office when Sadie leaned over the wall of her cubicle.

'Hey,' she said. 'I take it congratulations are in order?'

'What do you mean?' Emilia asked, though she knew exactly what Sadie meant.

'Your scare . . .?' Sadie said, pointing at the target's file still on her desk. 'You did scare him, didn't you? I saw it.'

Emilia frowned.

'What do you mean you saw it? What did you see?'

Sadie was equally confused, until she seemed to remember something.

'Oh, right,' she said. 'Researchers know the outcome of scare attempts that are made on targets that they have researched. You took one of my targets, so I got an email when you managed to scare him.'

She lifted her left hand and pulled down the sleeve of her jumper just past her wrist.

'I got some points, thanks to you,' she said.

Emilia baulked at the number on her wrist: 8,950.

'You have over eight thousand points,' she said, looking at the measly 100 on her wrist.

Sadie shrugged nonchalantly.

'Yeah, well, I'm a workaholic.'

'Didn't you join the Agency at the same time I did? We were in orientation together.'

'I'm really good at research. I've submitted more targets than I can count and none of them have missed getting scares.'

Emilia could hardly believe it. All this time she had wasted being a good-for-nothing agent, and Sadie was in the research department raking up points.

'Isn't that enough to get reincarnated?' she asked.

Sadie glanced at the number on her wrist, looking almost bored.

'Maybe, but I'm not doing this to get reincarnated. I don't care for that.'

Before Emilia could ask, she said, 'I'm only here because I'm not interested in finding out what comes after all this.'

Emilia had never thought of that before. From the beginning, her aim had always been reincarnation. Hearing Sadie candidly speak of life after the Spirit World made her realize that she, too, had no desire or curiosity to figure out its technicalities.

'Anyway,' Sadie continued. 'I came here to congratulate you on your first scare. I wasn't expecting to find you looking so glum. Did something happen?'

'Actually . . . You might have been right in warning me against scaring him.'

Sadie inhaled sharply.

'Something happened,' she said, and this time, it wasn't a question.

Emilia leaned forward slowly and lowered her voice.

'I didn't want to scare him. I just . . . I got curious and wanted to see what he was doing. The key led me to a secluded storage facility. I only wanted to take a little peek but . . .' She faltered for a moment before continuing, 'But then, he turned and . . . and he *saw* me, Sadie.'

'Okay . . . Why is that an issue?' Sadie said. 'I mean, I honestly didn't think you'd have it in you to let yourself be seen, but that's a good thing, right? You got your scare.'

'No, Sadie, you don't understand,' she said. 'I didn't do it. It wasn't me. I don't know how to channel my energy like that. I can't control who sees me and when. It just . . . happened.'

It took a while before her words registered.

'Oh,' Sadie finally said. 'Oh, no.'

Spirits were capable of doing a wide range of things, including being seen at will by the Living, but it was largely based on how well they were able to control their energies. A novice like Emilia who had not been dead for long and didn't have a lot of energy to begin with, could not have intentionally shown herself to the target even if she wanted to.

'And you're sure he saw you?' Sadie asked. 'You didn't, I don't know, assume he did or something?'

'He looked me right in the eyes, fell back, and screamed bloody murder,' Emilia said. 'So, yes, I'm sure he saw me. It freaked me out more than it freaked him out.'

Sadie scoffed.

'I doubt that. I'm pretty sure he was spooked. The man saw a *ghost*.'

'That's not the point.'

'All right, listen. If you're sure you didn't let yourself be seen and he still saw you, then that means . . .'

'He was dying,' Emilia said, her face paling. 'Isn't that against the rules? We weren't supposed to scare people who were dying! I'm in so much trouble.'

'Relax. It's not your fault.'

'*You're* in so much trouble,' Emilia said.

'Okay? It's not my fault either.' Sadie sounded mildly offended. 'Look, I did the research on him, and he wasn't vetoed. If anyone's to blame, it's the administration for approving his file. You're fine, all right? We're both fine. So just . . . calm down.'

'I don't feel fine at all. In fact, I feel so *not* fine, that I signed the contract Arthur gave me.'

'You what?'

Emilia showed her the signed contract.

'Are you sure about this?' Sadie asked, studying her with scepticism.

'I don't care. I really don't think I can keep scaring people. Just once is enough. I don't know why I was so sure I wanted to be an agent when all the signs were pointing me in the other direction.'

'Well, if you're sure then I guess I'm here to also congratulate you for coming over to our side,' Sadie said. 'Welcome to the research department.'

'Yay,' Emilia said, without a hint of enthusiasm.

6

Emilia sat in Arthur's office, the folder with the signed contract on her lap as she stared out the window at the streets of the Spirit World below. She'd dropped by to give him the folder but had unknowingly arrived at a bad time. His secretary informed her that he was in a meeting but would be back soon. When Emilia mentioned leaving the contract with her instead, the secretary was quick to refuse, claiming that Arthur had been intending to see her anyway so she might as well wait.

Emilia tapped her foot against the hardwood floor, her fingers drumming on the folder as she waited for Arthur to arrive. The door finally opened and he strode in, his expression unreadable as always, but she was certain she caught the hint of a smile tugging at the corners of his lips.

'Perfect timing, Emilia,' he said as he settled in his chair behind the desk. 'I was about to call you to my office.'

'Did you have something you wanted to tell me?'

Arthur looked somewhat confused.

'Yes, but . . . Don't *you* have something to tell me?'

It felt as though he expected her to be on the same page as him, but she had no idea what he was talking about. Instead, she said, 'I'm not sure if we're referring to the same thing but I came by to drop off the contract.'

'That wasn't exactly what I had in mind,' he said, taking the folder from her. 'You did not sign it, I presume?'

'Actually . . .' Emilia started but did not finish her sentence. She watched as his eyes widened a little at the sight of her name at the bottom of the contract. Hardly anything elicited a reaction from him, but remarkably, she had provoked a response from him in mere minutes.

'You signed it,' he said.

The air in the office was stifling as he exhaled and put away the folder. She fidgeted, an inexplicable urge to apologize gnawing at her. She bit down on the inside of her cheek to restrain herself.

When he spoke, his voice was level and bland. He sounded unimpressed and she knew that she had disappointed him yet again with her decision.

'I had intended to congratulate you on your success in acquiring a scare,' he said. 'I was not, however, expecting you to hand in your transfer papers.'

His gaze flitted to the folder once more before focusing back on her.

'What happened?' he asked. 'The last time you sat in that chair, you were desperate not to leave your role as an agent. But here you are, willingly transferring to the research department right after you secured your first scare.'

When she remained quiet, he said, 'Tell me what happened while you were in the Living World.'

Emilia no longer felt like a child being reprimanded. Now she felt like a prisoner locked in the interrogation room with the worse kind of inquisitor. On one hand, as her direct superior, she felt compelled to tell him the truth, but on the other, a part of her knew it would not be a good idea.

She was not technically at fault for scaring someone on the apparent verge of death—an assumption that had yet to be confirmed—but if she knew Arthur at all, she knew she would still be getting the brunt of whatever wrath he might rain upon her.

Considering her words carefully, she said, 'It wasn't what I envisioned it would be. My misconception painted the life of an agent as something grandiose, but reality shattered those illusions. I had such high hopes for it, only to be let down when I finally managed to scare my first target.'

'It wasn't what you were expecting?'

Emilia thought about it for a minute and realized it really wasn't.

'I didn't feel as accomplished as I thought I would. In fact, it made me feel quite miserable.'

'In that case, I'll approve your reassignment,' he said, signing his name adjacent to hers on the contract. He kept one copy and handed her the other before adding, 'If it's any consolation, I do think you deserve congratulations for your effort. It isn't easy being an agent. It might have only been for a moment, but you were still an agent, and I do appreciate you trying.'

A knock on the office door drew their attention, and his secretary appeared.

'Your afternoon appointment is here, sir,' she said.

'Send him in, we're about done here.' He turned to Emilia. 'You can start at the research department tomorrow. I'll let the head of the department know to expect you and to assign someone to show you the ropes.'

Emilia thanked him and stood. She heard the door opening and closing behind her, and the sound of footsteps approaching. She turned, expecting to see the face of a stranger, only to find herself staring once more at a gut-wrenchingly familiar pair of eyes.

Her mouth fell open in shock, as her copy of the contract fell from her grasp. The person standing before her looked equally aghast. Emilia couldn't move, nor could she bring herself to speak. She was frozen, rooted to where she stood. Her thoughts were running rampant in her head, but everything else seemed dull and slow. She was vaguely aware of someone—Arthur, likely—calling out to her, but even his voice sounded distant. It wasn't until she felt a hand gripping her shoulder that she snapped out of her trance and came back to her senses.

'Is everything all right?'

It was Arthur speaking.

Emilia ignored him. Her focus was entirely on the person who had entered the office.

'You . . .' she murmured. The one word sending a chill down her spine when she recalled that she had said the same thing back then too.

'*You*!' he echoed. Although, rather curiously, he sounded a lot more enthused than she did.

Arthur spoke again, 'Do you two know each other?'

Emilia was still too stunned to say anything more, but that was not the case for the person responsible for her state of shock.

He turned to Arthur and nonchalantly declared, much to her horror, 'She killed me.'

7

Emilia's chest was tight under the suffocating grip of invisible hands squeezing the very air from her lungs. The growing discomfort in her abdomen was back; the guilt, the fear, and the anxiety, all crowded the pit of her stomach, making her feel sick all over again. The rational part of her brain was urging her to apologize for being the direct cause of the man's death, but the subconscious lump that had lodged itself in her throat prevented her from saying a word. The colour had all but drained from her face and the only thing she could do was stare numbly at the familiar face of the man she had seen in the storage unit and whom she had, inadvertently, scared to death.

Arthur's silence stemmed from his perplexity and his inability to comprehend the current situation, but a glance in Emilia's direction pushed him to speak.

'You should sit,' he said, worried she might pass out.

When she remained frozen in place, he repeated in a much sterner tone, 'Sit down, Emilia.'

She collapsed onto the chair, her eyes reluctantly leaving the man to fixate on her quivering hands clasped tightly in her lap. Arthur, in an unusual display of tenderness, gently patted her shoulder. His voice was soft as he said, 'Breathe.'

Emilia willed herself to regulate her breathing, each inhale and exhale a deliberate effort to steady her nerves. That settled, Arthur shifted his attention to the man before him. He was unsure of how to begin the conversation, but before he could gather his thoughts, the man spoke first.

'I did not mean to cause such a commotion,' he said. He gestured almost timidly at Emilia. 'Will she be all right?'

'Give her a minute and she'll be fine. It seems you've given her quite a fright,' Arthur said, aware of the irony of his words.

'I'm Thomas, by the way,' the man said, looking every bit as apologetic as he felt. 'I'm here for the—'

'Interview,' Arthur interrupted. 'Yes, I'm aware. But right now, we have far more urgent matters demanding our attention. For instance . . . the two of you seem to be acquainted.'

Thomas glanced at Emilia again, a little uneasily this time.

'We are . . . but, not in the conventional sense . . .'

'Did she really kill you?' Arthur asked, getting straight to the point.

'Yes,' he said, at the same time as Emilia who mumbled, 'I didn't mean to.'

Arthur pinched the bridge of his nose in an effort to stave off an oncoming headache and gestured for Thomas to take the seat next to Emilia's.

'How did this happen?'

'I might have worded myself incorrectly earlier but it's not her fault,' Thomas said. 'She didn't do anything. I saw her and it was so sudden, my heart gave out.'

His explanation did little to ease matters. Rather than calming the situation, it appeared to escalate it, evident from the furrow on Arthur's brow. His eyes, usually sharp and discerning, now bore into Emilia with suspicion. Familiar with her skills, or lack thereof, he understood that she could not possibly have let herself be seen on purpose.

Arthur inhaled sharply before saying, 'Please, tell me you did not go after someone who had not been approved by the research and administration department.'

At this, Emilia immediately straightened.

'I swear on my honour that his file had been approved. I would never have done anything otherwise. If you don't believe me, you can look it up. The file and all the papers are there.'

He kept his gaze fixed on her for a few more minutes before nodding.

'And?' he said. 'Don't you have anything to say to Thomas?'

Emilia's face reddened. She disregarded her embarrassment and turned to Thomas, apologizing, and mentioning once more that she truly did not mean for it to have happened. Once the words had left her mouth, she found herself feeling much more at ease and soon, she had days' worth of apologies lined up as she repeatedly expressed her regret at what had occurred.

Her guilt could not be assuaged by mere words, however, and despite her endless apologies, she continued to feel terrible, blaming herself for his death. Certainly, she had harboured no intention of killing him, but he was dead anyhow and whether directly or indirectly, she was the cause. A part of her wondered if she'd feel better about the situation had she intended for it to happen. But that was a thought she was not willing to entertain.

'You don't have to bend over backwards apologizing,' Thomas said, his words and his manner both sincere. 'I'm not mad about what happened, and I don't hold you responsible. I've always had a bad heart. It was bound to have happened, sooner or later.'

Thomas was a blunt and practical man. He knew he was dead. And he also knew that dwelling on the circumstances that caused his death was pointless. He saw no meaning in holding contempt for something Emilia did not do intentionally. It was an accident and he would be a fool to hold it against her. Besides, as macabre as it might seem, there was a silver lining to his death.

Dying meant that he could see her. Not just in glimpses but actually *see* and talk to her. And he was glad for it. He had been at his wits' end when she had first appeared. Now, perhaps, something might come of his efforts. If only he could remember what it was that had him feeling such comfort and relief at seeing her.

'Be that as it may, I feel the need to apologize once more on Emilia's behalf. As her direct superior, I find myself partly responsible for her actions,' Arthur said. He appeared to be considering something, but then he continued, 'Seeing as how your death was the unfortunate doing of one of ours, I'd like to offer you a position here as compensation. That is, if all of this has not interfered with your intention to join us.'

Thomas smiled.

8

Thomas had adapted surprisingly well to life at the Agency. His week of orientation had followed the standard routine for newcomers: an introduction to the various roles, departments, and positions available within the sprawling network. Meanwhile, Emilia was preoccupied with her own form of orientation: familiarizing herself with the intricacies of her new placement in the research department.

By the fifth day, she had settled into a rhythm, her focus absorbed on reading the new materials she was meant to study. So, when she glanced up and saw Thomas standing there, his trademark easy-going smile firmly in place, it caught her off guard.

'Hey,' he said, giving her a casual wave as if it were the most natural thing in the world for him to show up in her workspace.

'Thomas? What are you doing here?' she asked.

His grin widened.

'I figured I'd stop by and see what all the fuss was about. I hear the research department is where the real brains of the operation hang out.'

'Are you here to learn what researchers do?' she asked. She was surprised he'd come to her instead of someone more attuned to the role.

'I heard from one of the others that you worked here, so I asked if I could shadow you,' he said.

Emilia raised an eyebrow, scepticism creeping into her expression.

'You do realize I'm just as new to this as you are?'

'That was mentioned as well,' he admitted with a shrug. 'But it's not important.'

She tilted her head.

'Then why are you here?'

'I'm not here to learn about what researchers do,' he said, his grin turning mischievous.

'You're not?'

Thomas shook his head.

'I just wanted to see you. Be with you.'

Emilia's eyes narrowed after his unexpected confession. Noticing her scrutiny, he rushed to explain.

'There's been something on my mind ever since I first met you,' he said. 'I wasn't lying when I said I didn't fault you for what happened. The thing is . . . I was relieved when I saw you. I think I felt happy, too. You feel familiar to me somehow. I don't understand it, but you just do.'

His response surprised her.

'Have we met before?' she asked. 'Before you, well, *we*, died.'

'I can't remember,' he said.

'Right. I forgot that you just died.'

'What do you mean?'

'Your memories are fuzzy, unreliable . . . You probably can't seem to remember much about anything, but remember some things in great and unnecessary detail, right?'

'How do you . . .?' he said and then paused. 'Is it the same for you too?'

'It's the same for everyone. Memories become useless once you're dead. There are some things I don't remember either but sometimes they come back in bits and pieces over time,' she explained. 'One thing I've learned is not to trust your memories until you're sure of them. The mind has an uncanny ability to twist things into whatever it wants and morphs it completely out of shape. I won't be surprised if we don't know each other the way you seem to think we do.'

'Maybe,' Thomas said, deep in thought. 'But the memories . . . They *do* return eventually?'

'I can't say for sure, but they do. Sometimes.'

He considered this and then asked, 'Do you remember how you died?'

She was taken aback by his brusque manner but was not particularly offended by it.

'It was a car accident,' she said. 'A hit and run. But that's pretty much all I remember about it.'

'Oh.'

Thomas frowned. Her casual mention of her demise caused a peculiar discomfort to creep into his heart as her words lingered in his thoughts. It stirred a sense of familiarity within him, a sensation he couldn't quite shake off. All he could do was offer his empathy.

'It must've been painful,' he murmured, the words feeling alien on his tongue, as if they were a language he had yet to grasp.

'I can't say,' she replied, shrugging. 'As I mentioned before, it's all a blur.'

'You were there right before I died,' he suddenly said, the realization settling in.

'Yeah . . .?'

'I can't remember much either, but did you see what I was doing?'

'You seemed deeply absorbed in something. It looked like you were working on some kind of project. There were documents and articles pinned to a mounted board, and you were writing something too. But that's all I saw. You saw me then and I fled the scene.'

'Why would I be working on a project in a storage facility?'

She opened her mouth to speak, but he cut her off.

'We should find out.'

'*What*?'

'We should find out what I was doing,' he repeated. Before she could question him further, he asked, 'How do you get to the Living World?'

'Through a door on the fourth floor.'

Thomas could not tell if Emilia was playing with him or being entirely serious. But given everything he'd failed to learn about the Spirit World so far, he figured she wasn't joking.

'I don't understand a word you're saying, but fine,' he said, standing abruptly and grabbing her hand. 'Let's go.'

'Go where?'

'To that door on the fourth floor so we can get to the storage facility,' he said, his tone laced with urgency.

She eased her hand out of his grasp.

'Yeah . . . Sorry to break it to you, but that's not how it works.'

'What do you mean? It's just a door. You walk through it. What's the problem?'

'You need a key to open the door,' she explained, her voice tinged with patience that was quickly wearing thin. 'And the key has to match the specific destination you're trying to reach. Without it, the door won't work.'

'Then, let's get the key,' he said simply, as though that solved everything.

'Again, not how it works. The keys are kept by the gatekeeper. He only loans them out in exchange for research files approved by both the research and the administration department. And even then, the key only opens doors to the location needed for the task. Not where you *want* to go.'

Thomas' enthusiasm visibly deflated, and he sank back into his chair.

'Okay, so . . . any chance you have an approved file that just so happens to be bound for the storage facility where I died?'

The silence that followed was all the answer he needed. Emilia didn't even bother responding, just shook her head with a wry smile.

He groaned, running a hand through his hair.

'Of course not. Because why would anything be easy in this place?'

'Welcome to the Spirit World,' she said dryly.

He leaned back and stared at the ceiling.

'I really should have read that manual.'

'Yes, Thomas,' she said with mock solemnity. 'You really should have.'

9

Thomas and Emilia crouched partially behind a pillar on the fourth floor with their eyes fixed on the Nameless Spirit seated behind the counter. Neither of them moved, riveted by the figure before them.

'Why are we hiding?' Emilia asked.

'I told you: reconnaissance. We're here to observe him.'

'I know, but we don't have to hide.'

Thomas turned to face her.

'It's *recon*. We have to hide. It isn't recon if we're not hiding.'

'I get it. But it's just—'

She stopped mid-sentence when she realized he wasn't listening any more. He had turned back around, resuming his watch on the Nameless Spirit. Emilia rolled her eyes. Straightening, she stepped out from behind the pillar, much to his alarm, and planted herself within the gatekeeper's line of sight.

'What are you doing?' Thomas hissed. 'Get back here. You're ruining our cover.'

Emilia shrugged and gestured towards the counter. 'He doesn't care.'

Thomas was about to argue, but the protest died in his throat when he followed her gaze. The Nameless Spirit was entirely unbothered, still as stone, his gaze fixed somewhere far beyond them.

Thomas frowned.

'What's going on? Why isn't he reacting?'

'I told you,' she said, crossing her arms. 'We could stand here all day, and he wouldn't care.'

Thomas stepped out from their hiding spot, still unconvinced, and cautiously approached the counter. As he got nearer, the Nameless Spirit remained unnervingly motionless, not even acknowledging his presence.

He leaned in, studying the gatekeeper intently. His expression tightened as he noticed the Nameless Spirit's eyes. They were completely blank: a pale, milky film obscuring the curve of his eyes, void of pupils or focus. The sight sent a chill crawling down his spine.

Thomas backed away slowly, his steps deliberate as he rejoined Emilia by the pillar.

'His eyes are . . .' he trailed off, gesturing vaguely in front of his own face as if miming an explanation.

'Yeah,' Emilia said. 'Creepy, right?'

'If he's blind, I'm pretty sure we can swipe the key before he even realizes it's gone.'

She tilted her head, peering past him towards the Nameless Spirit sitting rigid behind the counter.

'He's not blind. At least, I don't think so. He always looks over the files I hand him before retrieving the key I need.'

She motioned towards the endless wall of keys stretching upward and outward into what seemed like infinity.

'Even if he were blind, or we could somehow manage to steal a key, we have no idea which one to take.'

Thomas stared at the rows upon rows of identical keys.

'Then let's just grab any one and find our way to the storage facility from there.'

'Sure,' she replied with a sardonic grin. 'Except I have no clue how to get there, nor do I know the exact location of the place. That's fine by me if *you* know the way.' She paused, her eyebrows arched. 'Do you know where to go?'

'No . . .' he admitted begrudgingly, his shoulders sagging. 'I can't remember anything.'

She gave him a pointed look, her expression screaming, '*Exactly.*'

Thomas glanced back at the gatekeeper, and said, 'Okay, wait. Let me try something.'

He squared his shoulders and approached the counter, standing directly in front of the Nameless Spirit. His voice had an authoritative edge to it as he said, 'I need to get to the storage facility where I died. Can I get a key that goes there?'

The Nameless Spirit did not move. But then, slowly, the blank, milky eyes shifted towards him. For a fleeting moment, it almost looked as though the gatekeeper was contemplating his request. Hope flickered in Thomas' chest . . . until the Spirit's gaze slid away and fixed ahead once more.

Request denied.

'Okay,' Thomas muttered under his breath, refusing to give up. 'Let me try again.'

He cleared his throat.

'Please. I really need a key to that storage facility. Can you help me?'

This time, the Nameless Spirit didn't even look at him. In his low, sonorous voice that somehow managed to sound hollow, he said, 'File, please.'

'What?'

'You need a key, and I need a file,' the Nameless Spirit said. 'Do you have a file for me?'

'Well . . . no. But—'

'No file, no key.'

'Can't you make an exception? Just this once?' Thomas pleaded, exasperated.

'No.' The Nameless Spirit's voice remained monotonous. 'I don't know what key to give you if I don't have a file. Get me a file, and I will get you a key.'

Thomas was about to argue further, but before he could say a word, Emilia grabbed his arm and yanked him back.

'It's no use,' she said, steering him away.

'But he said he needs a file for the storage facility. We can give him my file. You still have my file, right?'

She stopped and turned to face him.

'You're dead. He can't find a key for that. He needs a file for someone still alive in the Living World to make the connection between the realms.'

Thomas bristled, on the verge of another argument, but she cut him off with a small smile.

'Come. There's someone I want you to meet. She might be able to help us.'

'Who?'

'You'll see,' she said.

Sadie blinked at Thomas, her mouth ajar and disbelief written plain on her face. Then she turned to Emilia, her expression tipping into something almost theatrical. Shielding her mouth from Thomas as though he couldn't hear her, she whispered, 'He died, and now he's *here*?'

Emilia shrugged, the corner of her lips tugging downward in a rueful gesture that said more than words could.

Sadie turned back to Thomas—her voice pitched somewhere between polite and incredulous.

'I'd say it's nice to meet you, but under the circumstances, I'm not sure that's appropriate.' She gave him a crooked smile, 'Still, for the sake of formality, it's good to make your acquaintance, though I wish it were under better circumstances. You know, without you being dead and all . . .'

'We're all dead,' Emilia interjected.

'Sure,' Sadie said, waving a hand dismissively. 'But the way he died was—'

'Okay, shush, Sadie.'

Thomas cleared his throat, visibly uncomfortable.

'Emilia says you might be able to help us,' he said, steering the conversation back on track.

'Maybe. What's the issue?'

He explained their predicament with the Nameless Spirit, recounting their failed attempts to procure a key. When he finished, Sadie laughed.

'That's it? *That's* your problem? Oh, please, that's nothing.'

Emilia and Thomas shared an uncertain look.

'You have a solution?' Emilia asked.

Sadie grinned and slid open the topmost drawer of the cabinet beneath her desk. From within, she retrieved a small, golden-wrapped piece of caramel candy. She handed it to Emilia with a flourish.

'Here's your solution.'

Thomas stared at the candy, confused.

'This . . . is supposed to help us? How?'

She propped her chin on her hand, her grin widening.

'The Nameless Spirit *loves* sweets. I found out by accident when I was handing out bonbons. Give him that, and he'll probably help you.'

Thomas squinted at the shiny wrapper.

'You were just giving these out? What was the occasion?' he asked.

'There wasn't one,' Sadie said, shrugging. 'Back when we were alive, there was always an excuse to celebrate something or the other. I liked that. People tend to forget these little things once they cross over. But I wanted to hold on to them. So in my first week here, I shared bonbons with everyone.'

Her cheerful demeanour faltered, the mask slipping for just an instant. Sadness threaded through her words, subtle but unmistakable. Then her smile returned, as bright and chipper as ever.

10

The Nameless Spirit's eyes shifted just a fraction when Emilia and Thomas stood in front of him.

'I have something for you,' Emilia said.

'A file?'

Emilia did not respond. Instead, she placed the candy on the counter before him. The Nameless Spirit stared at the offering but did not react. Thomas and Emilia glanced at each other, suddenly thinking the same thing: Had Sadie played them for fools?

But before either of them could voice their doubts, the Nameless Spirit swiped the candy and disappeared beneath the counter. They could hear the crunch of the foil being unwrapped and a moment later, just as Emilia was about to peer over in unrestrained curiosity, a little boy popped his head out, grinning at them.

Emilia staggered back in surprise.

'What—?' she mumbled, at the same time as Thomas, who said, 'How—?'

The little boy laughed at the stupid looks on their faces as he clambered onto the counter. He was small, with tousled brown locks and a very prominent gap between his two front teeth.

'Sadie gave you the candy?' he asked, sitting cross-legged on the counter so he could be at eye level. He rested his elbow on his knee and his chin on his palm as he stared at them. 'Got any more?'

Emilia ignored his questions, and said, 'You're the gatekeeper.'

It was more of an observation than a question, but the boy nodded anyway.

'Who else would I be?' he said.

Despite the childish excitement on his face, he appeared somewhat disinterested and bored, as though he would much rather be somewhere else and be doing anything other than having this conversation with them.

'You got any more candy?' he asked again.

'Maybe,' Thomas lied, ignoring the look Emilia was giving him. 'If you answer our questions.'

The gatekeeper sighed heavily, cementing his apparent boredom. Then he nodded unenthusiastically and gestured for them to speak. Thomas did not know what he wanted to ask, nor had he considered his method of negotiation thoroughly.

He had no idea where he was going with his line of inquiry, but he pointed at the wall of keys and said, 'I want to know how that works. There must be thousands of keys. How do you know what goes where and which key to take?'

The boy frowned.

'Is this about the thing you asked earlier?' he said, scratching his head as he tried to recall their conversation. His brow furrowed in concentration, struggling to remember, which was odd, considering it had happened hardly an hour ago. 'Going back to the place you died, or something like that . . .?'

'And if it is? Does that change your answer?'

The boy uncrossed his legs, swinging it over the edge as he leaned back on his hands and stared at the ceiling, pondering the question.

'I suppose I *could* help you . . . Though I'm not too sure if he would be a problem,' he muttered, almost to himself.

'He?' Emilia repeated, eager at the prospect of getting somewhere. 'Are you talking about the other gatekeeper? Are there two of you?'

'Two of us? Don't be silly. There's only one gatekeeper. Everyone knows that,' he scoffed. 'He and I are the same.'

'He's you?'

'He's like a placeholder. He holds my place here . . . and everywhere else I'm meant to be,' the boy clarified. The confused faces he was met with left him at a loss. 'You do realize this isn't the only gateway in the Spirit World, don't you? But there's only one gatekeeper: *me*. I can't be everywhere at once, so he's wherever I'm not.'

'But you're never here,' Emilia mumbled under her breath.

The boy raised his eyebrow at her impertinence. She had no business being this rude.

'I have no reason to be here. *He* does the job just as well. Besides, it's boring here. The only good thing about this place is Sadie,' he said. 'She gives me sweets. And *that's* the only reason you'll ever find me here.'

'Your sweet tooth keeps you coming here?' Thomas said. 'That makes no sense.'

'I stopped questioning things a long time ago. And I've been around for a *long* time,' the gatekeeper said. He glanced between them and then added, 'So, you want to know how the keys are sorted, huh? Let me guess, your grand plan is to steal the key you need and scurry off wherever you need to be?'

He continued without waiting for a reply. 'It's not going to work. The keys don't number in the thousands. They go up to the millions. There's a key for every possible location everywhere in the Living World. I don't know the exact number, but there's a lot more than I can keep track of. And, unfortunately, the keys aren't sorted in any order. They shuffle around every so often.'

Emilia craned her neck, taking in the seemingly endless rows of keys behind the gatekeeper, stretching back to where the timber key shelves climbed into the rafters. It wasn't logically possible, of course. They were in an office building. And yet somehow, it *was* possible, for reasons she could not discern. She was starting to see sense in the gatekeeper's wisdom. The rationality behind the Spirit World's illogicalities was sometimes better left as it was. Trying to search for rhyme or reason would only give her a headache.

'You said you could help us,' Thomas reminded him.

'I might have a way . . . But I see no reason to help you,' he said, cutting off their protests by adding, 'Why *should* I help you?'

'There's something I have to do in the Living World. I'm not sure what, exactly, but the feeling is gnawing at me.'

'Everyone has unresolved business with the other side. That's the whole point of this place,' the gatekeeper said, unimpressed with his weak reasoning. 'You may not know this because you've only been here a while, but despite everyone's common goals of reincarnation, it is highly frowned upon to dwell on the Living.'

Emilia cringed. She had heard those words far more often than she cared to admit, and the fact that they had once come from Arthur only made it worse. But hearing them now from the gatekeeper, whose current appearance was that of a little boy, made her deeply uncomfortable. The dissonance between his words and the way he looked was unsettling.

Thomas, unfazed, said, 'My reasons shouldn't matter as much if we agree to get you more sweets in exchange for allowing us passage to where we need to be.'

Emilia didn't intervene. She wasn't sure if such a bargain was even possible, but at this point, it was worth a try. Unlike Thomas and herself—regular spirits who no longer required sustenance and couldn't eat even if they wanted to—the Nameless Spirit was unique. He was tethered to the Spirit World in ways others weren't, likely having existed as part of it since the beginning.

There were many things he could do that others couldn't, and many restrictions he endured that others didn't. One of those restrictions, Emilia knew, was his inability to leave the Spirit World for longer than a certain amount of time. That difference made him an enigma, and in moments like this, a frustrating one.

Still, Thomas' suggestion wasn't entirely foolish. If anyone could be swayed by confectionery, it was the Nameless Spirit. Whether he would take the bait remained to be seen.

Spirits did not need to eat, so there were no sweets or other foods in the Spirit World. Any treat the Nameless Spirit might want would have to come from the Living World. And since his time there was limited, the candy he craved was the perfect bargaining tool.

When he remained unconvinced, Emilia added, 'I'll tell Sadie not to give you any more of her leftovers.'

'You're so annoying!' he huffed. Between the disgruntled look, the whining, and his obvious love of sweets, it was clear he was still, after all, a child.

'Well? Do you want your sweets or not?' Thomas asked, feigning impatience to get him to cave.

The Nameless Spirit frowned as he chewed on his bottom lip.

'Fine, I'll help you,' he said, though the prospect didn't seem to please him.

He paused, staring at the wall of keys as if weighing his options, then turned back.

'You haven't used the gateways yet,' he said to Thomas. His gaze found Emilia's. 'But *you* have. You know how it works, don't you?'

'I understand how it works, but not *how* it works,' she said.

'Naturally. But few do,' he said. His expression was now blank, serious. 'The keys are all skeleton keys. They fit in any lock, in any door, but they open only to where they're supposed to go. Nowhere else. No matter the times you use and reuse the key, it will always lead you to the same destination and back again.'

The wall of keys behind him looked all the more daunting now as Thomas said, 'Finding a specific key would be an impossibility.'

'It is an impossible task, yes. But not entirely unachievable.'

'There is a way to locate the key we need?'

'Not without a file. But there *is* a way to get you where you need to be. These are all skeleton keys to specific locations. You don't need to find the key that will lead you to one destination. You need to find the key that will lead you to *all* the destinations,' the Nameless Spirit said. 'You need to find *the* skeleton key.'

11

The existence of a master skeleton key came as a surprise. Spirits were not permitted to leisurely travel between realms, hence, the unyielding presence of the gatekeeper at every gateway in the Spirit World. The fact that such a key existed was cause for concern—at least to certain groups of people. Even if Emilia did not necessarily fall into this category, the potential danger was enough to nag her.

She'd naturally assumed such a key to be of import, which would explain the Nameless Spirit's apparent hesitance in telling them about it. But the longer she considered it, the more she realized that her initial assumptions might not be true after all. It was certainly suspicious how willing he had been to loosen his tongue and so easily convinced to do so for something as inconsequential as *sweets*.

She'd been largely preoccupied by the thought of the master skeleton key, but at the forefront of her mind was the more troubling notion of the person who had it. It wasn't the Nameless Spirit.

It was *Arthur*.

The Nameless Spirit had deemed his part of the deal complete when he'd told them that it was the head of the Agency who had the key. He hadn't waited around for them to hit him with a barrage of questions, which they no doubt had. He had immediately disappeared, the other version of him taking his place soon after.

Reality seemed to come crashing down on Emilia upon hearing of Arthur's involvement. All of a sudden, the notion of helping Thomas to investigate the storage facility where he'd died did not seem as appealing as it had before.

'Let's go,' Thomas said, tugging on her arm to get her moving as she stood rooted to the spot, hesitant and unwilling.

'Go where?'

'To see Arthur,' he said, his tone implying that the answer should have been obvious.

Emilia tried to pry his hand from around her wrist and was glad when it slackened and fell away.

'Is something wrong?' he asked, confused.

'I don't think this is a good idea,' she said. When he appeared nonplussed at her refusal to cooperate, she continued, saying, 'What is so important that you need to go back to the storage facility? Your memories will come back with time, and you'll eventually find out what it was that you were doing there. Let's just wait—'

'I don't want to,' Thomas said, cutting her off.

His brow was drawn tight, his jaw set, and every word he'd just spoken hung between them like a challenge. He wasn't backing down. For a moment, neither moved. Then his shoulders slumped, and the sharp edge in his voice softened, almost hesitant, as if he regretted what he was about to say.

'Look, Emilia. I don't know why I feel so strongly about this, but I just do. This is important to me. Something is telling me that I *have* to do this, all right?'

'Good luck,' she said.

That was not what he'd expected to hear from her.

'What do you mean?' His frown deepened. 'You're coming with me, of course.'

'No way,' she said. 'You're crazy to think you can somehow get that key from Arthur. I'm not going to get into unnecessary trouble with him.'

Thomas gave her a long, deadpan look.

'You killed me,' he reminded her, voice flat and without malice.

She groaned, throwing her hands up.

'Fine!'

'This is a terrible idea,' Emilia muttered for the tenth time as they were ushered into Arthur's office.

Thomas gave her a cheeky grin and whispered, 'Don't worry. I just need you here for moral support. I'll do all the talking.'

Arthur didn't so much as glance up when they entered, too absorbed in his work. He waved vaguely towards the guest chairs, attention still fixed on the document he was reading. Emilia slid into her seat a fraction too quickly and Thomas dropped into the other chair with ease. When their eyes met, he winked and mouthed, 'It'll be fine.'

She resisted the urge to reach out and smack him in the head. She didn't know where he got the gall to treat Arthur like he was one of his friends and not the stern superior everyone knew him to be. She supposed it had to do with how recently Thomas had joined the Agency. If he'd been here longer, he would, like Emilia, be unable to find a single person in the entire Agency who was not mildly afraid of Arthur.

'I do not recall us having an appointment,' Arthur said, his eyes still glued to his work.

It wasn't a question, but his meaning was clear.

'I needed to see you,' Thomas said, calm as ever. 'Well, *we* needed to see you.'

Arthur looked up at this. His gaze met Thomas' first before it flickered ever so slightly in Emilia's direction. She could see the curiosity there. He was not expecting either of them and certainly not together.

'You still have two days of orientation left.'

'I'm shadowing Emilia to learn about what researchers do,' Thomas said easily.

Arthur raised an eyebrow.

'Huh,' he muttered, but said nothing else.

Heat rushed to Emilia's cheeks, and she ducked her head, wishing the floor would swallow her whole. She was never on the list to be shadowed and she herself was new to the research department. They all knew it, which made the silence even more embarrassing.

'I met the Nameless Spirit,' Thomas said. This earned him another look.

'You did, did you? What could have spurred your early introduction to the gatekeeper, I wonder?'

Emilia could have sworn that Arthur's gaze seemed to find her once more as though he *knew* that her being there was the very reason for Thomas' unorthodox behaviour. Because firstly: no one was allowed to meet the gatekeeper nor learn about the gateways until they'd chosen a department to work in. And secondly: Emilia seemed to be the cause of all of Arthur's problems as of late, and he would not be too surprised if she was the cause of this one as well.

'Nothing too important,' Thomas said. 'But he did tell me something interesting.'

'Unfortunately, I do not have the time for idle chatter,' Arthur said. He had deemed, within these short few minutes, that this meeting was a waste of his time. 'Come back to see me when your orientation is over and perhaps, we might have a more fulfilling conversation then.'

'I need the master skeleton key,' Thomas said, ignoring his words and jumping straight to the point.

The silence that followed his sudden declaration was even louder and more palpable than the one from earlier. Was *this* his plan? To go right up to Arthur and ask? But then she remembered how he had done the same thing to the gatekeeper and she chastised herself for not realizing this sooner. Thomas was too straightforward for his own good and so were his mannerisms. Emilia contemplated getting involved, but she knew Arthur well enough to know that the best course of action was to stay silent.

When it seemed as though Arthur was waiting for him to elaborate, Thomas took the opportunity to say, 'I need to go back to the place I died.'

This garnered a reaction out of Arthur who immediately said, 'No.'

'But—'

'You are not allowed to use the gateways as and when you please,' Arthur said. Emilia couldn't tell if he was actually mad at them, or if it was just misplaced anger. But she wasn't too sure she even wanted to know.

Thomas was about to argue when he was cut off a second time.

'No good comes from dwelling on the Living.'

The familiar words made Emilia wince. She felt Arthur's gaze on her once more and when she dared herself to look up, he said, 'You should know better than to encourage such behaviour.'

This seemed to push Thomas to anger and he snapped, 'I have unfinished business—'

'*Everyone* has unfinished business,' Arthur said. He did not raise his voice, but his words were said with such force that it silenced Thomas. 'Why do you think they are here? Why do you think this place even exists? This world? You are not the only one. And if I give in to every person who comes here wanting to argue their case, there would be no end to it. It is unfortunate that you found out about the master skeleton key. I don't know why the gatekeeper would let you know of it, but I cannot give it to you. I will, however, implore that you keep its existence a secret.'

When neither Emilia nor Thomas had anything else to say, he added, 'You are dismissed. Both of you.'

The finality in Arthur's voice was unmistakable, leaving neither of them with the nerve to argue further. Emilia shot Thomas a pitying glance, her expression a silent acknowledgment of the situation. This was precisely why most people were wary of Arthur and it was also the reason behind her reluctance to involve him from the start.

Arthur had a knack for putting people in their place. Not through cruelty, but with cutting honesty that often stung more than it soothed. This moment was no exception, and his words lingered like an echo that neither Thomas nor Emilia could shake.

12

Emilia did not see Thomas for two days after the confrontation with Arthur. She tried to focus on her work, but no matter how hard she tried, she couldn't keep him out of her mind. Worry crept in despite her attempts to brush it off. She considered searching for him but realized she hadn't the faintest idea where to begin. Without a chosen department or an assigned desk, Thomas was impossible to pin down.

On the third morning, however, she was startled to find him waiting for her when she arrived at work. She had prepared herself for the worst, expecting him to be sullen, frustrated, or even angry after the ordeal with Arthur. In fact, she had spent much of the previous nights rehearsing ways to console him. Instead, she was met with an entirely unexpected sight: Thomas, grinning brightly, as though the events of the past days hadn't phased him in the slightest.

'Morning!' he greeted, his tone light and cheerful.

Emilia blinked, her rehearsed words scattering like dry leaves in the wind. Whatever she had planned to say no longer seemed necessary.

'Are you all right?' she asked instead.

He nodded.

'If you want to talk about what happened with Arthur—'

'I don't care about that,' he cut her off briskly. '*Look.*'

He reached into his pocket and pulled out a key that looked like any other skeleton key except this one had an ornate skull woven into its design.

'The master skeleton key?' Emilia gasped, somehow already knowing what it was.

Thomas nodded, and her questions spilled out in a rush.

'How did you get that? Did you steal it? From *Arthur*?'

'What? No!' he exclaimed, looking genuinely offended. 'It was on my desk when I came to work this morning.'

'How? And desk? Since when do you have a desk? What department are you even in?'

Everything was moving far too quickly for her to process.

'I figured that since you're already a researcher, I might as well be an agent. It makes sense, right? That way, we can work together.'

His grin widened and he gave her a triumphant thumbs up as though he had just solved the world's most complicated puzzle.

'You do realize that's not how it works, right?'

He shrugged with maddening nonchalance.

'Don't care.'

Before she could say anything else to refute him, he clapped his hands together and declared loudly, 'Anyway! We've got the key. Now we can go to the Living World. So . . . what do you want to do?'

Emilia hesitated, caught in the pull of two opposing instincts.

On the one hand, returning the key to Arthur seemed like the responsible thing to do. He was her superior, after all, and the master skeleton key clearly wasn't something to mess around with. On the other hand . . . she couldn't shake the bitterness she'd felt at Arthur's cold dismissal. She had known Arthur long enough to understand that blunt honesty was simply his way of expressing himself, but she couldn't help feeling that he had been unnecessarily harsh, especially when Thomas was still figuring things out.

A flicker of rebellion sparked within her.

'Fine,' she said finally. 'Let's go.'

Thomas' entire face lit up.

'Really?'

For reasons she couldn't quite explain, seeing him smile like that made her doubts disappear.

'Yes. Before I change my mind.'

As they ascended to the fourth floor to see the Nameless Spirit, a thought struck Emilia. Today was Thomas' first official day at the Agency. Just two days ago, he had still been going through orientation, undecided about his position.

'Don't you think this is strange?' she asked.

'What's strange?'

'Two days ago, you didn't have a permanent position or even a desk. Now, on your first day, the master skeleton key just happens to find its way to you? It's suspicious. When did you even put in your request to become an agent?'

'Yesterday,' he replied casually. 'Right before the end of the workday. I dropped off the application on my way out. When I came in this morning, and was shown to my desk, there was already an envelope pinned to the divider with the key inside.'

Emilia frowned.

'You don't find that odd? It's way too convenient.'

He shrugged, not wanting to read too much into it.

'Maybe it's just the Agency being efficient. Lucky for us, right?'

'It's strange,' she repeated firmly. 'Too coincidental for it to be chance.'

'Who cares?' he said as they reached the fourth floor. 'We got what we needed. Let's not dwell on the hows and the whys.'

He jerked his head in the direction of the counter and to her surprise, Emilia saw the Nameless Spirit in his child persona. He was sitting on the countertop, leaning back on one hand, the other holding on to a piece of lollipop as he swung his feet in glee.

'Yo,' he said, his white eyes staring straight ahead.

'You're a boy again today,' Emilia commented.

'Sadie gave me this lollipop,' he said without elaborating. Then added, 'You have the master key, yes?'

Thomas took it out from his pocket and handed it to him. The Nameless Spirit held the key to the light and hummed softly to himself in thought before giving it back.

'I haven't seen this in years. I'm surprised Arthur gave it to you.'

Emilia and Thomas exchanged a look, coming to an unspoken understanding. They hadn't discussed this earlier, but with a single glance, they reached an agreement.

'Yeah, well, who knows what Arthur's thinking,' Emilia said, lying with ease.

They didn't know who had left them the key, and for now, it felt safer to keep that secret to themselves. They couldn't fully trust the Nameless Spirit either. He might report them the moment they revealed that Arthur had no idea the key was in their possession.

Better to play it safe.

The Nameless Spirit said nothing. With the lollipop in his hand, he pointed towards the gateway.

'Go ahead. It works the same as all the other keys, except the person holding the key has to think of the destination—picture the place in your mind or say its name. But remember to think hard and keep a clear mind. Distractions affect destinations.'

Then as an afterthought, he added, 'Oh, and don't forget to hold hands. It'll be terrible if one of you gets left behind, or torn to shreds, in the void of nothingness.'

Despite his warning, there was a mischievous glint in the white of his eyes, as though he wouldn't necessarily feel all too terrible if such a thing were to happen.

'Bye, have fun,' he said, waving them off. Before they could even respond, he was already gone, and in his place stood the bored-looking spirit.

'Here,' Thomas said, handing her the key. 'I can't remember where I was when I died. You have to do it.'

Emilia took the key, and was it her imagination, or did it feel heavier than all the other keys? Thinking nothing of it, she said, 'We should get something to secure the key. If we lose it on the other side, we have no way of getting back.'

She explained how she'd use strings to cord through the keys and wear them around her neck, but she didn't have anything on her right now. Thomas disappeared and came back a while later with a length of twine.

'Borrowed it from the office below,' he said. Again, with that easy-going smile on his face.

Emilia threaded the twine through the key before pushing it into the keyhole. She turned it, hearing the distinct sound of a lock clicking. With her right hand on the doorknob, she held out her left for Thomas to take.

'You ready?' she asked.

'As I'll ever be.'

His hand was much larger, easily engulfing hers in its warmth and reassurance.

She faced the door, exhaled, and closed her eyes. She pictured the storage facility as she'd seen it not so long ago. The image in her mind's eye was fuzzy at first, but the more she concentrated, the clearer she was able to see the place as it slowly came into focus.

Then, she pushed the door open.

13

Emilia stepped across the threshold of the door into nothingness and was immediately met by a rush of wind against her face, as if she were plummeting through the void. She had grown used to this peculiar sensation, though familiarity did little to lessen the discomfort. If she had been travelling alone, she would have been flailing helplessly, but with Thomas beside her, she was anchored as she squeezed his hand tight.

If they had been using one of the many keys from the gatekeeper's timber key shelf, the journey would not have been so nerve-racking. Those keys had fixed destinations, and it wouldn't have mattered if she had panicked because she would've still stumbled out on the other side eventually. But this was different. They were using the master skeleton key, and reaching their destination depended entirely on Emilia staying calm and keeping her mind sharply focused.

She tried her hardest to block out the mounting anxiety, but her thoughts spiralled regardless. Had they been falling for too long? It shouldn't have taken them this much time to reach the other end of the door.

Was it her fault? Had she somehow botched the process? Her heartbeat quickened as dread took hold.

Oh, no. Oh, no. Oh, no, she thought in a frantic loop, berating herself.

Wait.

She shouldn't be thinking like this. *Focus, Emilia. FOCUS.*

She strained to conjure a clear image of the storage facility as it had appeared the day that she first saw Thomas. But her thoughts betrayed her, splintering into a thousand directions. She was thinking about the storage facility . . . and everything else all at once. Why was it that at the precise moment she needed to focus, her mind refused to cooperate? The harder she tried, the more her panic grew. They had been falling for far too long. This couldn't be normal. They were lost, plunging into an endless abyss. And it was all her fault.

Just as she was on the verge of giving in to despair, her feet struck solid ground with a jarring thud. Before she could process what was happening, she was hurled forward, slamming face-first into an unforgiving surface. A moment later, Thomas landed beside her in a graceless heap, both of them groaning in pain.

Despite the chaos, their hands remained clasped. Emilia felt as though they'd been tossed about in a giant washing machine, only to be spat out at the end of a brutal spin cycle. Her head throbbed, her limbs ached, and she was too disoriented to even think about moving. For now, all she could do was lie there, catching her breath and silently cursing the ordeal they had just endured.

'Is it always like this?' Thomas asked as he sat up, looking a little pale.

'Not really,' Emilia said, pressing her temples with the heels of both hands when he finally let go of her. 'It's easier when we're not using the master key.'

She hung the key around her neck, letting it dangle against her chest as she took a moment to steady herself. Lifting her gaze, she was met with a familiar sight: the long, dimly lit corridor of the storage facility. The air was thick with silence, and the flickering lights cast unsettling shadows on the walls. It was exactly as she remembered.

'We're here,' she said, unable to keep the relief from her voice. She pushed herself to her feet and extended a hand to Thomas, who took it and pulled himself up with a groan.

As they walked down the corridor, a wave of déjà vu washed over her. Everything looked the same: the deserted hallway, the rows of metal shutters drawn tightly over the storage units, and the oppressive stillness that made every sound feel amplified. Her footsteps echoed faintly, a sharp contrast to the uneasy quiet.

'You found me here?' Thomas' voice broke the silence, bouncing off the walls and making her flinch. His tone was soft, almost uncertain, as though he was trying to place himself in the context of this eerie place.

She didn't immediately answer. Instead, she let the question linger, her thoughts distracted by the chilling atmosphere. They were both dead, they had accepted that fact. Yet the storage facility's desolate emptiness still managed to send a shiver down her spine. It felt wrong, more unsettling than it had any right to be. Was it the oppressive quiet? The flickering lights? Or perhaps something deeper, something unspoken that hung in the air like a threat?

She stole a glance at Thomas. His face was a canvas of conflicted emotions: confusion, curiosity, and an undercurrent of apprehension. He was grappling with the questions that must have been swirling in his mind. What had brought him here? What did this place mean to him? And why couldn't he remember?

'Nothing comes to mind?' Emilia asked. She was curious and sceptical all at once. She wondered if it was possible for their memories to return so easily.

She had been dead for months now, and still nothing surfaced when she thought of her own death. The only detail she could recall with certainty was that she had been hit by a car. A jeep, to be precise. But beyond that, her mind was a blank.

She hadn't bothered piecing together the rest, not in the way Thomas seemed intent on doing. She didn't see the need. Her priority had always been to return to the land of the Living as quickly as possible, gathering whatever fragments of her memories she could along the way. Not the specifics of her death, though. That part of her past felt irrelevant.

Thomas shrugged, his movements slow and uncertain.

'None of this makes any sense to me, and nothing seems familiar.'

The disappointment in his voice was obvious, and for a fleeting moment, Emilia thought she saw dejection flash across his face. She'd only known him for a few days, but even she could tell that such an emotion didn't suit him. She had grown used to seeing him as the lively, cheerful presence that she herself was not.

'I'm sure something will come back to you soon,' she said, her words a weak attempt at consolation.

Thomas offered her a small smile, but it didn't reach his eyes. His usual brightness was dimmed, shadowed by doubt. He gestured towards the rows of metal shutters lining both sides of the corridor, drawing her focus back to their surroundings.

'Where do we go from here?' he asked.

Emilia paused, trying to gather her thoughts. The last time she had been here felt like a lifetime ago. Back then, she hadn't known where to look either, but by chance, she'd found him inside one of the units, the lights within catching her attention. Now, there was nothing. No lights, no sign of activity.

'Let's just keep walking,' she said, hoping to mask her uncertainty. She didn't want to dampen his mood further by admitting she had no idea what they were doing.

As they neared the end of the corridor, something caught her eye. Movement. She squinted, the dim light making it difficult to discern what it was. Then she saw it: a piece of police tape, fluttering loose from one of the units.

'There,' she said, pointing at the shuttered unit with the tape.

'It's shuttered.'

Emilia tilted her head, incredulity written in every line of her face.

'You're *dead*,' she said matter-of-factly. 'The only doors we can't walk through are gateways. This isn't an obstacle.'

He stared back at her, blank and unresponsive. She sighed.

'Just walk through it. Watch.'

She stepped forward, disappearing through the metal shutters as if they weren't there. Thomas stood rooted to the spot, his mouth slightly agape. Moments later, Emilia's head popped back out, startling him.

'Come on,' she urged. 'Get in here.'

'But . . . *how*?'

'I already told you how. Just walk through it.'

When he hesitated, she reached out, grabbed his wrist, and yanked him forward. He braced for impact but to his surprise—and relief—he passed through effortlessly. The sensation was strange but not unpleasant, like stepping through cool water.

Emilia was already giving him a look that said, '*That wasn't so difficult, was it?*'

Thomas offered a sheepish laugh in return.

Inside the unit, she felt another wave of déjà vu. The space was dark, but as a spirit, her vision adapted quickly. All she had to do was concentrate, and details began to emerge from the shadows. The room was mostly empty except for a table pushed against the far wall and a cork board, now dislodged and hanging haphazardly. She remembered it being covered in articles and notes, but it was bare now. The table had also been cleared of anything significant.

Thomas, still coming to terms with his ability to walk through solid objects, looked like a fish out of water, and Emilia had to resist the urge to laugh. She was about to say something to him when he said, 'Where are you? I can't see a damn thing.'

'Give it a moment,' she said. 'If it helps, try to squint. That's what I do.'

He squinted, clearly struggling to adjust to the darkness, and said with dismay, 'There's nothing here.'

While he continued fumbling around, Emilia surveyed the room more thoroughly. It was as empty as it had appeared at first glance, save for two notable details. The first was a fading chalk outline on the floor, one she intentionally avoided and didn't mention, unwilling to confront the memory of her role in his death. The second was a piece of paper near the entrance, lying crumpled on the floor. It must have fallen from the wall.

She recalled the police tape she had seen outside. Of course. The *police* had been here.

'They must've cleared out the place,' she said.

Someone had reported him missing perhaps, and they must have traced his location here only to find his dead body.

She crouched by the fallen piece of paper. It was a printed notice left by the police, informing anyone who entered that the unit's contents had been seized as evidence. Most of the details were unimportant, but the official letterhead caught her attention. It listed the location where the seized items had been taken.

'What is it?' Thomas asked, finally managing to focus on her.

She stood and pointed to the paper.

'Our next destination. It's where they've taken everything from this unit,' she explained.

'And where's that?'

'The Aspen Hollow Police Department.'

14

Emilia and Thomas landed with a graceless thud on the road, their groans of discomfort breaking the stillness around them.

'We really need to fix our landings,' Thomas muttered, pushing himself up with a wince. He brushed gravel from his hands and shot her a disgruntled look. 'Why is it that I can actually feel all this? We're supposed to be dead.'

Emilia rolled over onto her back and stared at the soft hue of the evening sky, wispy clouds catching the fading light as they drifted across the stretch of indigos and violets. She could hear Thomas rambling next to her, but his words sounded muffled and far away. An ache was blooming in her chest that made her sick with longing.

The scene felt. . . familiar. Wasn't this how she'd died? On a gravel road, staring up at the sky? But this sky . . . this mess of pinks and blues and purples wasn't the right colour. The day she'd died, the sky had been the brightest blue, not a cloud in sight.

Emilia stretched her arm high above her, the setting sun casting a warm, orange glow through the translucency of her skin. She hadn't gotten used to how strange spirits looked in the light. The shimmer and ripple of her form, like moonlit waves, was an undeniable reminder that she didn't belong in the Living World any more. They were visitors, fleeting and out of place.

Spirits didn't always look this way, though Emilia hadn't figured out when or why they transitioned between states. She suspected it had something to do with their ability to pass through solid objects or interact with the world, but there was so much about being dead that remained a mystery. Questions she hadn't dared to ask piled up in the back of her mind, the answers likely as elusive as the Spirit World itself.

Her musings were abruptly interrupted by Thomas' ear-splitting shriek. Emilia winced, her hand covering one ear as she turned to face him.

'You—! Why do you look like that?' he stammered, teetering on the edge of hysteria.

Ah. So, he'd finally noticed. Emilia's brief relief at his obliviousness vanished, replaced by mild annoyance.

'*You* look like that,' she pointed out flatly.

'No, I—'

He cut himself off, glancing down at his own shimmering, translucent body. A second louder scream erupted from him as he stumbled back, his hands flailing.

She winced again.

'Would you stop screaming?'

'Why do I look like this?' he yelled, panicked.

'It's fine. Calm down,' she said as she sat upright. 'We all look like this sometimes. It's not a big deal.'

Thomas continued to gape at her, like he'd forgotten how to speak. When the screaming resumed, Emilia's patience snapped. Without thinking, she balled her hand into a fist and gave him a solid thwack on the head.

Thomas' yelling was cut off the minute her fist made contact, his hands flying to the side of his head as he turned to her, eyes brimming with disbelief and betrayal.

'That *hurt*,' he said, his voice filled with indignation.

'I'm sorry,' Emilia said, though she didn't sound particularly apologetic. 'But you wouldn't shut up.'

Thomas grumbled under his breath, rubbing his head and pouting like a child. Emilia wasn't sure which was worse: his screaming or his sulking.

Sighing, she tried a different approach.

'Look, there are a lot of things about the Spirit World that don't make sense. Questioning them doesn't guarantee you'll get any answers. Trust me, I've learned it's better not to be too curious.'

He scowled, clearly finding her answer lacking.

'Doesn't it bother you that you're see-through? Or that we can feel pain while looking like . . . jellyfish?'

Emilia shrugged.

‘I mean, we’re dead. Anything’s possible at this point. I get that it’s a lot to take in, especially for someone new to this, but it gets worse.’

‘Worse?’ Thomas’ voice cracked at the implication.

‘Come on,’ she said, offering no further explanation as she started walking.

The master skeleton key had deposited them on the road in front of the headquarters of Aspen Hollow PD. The two-storey building stood on its own lot and was surprisingly modern—its sleek facade of glass and steel glistening in the fading sunlight. Emilia had been expecting something else, something different, something, perhaps, a bit shabbier, and was taken aback by such exuberance.

They approached the entrance, a pair of polished glass doors emblazoned with the proud emblem of the police department and slipped right through. The spacious lobby hummed with purposeful energy. The place was quieter now that the sun was setting, but there were still a few visitors and uniformed officers lingering about.

To the left of the reception desk were a series of wide glass panels, giving them a glimpse of the bustling activity within, a contrast to the quiet of the lobby. It was an open workspace, the night duty staff starting their shifts just as the morning staff said their goodbyes.

‘I reckon whatever we’re looking for is somewhere in there,’ Thomas said. ‘The evidence would have been logged by now and brought to the locker. That’s where we need to be.’

Emilia turned to look at him, impressed.

'You know your stuff.'

Her comment seemed to give him pause. She hadn't questioned him, but he felt the need to say, 'I have no idea how I know that.'

'Maybe—' Emilia started, but her words were cut off when two men passed directly through her.

Thomas' mouth fell open as he watched her dissipate like smoke. She reformed just as quickly, her face contorted in discomfort as her shimmering, translucent blue hue briefly intensified.

'Ugh,' she groaned, brushing her arms and trying to shake off the sensation. 'I hate when that happens.'

The experience was an unpleasant reminder of why she avoided crowded places in the Living World. Walking through Spirits felt like nothing for the Living; for the dead, however, it felt like being tugged by an invisible string tied to their core and yanked into nonexistence.

'You look like a jellyfish again,' Thomas whined, cringing at the sight of her.

'Stop it,' she said.

'What *was* that?' he asked, stunned by what he had seen.

'The joys of being dead,' Emilia said, shaking off the residual wisps of smoke from her hands and feet. 'The Living can't see us, and it's not fun when they walk through us.'

'It looked like you just . . . evaporated.'

'Felt like it too,' she admitted, grimacing. 'It's like being pulled out of yourself for a second. You get used to it, though.'

'I'd rather not,' he muttered, still watching her warily as if expecting her to vanish again at any moment.

'It's easier to just stay out of their way,' Emilia advised, nodding towards the steady stream of people entering and exiting the workspace.

The men who had walked through her were whispering harshly to one another, their voices low but laden with urgency. The taller man, a blonde with sharp features, looked impatient, his hand gripping the arm of his shorter companion. As they disappeared around the corner, Emilia caught a glimpse of him dragging the latter towards a stairwell on the far side of the lobby.

How intriguing.

Her curiosity piqued, Emilia trailed after them. She slipped through the stairwell door just in time to hear the tail-end of their hushed argument. '*—calm down*,' the blonde hissed.

'Calm down?' the shorter man—dark-haired and jittery—nearly shouted, his eyes wide with panic. 'How can I be calm when everything's falling apart?'

'You're blowing this out of proportion, Marcel,' the blonde snapped. 'Detective Alexander is dead. The evidence has been logged and cleared. We're fine.'

Emilia noticed the badges slung around their necks and realized they were police detectives. Thomas appeared beside her, his expression mirroring her curiosity.

'Who's Detective Alexander?' he whispered.

Emilia shrugged, motioning for him to be quiet as the dark-haired man, Marcel, spoke again.

'I can't do this, Blake. Did you see the captain hovering near Alexander's desk? He's suspicious. If we don't handle this carefully—'

His words cut off with a strangled gasp as Blake grabbed him by the collar and slammed him against the wall. The sound echoed in the empty stairwell. Blake's calm facade cracked, his eyes blazing with barely restrained fury.

'Listen to me, Marcel, and listen well,' Blake growled. 'Alexander wasn't killed. He *died*. Conveniently, yes, but that's it. We had nothing to do with it. Got it?'

Marcel nodded frantically, his face pale.

'Good.' Blake released him, smoothing the front of Marcel's jacket with practised nonchalance. 'Don't go mouthing off and saying the wrong thing. Keep your head down and your mouth shut. Understood?'

Marcel nodded again, his hands trembling as he straightened himself. After a pause, he said in a much softer voice, 'I know you're not worried, but the captain . . . he's suspicious, Blake. If he decides to dig into Alexander's investigations . . . it could spell trouble for us. We need to act.'

'Tampering with evidence after it's been logged will only get us in more trouble,' Blake said, his tone clipped. 'Leave it alone. Don't be difficult.'

'I'm not saying we should erase everything,' Marcel protested, wringing his hands. 'Just enough to make sure we're safe. If the captain reopens the case—'

‘Enough,’ Blake interrupted. ‘The case is closed. We’re not touching it. Snooping around will only draw more attention. Do as I say and leave it.’

With that, Blake turned on his heel and strode away, the stairwell door slamming shut behind him. Marcel’s face burned red with humiliation and frustration.

‘Shit,’ he muttered, kicking the railing with enough force to make it reverberate. The metallic clang echoed in the silence, a stark reminder of his simmering rage.

15

‘Who’s Alexander?’ Thomas asked again, poking her repeatedly on the shoulder.

Emilia swatted his hand away, irritation flashing across her face.

‘I told you, I don’t know.’

‘Then what are we doing here? Shouldn’t we be going to the evidence locker?’

She shot him a sharp look, then turned her attention to Marcel, who had stormed off shortly after Blake. His tense posture and frustrated expression stuck in her mind. Something about the interaction between the two detectives and their conversation had concerned her.

Marcel had returned to his desk in the open workspace, but his behaviour was far from composed. He fidgeted incessantly, perspiration dotting his brow. His fingers tapped erratically on the desk, and his eyes darted nervously around the room. When a colleague called his name, he flinched so hard he nearly fell out of his chair.

While Marcel’s agitation was impossible to miss, Blake was a picture of calm. He moved through the room with ease, exchanging pleasantries with coworkers as he packed up for the day. But when he passed Marcel's desk, his friendly demeanour vanished. His expression turned cold, his gaze sharp with unspoken warning. Marcel visibly recoiled, his already pale face losing even more colour. Blake exited the building without a backward glance. Marcel stayed seated at his desk until he was certain Blake wasn't returning anytime soon, then rose quickly.

'Let's go,' Emilia said, weaving through the space with her eyes locked on him.

Thomas followed, grumbling under his breath about wasted time. Emilia ignored him, confident Marcel's actions would lead them somewhere important. Her intuition proved correct when Marcel walked to the back of the room and slipped through a door marked 'Evidence'.

Thomas' protests ceased immediately when he realized where they were going. They phased through the door to follow Marcel and watched him exchange words with the officer stationed at the counter. The conversation was brief and when it was over, the officer unlocked a second door, leading him into the evidence storage area. Marcel retrieved a cardboard box from one of the shelves and set it on the floor. Once the officer left, he began rifling through the bagged contents.

Emilia crouched beside him, hugging her knees as she observed the growing assortment of items he pulled out: documents, newspaper clippings, and photographs. She recognized what they were instantly.

'Thomas,' she said, beckoning him closer. 'These are the things you were poring over before you died. This is your research!'

Thomas scanned the papers. But as his eyes roved over the items, no memories surfaced. The absence of recognition gnawed at him, a bitter reminder of how much he'd lost. He shook his head, frustration clouding his features.

'Nothing?' she asked.

'It's fine. It'll come to me eventually.'

Marcel continued sifting through the evidence, oblivious to the two spirits hovering nearby. Emilia's mind churned, piecing together fragments of the detectives' earlier argument. Blake and Marcel had spoken about Detective Alexander—how his death was 'convenient' and how tampering with evidence might feed into their captain's suspicions. The tension between them hinted at deeper involvement in Alexander's investigation. Marcel's unease suggested guilt, while Blake's composure masked a dangerous resolve.

A chilling thought took shape in Emilia's mind.

'Thomas . . .' she said slowly. 'I think you're Detective Alexander.'

Thomas stared at her, uncomprehending.

'What?'

'Your name,' she pressed. 'What is it?'

'Thomas Alex—' He stopped short, realization dawning. 'Oh my god. *I'm* the Detective Alexander they were talking about?'

Emilia nodded eagerly, barely able to contain her excitement.

'This investigation was yours. Your research and the evidence here . . . they're the same thing! It all makes sense now.'

Her enthusiasm faltered as she shot him a scowl.

'We could've figured this out sooner if you didn't have a first name for a last name. I thought Alexander was a first name!'

'Well, *sorry*! How was I supposed to know I was a detective? I didn't exactly wake up with a badge.'

He gestured at the evidence laid out on the floor.

'And this? What's he doing with all this?'

'More importantly, why were they so relieved you died? It's troubling. Your investigation was clearly a threat to them. Are you sure none of this looks familiar?'

Thomas shook his head, then repeated, 'What is he doing?'

'Tampering with evidence, most likely,' Emilia replied. She watched as Marcel pulled out a case file. As he flipped it open, a photograph fluttered to the floor and landed next to Thomas' feet.

'Uh, Emilia?' he said. 'You might want to take a look at this.'

She leaned over, and her insides immediately turned to ice.

It was a picture of *her*.

16

They stared at the photograph that was unmistakably of Emilia, comprehension slipping through their grasp. Though confusion clouded their thoughts, one fact stood out: Thomas, or rather Detective Alexander, had been investigating a case involving Emilia just before his death. The details, however, eluded them both.

'You were investigating *me*?' Emilia asked, once the shock of seeing the photograph subsided.

'Apparently,' he replied with a shrug. Turning to her, he asked almost warily, 'You're not a criminal, are you?'

'What? No,' she answered quickly. 'At least, I don't think so. I can't remember.'

Her gaze shifted back to Marcel, her expression tightening in distaste. Her inability to remember her life before her death had never troubled her much before. She had simply accepted that she'd died in a car accident. But now, she doubted even that. Could it really be that simple? Not when she was somehow connected to a police investigation.

She tapped her fingers irritably. As if reading her thoughts, Thomas asked, ‘Are you sure you died in a car crash?’

She nodded.

‘I can’t remember the exact details, but there was a car involved, and it hit me. That much I’m certain of.’

They watched as Marcel turned his back to the security cameras in the room. With deliberate movements, he grabbed several pages from the case file, stuffing them into his pocket before putting the rest back in the box.

Emilia and Thomas sat huddled on the floor of the evidence locker room long after Marcel had left. The steady whir of the ventilator filled the space between them, but it wasn’t enough to drown out the weight of their spiralling thoughts.

‘We should tell Arthur about this,’ Thomas said.

‘*No*,’ Emilia retorted almost immediately. ‘Are you out of your mind? Have you forgotten we’re not even supposed to be here? And now you want to tell him about this? Don’t be ridiculous.’

‘Emilia, *think* for a second. We’re in over our heads here. I don’t know what’s going on, but . . . I don’t think you died the way you think you did,’ he argued.

Her eyes narrowed.

‘What are you trying to say?’

‘All I’m saying is . . . I think you were murdered.’

Emilia held his gaze but said nothing. Sensing her hesitation, Thomas pressed on.

‘We need a second opinion. Who else can we turn to that knows more about this than we do?’

‘Not the Nameless Spirit,’ she joked weakly.

'Exactly,' he replied. 'Since we don't have a clue how to proceed . . .' He shrugged, as if to say, '*Why not?*'

'He's going to kill us,' she mumbled.

'Doesn't matter. We're already dead,' Thomas said, flashing her a grin.

When Emilia tried to justify their actions to Arthur, the words came out uneven and rushed—slipping into the Living World without permission, crossing a boundary they knew better than to test, and meddling in the affairs of the Living. She'd barely managed to explain what they had found when her courage had faltered, her hands clenched tight at her sides. She had expected Arthur to erupt in a rage the moment they'd admitted their mistakes, but he merely acknowledged them with a brief, unreadable look before returning to his work.

He continued examining his paperwork in silence as though her confession had not unsettled him in the slightest. The sound of his pen scratching against the paper grew gratingly loud in her ears. Emilia clenched her teeth, resisting the urge to snatch it from his hand. From the corner of her eye, she caught the helpless look on Thomas' face. He didn't seem to know what to do either.

'Arthur,' Thomas began, but Arthur raised a finger to stop him.

Without sparing them a glance, Arthur continued writing, the scene striking Emilia with an uncanny sense of déjà vu. It reminded her of the time they'd asked for the master skeleton key. She braced herself, knowing that the moment Arthur set his pen down, the argument would begin. The familiar sound of scratching continued for a while before it stopped. Arthur capped the pen and set it aside. Emilia exhaled sharply.

When he finally looked at them, Arthur's features were blank, his face disturbingly impassive.

'So, you've come here to proudly inform me that you've broken the rules,' he said.

Emilia stiffened, but said nothing.

'Surely you haven't come to your senses only to confess, hoping I would forgive you?' His tone dripped with sarcasm that disappeared entirely when he was met with silence. 'Tell me.'

It was Emilia who finally spoke.

'I want to know how I died, Arthur,' she said.

'In a car accident. You know that,' he replied, his tone flat. Yet something felt off. His words were too measured, and his face impossibly calm, as if he were holding something back.

'*Bullshit*,' Thomas muttered under his breath.

Arthur ignored him.

'I don't think that's true,' she said. 'If it was just an accident, why would Thomas have been investigating my death?'

'The authorities handle hit-and-runs all the time. It's hardly unusual. And even if he was investigating, why does it matter? You're dead, Emilia. How many times must I emphasize that the dead should not meddle in the affairs of the Living, whether it concerns your life or others'?'

This was why Emilia hated going to Arthur for anything.

'You won't help us?' she asked, voice taut with frustration.

'No,' he said firmly. 'I won't ask how you got hold of the master skeleton key either, but if you return it and drop this matter, I will overlook your actions and spare you any punishment.'

Emilia's anger surged. Before she could stop herself, she blurted, 'Then I quit. There's no point in working here if it will only hinder what I need to do.'

Arthur scoffed.

'And what exactly *are* your priorities, Emilia? Not long ago, you sat here terrified that I would fire you for neglecting your duties. As I recall, your priority was to accumulate as many points as possible in the shortest time. Has that changed? And for what?'

Emilia paled. His words landed hard, sharp as a whip. She had been so focused on helping Thomas that she'd forgotten her original purpose. Her gaze dropped to the inked number on her wrist. She hadn't been collecting points at all. But somehow, uncovering the truth about her death felt more important.

She took a deep breath and steadied her expression. 'My priorities have changed.'

The room grew tense, the silence suffocating. Emilia refused to waver, meeting Arthur's steely gaze with her own. A minute passed, then another. To her astonishment, his eyes softened, and his shoulders sagged ever so slightly.

'Fine,' he said at last. But his words were directed at her alone, his focus entirely on Emilia. Thomas seemed forgotten in the confrontation.

'If you insist on this path, I won't stop you,' Arthur continued. 'I'll even help you, if that's what you really want.'

'Help me?' Emilia repeated, startled. Her initial reaction was confusion, but it quickly morphed into wariness. Arthur had been steadfastly opposed to aiding them, his resistance unyielding. The abrupt shift in his stance didn't sit right with her.

She studied him closely, searching for a sign of his true intentions. His face was still calm, but his eyes held an intensity that made her feel scrutinized.

'Why the sudden change of heart?' she asked.

Arthur shrugged.

'I've reconsidered. Perhaps your determination has convinced me. Perhaps if I let you do this, your appetite for the Living World will finally be satiated and you will no longer feel the need to keep meddling when I have expressly told you not to.'

He was obviously miffed, but Emilia would take any opportunity she was given and was not one to look a gift horse in the mouth.

'All right,' she said. 'If you're willing to help, I won't turn you down.'

She saw a faint tilt at the corner of his lips. It wasn't quite a smile, but it was enough to make her heart lurch unexpectedly. Arthur's stern facade had cracked, however briefly.

'Good,' he said. 'Then let us learn the best defence a spirit has in the Living World.'

17

Scaring the Living had always been hard work. Emilia knew this all too well. It had taken her months to secure her first scare, and even then, it had been accidental rather than a testament to any natural talent she possessed. She struggled to see how learning to scare the Living was relevant now, especially when she was no longer an active agent. The idea that it could be considered a form of self-defence eluded her. Arthur seemed resolute, an unusual trait for someone who rarely went beyond fulfilling the bare minimum of his duties as the spirit in charge of the Agency.

When she voiced her scepticism, Arthur's response was straightforward enough to leave her wondering why she hadn't thought of it herself. He explained that if they were serious about investigating the suspicions surrounding their deaths, they would likely need to interact with the Living. Such interactions might involve uncovering hidden secrets or gathering critical evidence, tasks that were almost impossible for spirits to do without employing the tactics of a haunting.

'Besides,' Arthur added, turning to Thomas, 'you're still a Scare Agent. Practising in this way will benefit both your official work and your extracurricular activities.'

At the mention of work, Arthur continued, 'I would also advise against quitting the Agency. Investigating one's own death is generally frowned upon. At the very least, the Agency can offer you some protection should word get out.'

'How?' Emilia asked. The idea that the Agency would shield them seemed far-fetched.

Arthur considered this for a moment. Then, turning to face her, he amended his statement.

'*I* could protect you.'

The sincerity in his words was disarming, and she quickly forced a frown to mask her reaction, averting her eyes.

When Arthur had offered to teach them the ways of a Scare Agent, Emilia had not assumed it would involve a field trip to the Living World. Yet here they were, standing in front of a large suburban house beneath a sky strewn with stars.

Emilia had now seen Arthur acting unlike himself not once, but twice. It was more than enough times to raise alarm bells in her head. She found it unusual that he could bring them to a target without following the Agency's orthodox procedures. Arthur had neither retrieved a file from the Nameless Spirit nor had he used the master skeleton key, or any key for that matter, to get them here.

Instead, he had instructed them to hold on to him as he stepped through the gateway. And in an instant, they had appeared in the Living World. She chose not to question him on this, suspecting he would not offer any real answers even if she did. But she had asked about the target, and he had simply said that there were some perks to being the spirit in charge of the Agency. One of which was that you were trusted to make decisions that would otherwise need approval from the bureaucratic channels.

The stillness of the night was punctuated by the occasional rustle of leaves, the distant hum of crickets, and the soft whisper of a breeze. A sense of calm pervaded the air, mingling with a hint of anticipation, as though the house itself was holding its breath, waiting for some unseen event to unfold.

Thomas and Emilia stood on either side of him, staring up at the house and its white clapboard siding that seemed to glow faintly in the moonlight.

'Our target is eighteen-year-old Dean. His curiosity has recently led him down unfavourable paths, dabbling in dangerous occult practices,' Arthur explained. 'Nothing has come of it. *Yet.* But let's not wait until it does. I want you to scare him enough to make him stop messing with things he does not fully understand.'

'I have to do it, too?' Emilia asked, looking uneasy.

'You don't have to if you don't want to. But this is mostly a way for me to gauge how well Thomas can fare on his own.'

Right, she thought. *Because he already knows that I cannot be relied upon to scare anyone.*

With a heavy sigh, Emilia followed them through the front door and into the house. Dean's room was dimly lit, the boy himself hunched over what appeared to be a makeshift altar tucked at the back of his cupboard. Clothes were strewn across the room, most piled in a heap at the foot of his bed. Flickering candles adorned the altar's surface, their light illuminating the intricate symbols drawn upon it. Dean was engrossed in reading a thick leather-bound book, the pages filled with ghastly sketches that made Emilia shudder. His headphones blasted music loud enough for her to hear the muffled rhythm.

Emilia leaned forward and peered over Dean's shoulder, squinting at the disturbing images in the book.

'He's really into this stuff,' she murmured.

Thomas, aware of Arthur's watchful presence nearby, felt nervous. This all seemed less like a lesson and more like a test. Arthur wasn't interfering but observing him silently.

'Should we try to move something?' Thomas asked, glancing at Emilia for suggestions. 'He has his headphones on, so there's little we can do about sounds.'

She nodded, offering him an encouraging smile. She looked around the room and pointed at the pencils scattered across Dean's desk, near his computer.

'Try to focus your energy on rolling those off the table. It should catch his attention.'

Thomas inhaled deeply, attempting to focus. He stared intently at one of the pencils. The mechanics of haunting were still foreign to him, but he figured it might be like willing an object to move in a dream. If he just concentrated enough . . .

The pencil jolted upward, shooting straight into the ceiling with a loud *thunk* before ricocheting into the laundry basket and vanishing from sight. Thomas' hands dropped to his sides, determination slipping into dismay.

Undeterred, he tried again, this time directing his energy towards the overhead light fixture. He aimed to create a subtle flicker but overcompensated, plunging the entire house into darkness. The room's candles cast an eerie glow, the only source of illumination now.

Dean pulled off his headphones, glancing around with a frown.

'A blackout . . .?' he murmured, his voice barely audible over the din from his headphones.

Emilia noticed the disgruntled look on Thomas' face.

'You're getting there,' she whispered, attempting to keep his spirits up. Haunting wasn't easy. She knew that better than anyone.

Panicking slightly, Thomas tried one last thing. Focusing his energy, he attempted to project a ghostly wail. The sound that emerged, however, resembled off-key singing, warbling and uneven. Dean paused for a moment, then shrugged, assuming someone had left a radio on in another room.

Emilia cringed but quickly hid her reaction.

'You're not bad at this,' she reassured him. 'Seriously. You moved the pencil, turned off the lights, and even managed some sound projection. That's a lot more than I could do.'

Thomas exhaled, frustration evident.

'But it's not enough to scare him.'

'It's your first time,' she said. 'You'll get the hang of it.'

Arthur stepped forward to join them.

'You set the stage well with the blackout,' he said. 'Now let's take full advantage of it before the lights come back on. Watch closely.'

With a wave of his hand, Arthur made the curtains billow dramatically despite the absence of wind or open windows. The temperature plummeted, and an unnatural chill swept through the space. On the wall opposite Dean, a shadowy figure began to form. It loomed ominously, its shape growing larger and more grotesque with every passing second. Horns jutted from its head, twisting as the shadow shifted.

By the flickering candlelight, they saw Dean's face drain of colour. His previously unbothered demeanour was gone, replaced by wide-eyed terror. He stumbled backward, falling onto the floor as he gawked at the looming figure. The shadow seemed to breathe, expanding and contracting as if alive.

Dean scrambled onto his hands and knees, frantically smudging the symbols on the altar with his sleeve. He blew out the candles in rapid succession and hurled the occult book away as though it had burned him. Moments later, he bolted from the room, his panicked shouts echoing down the hallway as he screamed for his mother.

The house settled back into stillness.

'You did well,' Arthur said, turning to Thomas.

Thomas frowned, shaking his head.

'I didn't do anything.'

'I wasn't expecting you to get everything right on your first attempt. That's why I'm here.' He gestured around the room, now eerily quiet. 'Scaring isn't just about raw power or perfect control. It's about *understanding* your target.'

He paused, giving Thomas a moment to absorb the words. 'The Agency's researchers gather detailed information about each target for a reason. An agent's job is to use that knowledge to craft the most effective scare.'

Realization dawned on Emilia just then. She had been wrong about Arthur's intentions. She'd assumed this exercise was meant to highlight her failings as an agent—her inability to frighten the Living. But Arthur's point wasn't about failure; it was about partnership.

The Agency thrived on the collaboration between its agents and researchers. Researchers unearthed the critical details, and agents brought those findings to life. One couldn't succeed without the other.

Arthur's gaze shifted to Emilia.

'Dean was dabbling in the occult, trying to summon something from that book. I used the imagery from his own mind to terrify him. The shadow I conjured was straight out of one of the sketches you saw.'

The figure had convinced Dean that his ritual had succeeded, and the realization had scared him far more than any random haunting would have.

Arthur addressed Thomas again.

'Practise channelling your energy. Control will come with time. But remember that knowing your target will always make the difference.'

To Emilia, he said, 'You have the instincts of a researcher. Out here in the field, there's rarely time for deep dives into information. But you notice the details that matter. Trust that.'

He stepped back, looking at both of them.

'The two of you are capable of investigating the Living World effectively. Keep honing your skills—you'll need them.'

18

'Emilia,' Arthur called as they stepped outside the house. 'There's something I want to give you.'

From his inner pocket, he retrieved a delicate bracelet that shimmered faintly in the moonlight. It was crafted from thin, interwoven strands of silver and onyx, intricately braided together. The metal band seemed almost alive, pulsing with an ethereal glow that shifted from a deep, shadowy black to a bright, silvery white as it caught the light. At the bracelet's centre rested a single, round gemstone. It was an opal, but unlike any Emilia had ever seen. Within its depths swirled a myriad of colours, constantly shifting and changing like a miniature galaxy. Tiny specks of light darted through the gemstone, giving it a mesmerizing, almost hypnotic quality.

Arthur stepped closer and gently clasped the bracelet around her wrist. The metal was cool to the touch, sending a shiver up her arm. As soon as it was secured, the bracelet adjusted itself, fitting perfectly and comfortably. His fingers lingered briefly on the inside of her wrist before he pulled away.

'This bracelet holds a fraction of my energy,' Arthur explained, his voice softer now. 'It will aid you in your tasks and grant you abilities beyond what you can currently muster.'

Emilia stared at the bracelet, enraptured by its beauty and the thrumming of the energy she could feel emanating from it. But something was not right. Spirits did not have the capacity to transfer their energy into objects. They could use their energy to manipulate the things around them, yes, but not in the way Arthur was doing it. Not like this. Unease crept over her. This wasn't the first time Arthur had acted unlike himself, and now her suspicions solidified into certainty.

Arthur was not a spirit.

It would explain his ability to travel to the Living World without the master skeleton key, his effortless rule-bending, and now this. But if he wasn't a spirit, then what was he?

'Why are you giving this to me?' Emilia asked with caution.

'Because I believe in your potential,' he said simply. She noticed that the severity in his eyes faded when he looked at her. 'This bracelet will help you. But I must warn you: the energy within it is not limitless. Use it wisely and within reason.'

Emilia glanced at the bracelet again. It pulsed gently, a steady reminder of the strength he had entrusted to her. She could feel the weight of his faith in her, but the questions swirling in her mind dampened her awe.

'I know you're not particularly well-versed in hauntings,' Arthur continued, his tone matter of fact. 'The energy within this bracelet can assist you if the need arises. But for now, Thomas seems to be making steady progress with his abilities. I trust he can be relied upon.'

Louder, so Thomas could hear, he said, 'I must return to the Spirit World, but remember what I said. If you encounter any trouble, go back to the Agency immediately.'

Before either of them could respond, he vanished, leaving behind only a faint ripple in the air. Thomas stared at the spot where Arthur had been, his brow furrowed in confusion.

'How does he do that?' he murmured.

Emilia didn't have an answer for him. She was still entranced with the bracelet on her wrist, its faint glow a reminder of Arthur's strange abilities. As dawn began to break, the soft light of the rising sun painted the front lawn in shades of gold and amber. Emilia and Thomas walked across the grass, their steps slow and aimless. They had permission to continue their investigation, but neither had a clear idea of where to begin.

For Emilia, the silence was filled with thoughts of Arthur. His recent behaviour gnawed at her. He had been more lenient, more concerned, and far more protective than she had ever seen him be. In all her time with the Agency, he had never shown such consideration. The shift in his manner was unsettling, and she couldn't shake the feeling that something fundamental had changed between them.

Lost in her thoughts, Emilia wasn't paying attention to her surroundings. She stepped off the curb and crossed the empty street, only to recoil as an intense, unfamiliar sensation ripped through her. Her body dissipated into smoke, a reflexive reaction to the sudden shock. She collapsed onto the asphalt, slowly reforming into her solid shape. Her wide eyes stared unseeing, memories flashing vividly before her mind's eye.

She heard Thomas' voice calling her name, his face coming into focus through the haze of images. Yet her body betrayed none of the terror coursing through her. She felt calm, unnaturally so, despite the flood of memories overwhelming her.

It felt wrong.

But it wasn't.

This was how it felt to be *dead*.

She turned her head just in time to catch the fading taillights of a car disappearing around the bend. She closed her eyes and exhaled shakily.

'Emilia! What happened? Are you okay?' Thomas' words came in a rush as he crouched beside her, each syllable tinged with panic.

She eased herself into a sitting position, her breathing slowly levelling out.

'I . . . I know where we have to go.'

'What? What are you talking about?'

She remembered.

'I know where we have to go,' she repeated.

'Where?'

'Hope Spring Memorial.'

'Okay, fine. But are you sure you're all right?'

Emilia brushed off his concern, mumbling almost to herself. 'I was hit by a jeep in the parking lot of that hospital. I was on my way to visit my brother. I couldn't remember the name of the place before but seeing that car just now . . . it triggered something. I think we finally have a lead.'

19

Thomas groaned as he lay sprawled on the ground. Agreeing to accompany Emilia to the hospital had seemed like a good idea at the time, but he'd conveniently forgotten what travelling with the master skeleton key entailed. The void they had fallen through had left him disoriented, and the landing had been as unceremonious as always. Rolling onto his back, he took a moment to stare at the overcast sky before forcing himself upright.

Hope Spring Memorial Hospital loomed before them, an imposing structure of concrete and glass. Thomas vaguely recognized the building, having visited it once or twice before, but it held no real significance to him. For Emilia, however, the sight of it sent a shiver through her. This place was steeped in memories she'd rather not revisit, yet it was also central to everything she was trying to uncover. Her brother's admission here had tethered her to it, even after death.

A chunk of her memory had been missing since she'd died, leaving her with gaps she couldn't fill.

She'd known her brother was unwell and that she'd been working to help him, but the name of the hospital and the details of his condition had remained elusive. Until now. The sudden return of her memories felt like puzzle pieces snapping into place, yet the clarity came at a price. Alongside the images of her brother came the ache of grief and pain she'd tried to suppress. He hadn't merely been unwell; he'd been in a coma for months. Her last visit had been marked by the doctor's grim prognosis: his chances of waking were slim.

The air inside the hospital was heavy with the sterile, antiseptic scent Emilia knew all too well. It mingled faintly with the aroma of coffee wafting from the vending machines lining the hallways. Overhead, fluorescent lights bathed everything in a harsh glow, the artificial brightness contrasting sharply with the dim natural light filtering through narrow windows.

Emilia led the way through the corridors with an ease born of repetition. Her steps were automatic, guided by the muscle memory of someone who'd walked these paths countless times. Faded posters promoting health and wellness lined the walls, the cheerful slogans at odds with the tension that seemed to hang in the air. She weaved through nurses and doctors with practised agility, determined to avoid collisions that would cause her to dissipate into mist.

Room after room passed in a blur of quiet activity. The muted symphony of hospital life surrounded them: the rustle of bedsheets, the low hum of conversations, the steady beeping of monitors. In one room, a newborn's cries filled the air, mingling with the whispered relief of exhausted parents. In another, a family huddled close, their shared grief palpable even through closed doors. The juxtaposition of life and loss was a reminder of the fragile balance this place represented.

Emilia's grip on her emotions tightened as they neared their destination. The memories resurfacing in her mind were relentless, but she forced herself to focus.

The farther they ventured, the quieter it became, until Emilia came to a stop in front of a room adjacent to the nurses' station. From inside, the muted beeping of monitoring equipment and the soft hum of ventilators formed a steady rhythm, muffled by the closed door. A nameplate affixed to the wall read, 'E. Elliot'.

Thomas leaned closer to peer through the rectangular glass pane on the door.

'Your brother?' he asked.

Emilia nodded.

'Eldon.'

'What happened to him?'

For a moment, she was silent, her gaze fixed ahead as though lost in her own memories. Thomas waited, sensing the difficulty of whatever she was about to say. When she finally spoke, her voice was soft, almost a whisper.

'He jumped.'

Thomas' eyes flicked back to the room beyond the glass. If her brother's circumstances were somehow connected to Emilia's death, then it seemed unlikely that Eldon had jumped intentionally. But he kept his thoughts to himself. The topic was delicate, and he had no desire to speculate without more information.

Instead, he asked gently, 'Do you know why he did it?'

Emilia shrugged, her movements small and uncertain.

'The police said he jumped. That's all I know. They never gave me any details.'

He mulled this over before speaking again.

'Was he acting strange before it happened? Different?'

Emilia's expression shifted, as though she was trying to pull a buried memory to the surface. Slowly, she nodded.

'He called me a few days before it happened. He sounded . . . panicked. Distracted. It wasn't like him at all. Usually, we'd meet once a week for dinner, but this time, he insisted on coming over to my place. I agreed because he seemed so shaken.'

'Did he say what was wrong?'

'Eldon's an investigative journalist, and he never shares details about his work, especially when it's ongoing. But that night, he couldn't stop talking about an article he was working on.'

'What was the article about?'

Emilia frowned, her fingers twitching slightly as she tried to recall.

'It was about a tech company. What was it called again . . .? Tech Inc . . . EverTech . . . no, it was J.Tech, I think.'

J.Tech.

The name hit Thomas like a bolt of lightning, sending a jolt through him. His eyes widened as a flood of memories cascaded back, vivid and undeniable. The sterile hospital corridor seemed to fade around him as he was transported to another time and place—a storage unit filled with stacks of documents, the glow of a desk lamp illuminating the scattered evidence before him. He could almost smell the stale coffee and hear the rustle of paper as he sifted through records, the shape of a dark conspiracy slowly emerging.

He remembered everything now: the suspicious transactions, the invasive surveillance practices, the encrypted emails, and the elusive CEO who seemed to operate above the law. J.Tech had been at the centre of his final investigation. He had been close to uncovering something monumental when his life had been cut short.

Thomas drew in a sharp, shaky breath as the realization settled over him. He glanced again at Eldon's room, his mind racing. Had Eldon's investigation into J.Tech been connected to what had happened to him? The implications were chilling. The name J.Tech had unlocked a door, and beyond it lay a path Thomas knew he had to follow, no matter the cost. He remembered everything now, including his misgivings about Marcel and Blake. Before his death, he'd long suspected that the two were somehow involved with the tech company but he hadn't been able to prove it.

'J.Tech,' he murmured, his voice hoarse.

Emilia turned to him. 'What is it? Do you know the company?'

Thomas swallowed hard.

'I was investigating your death in connection to J.Tech before I died. I don't know everything yet, but I was onto something big.'

'The same company my brother was looking into?'

Thomas nodded grimly.

'They're at the centre of everything. Your brother probably dug too deep, and now he's in a coma. You heard about his investigation, and now you're . . . dead.'

Emilia's voice trembled.

'Wait. Are you saying . . .?'

'Yes,' Thomas said, his tone heavy with certainty. 'You weren't in an accident, Emilia. You were *murdered*.'

20

Emilia felt as though she were in a dream she couldn't wake from as she stood in the hallway outside her brother's hospital room. The muffled beeping of monitors inside seemed distant, almost muted, as her mind buzzed with Thomas' revelation.

She had always believed her death was an accident, a cruel twist of fate. But now, the truth hit her like a tidal wave.

It hadn't been an accident.

It had been *murder.*

A cold, creeping sensation spread through her, a chill that no warmth could dispel. Her mind reeled, struggling to comprehend the implications.

Murder.

Someone in J.Tech had wanted her dead. But, *why*?

Her gaze drifted to the glass panel on the door, through which she could see her brother's still form lying on the hospital bed. Fear and confusion twisted in her chest. What had he been investigating that was so dangerous that it had cost both their lives? She rued the day she hadn't paid more attention to his panicked ramblings. If she had, maybe they wouldn't be as clueless as they were now.

Her fingers brushed against the bracelet on her wrist, the slight warmth of its energy grounding her. The rhythmic thrumming reminded her of the person who had given it to her, allowing her a moment to think.

If someone had gone to such lengths to kill her, what else were they capable of? How long would her brother remain safe while unconscious? It seemed they had left him alone for now, but for how long? The questions ran rampant in her head, each one more urgent than the last.

She clenched her jaw, feeling a surge of unexpected determination. Whoever had done this had to be stopped. She would unravel the tangled web that, according to Thomas, surrounded J.Tech. She had to protect her brother from the dangers he had unknowingly invited and see her murderer punished.

'What should we do?' she asked.

Thomas regarded her, his own expression grim but resolved. Before he could respond, Emilia straightened her posture. Even as the words left her mouth, she realized she already knew the answer. She would discover the truth—no matter the cost.

'You're back sooner than I expected,' was the first thing Arthur said when they arrived at the Agency. 'Is everything well?'

Emilia and Thomas exchanged a glance. He gave her a small nod of encouragement, which she returned before addressing Arthur.

'I found out how I died,' she began. 'And . . . you were wrong. I didn't die in a car accident.'

'Oh?'

Arthur's expression remained impassive, his curiosity betrayed only by a faint glimmer in his eyes. He leaned back slightly, waiting for her to continue, his demeanour calm and unreadable. He showed no sign of surprise or distress at her words.

'I was—' She faltered, the admission sticking in her throat. The truth was a bitter pill, much more difficult to speak than she had anticipated.

'Emilia.'

Arthur's voice was low and measured, cutting through her hesitation. There was no question in his tone, only a quiet insistence that drew her back from the haze of her thoughts. She blinked, then shook her head as if to dispel her uncertainty, embarrassed by her inability to continue. Dead was dead, regardless of how it had happened. Nothing would change that.

'Emilia,' he repeated. 'What is it?'

This time, she did not hesitate.

'I was murdered,' she said.

The room fell silent. Arthur's expression was unflinching, the gravity of her words seeming to slide off him like water off stone.

'Well,' he said at last. He glanced between Emilia and Thomas. 'You've accomplished what you set out to do. Are you ready to return to your work at the Agency now?'

Thomas frowned, his brows knitting together in confusion. Arthur's dismissal of such a significant revelation struck him as odd, even callous.

'No, we came to—'

'No?' Arthur cut him off, his voice edged with irritation, the first emotion he had shown since their arrival.

'No,' Thomas repeated firmly. 'As I was about to say, we came to update you on our findings and to inform you of our plans to proceed.'

A shadow passed over Arthur's features, and his gaze snapped to Emilia.

'I'm afraid I don't follow. You came to me with a request to investigate your death. You've investigated, and now you know how you died. That concludes your investigation, does it not? There is nothing else to be done.'

His words were clipped, dismissive. The indifference grated on Emilia, a sting of regret blooming within her. How foolish she had been to think he would care, to believe that sharing this news with him would elicit something more than cold pragmatism. If she had known this would be his reaction, she never would have chosen to return to the Agency first or confide in him at all.

Thomas explained the rest of what they had discovered. When he finished, he said, 'We're going to continue the investigation. I want to finish what I started before I died.'

Arthur nodded but did not respond immediately. Thomas felt compelled to remind him of their agreement and said, 'You permitted us to investigate.'

'I agreed to let Emilia discover the reason behind her death, that is all,' Arthur corrected. 'But I cannot permit you to continue now that the objective of your involvement has changed. I have told you time and time again that the dead do not interfere with the life of the Living, and I cannot agree to what you have in mind.'

'How is this any different from looking into Emilia's death?' Thomas protested.

'You are asking to bring down an entire organization in the Living World. It is not the same,' Arthur said. 'Interference of this magnitude cannot be allowed. I will say it as many times as it takes for you to understand: the dead do not intrude upon the life of the Living.'

Thomas clenched his fists at his sides, the simmering frustration threatening to boil over. This was more than just a mission; it was something he needed to do. He had to expose J.Tech, bring them down, and reveal their wrongdoings. It was a task he had dedicated months of his life to, and though he wished he could let it go, he couldn't shake the bitterness that clung to him. A small, unkind part of him blamed Emilia for his untimely death. Rationally, he knew it wasn't her fault. He had already been in a precarious position, but his anger, raw and restless, found an outlet in her.

He exhaled slowly, trying to redirect his anger into a more productive channel. Why had Arthur been so willing to allow Emilia her investigation yet stood so resolute against his desire to continue? It was a question that gnawed at him, the answer just out of reach.

Then, he recalled the subtle moments when Arthur seemed to soften around Emilia. An uncharacteristic tenderness lingered in his voice and in the brief glances he stole at her, details that Thomas had noticed only because he had been watching from the sidelines. Time and again, Arthur's usual sternness had wavered when Emilia had been involved.

Emilia, with her gentle smile and unassuming charm, had a way of lowering Arthur's defences. It was not deliberate on her part, yet it was undeniably effective. Thomas faltered, recognizing the line he was about to cross. He was teetering on the edge of manipulation, but desperation overrode his scruples. If he couldn't appeal to Arthur directly, perhaps he could use the one person who seemed to hold sway over him.

'Emilia needs this too,' he said. The words came out in a rush, almost before he had the chance to think better of it.

Arthur's eyes met Emilia's, and the iron in his expression cracked for a moment. A flicker of confusion and uncertainty crossed his features. Sensing his opening, Thomas pushed forward despite the guilt gnawing at him.

'Her brother was involved with J.Tech,' he said. 'She was likely killed because of them too. She wants to see them taken down just as badly as I do. As long as the people behind J.Tech aren't dealt with, her brother will always be in danger. Don't you see that? We have to do this.'

The rigidity in Arthur's posture loosened as he processed Thomas' words. The mention of Emilia's brother seemed to give him pause, and her supposed motivations added gravity to the situation.

'Is that true?' he asked her. 'You want to see this through because of your brother?'

Thomas' heart raced. He stood motionless, silently pleading with Emilia. He hoped she would back him up, knowing full well how much depended on her response. He braced himself, ready to intervene if she said anything to undermine his argument.

Emilia hesitated, her thoughts racing. Her reasons for wanting to investigate J.Tech were deeply personal, rooted in fear for her brother's safety and a need to uncover the truth. And though Thomas had never said it outright, she felt responsible for his death. If she hadn't gone to the storage facility, he might still be alive, possibly even on the verge of taking J.Tech down himself. It was an unspoken burden they both carried, one they had agreed not to dwell on. But now, standing under Arthur's scrutiny, she saw how desperately Thomas needed this.

'I'm dead because of J.Tech, but this isn't about me any more,' she said. 'Thomas is right. I am worried about my brother. And I will be as long as J.Tech still poses a threat to him. I don't want him to end up here too.'

A wave of relief washed over Thomas as he caught her gaze and mouthed a silent ‘thank you’. She gave him a small nod in return. But their hopes were shattered instantaneously when Arthur spoke.

‘I’m sorry,’ he said. ‘But I cannot agree to this. It’s too risky.’

They felt the finality of his words like the blow of a hammer. Thomas’ relief turned to agitation in an instant, but Arthur’s answer left no room for argument.

It was a resolute *no*.

21

Thomas had been confident his ploy would work, and Arthur's swift dismissal caught him off guard. His stomach churned as Arthur's disapproval settled heavily on him, irritation and unease threatening to fracture his composure.

'No?' Thomas repeated, his voice strained with disbelief.

'You must not interfere with the lives of the Living,' Arthur said, his tone maddeningly calm.

The measured response grated on Thomas' nerves.

'You're starting to sound like a broken record,' he snapped.

That steely determination, the kind born from sheer stubbornness, was something Arthur knew well. Thomas wasn't going to back down. Not this time.

'Arthur, you have to understand. These are not good people. I've been working on this case for months, gathering evidence to bring them down. Now it's all gone, destroyed. If I don't act, they'll continue to wreak havoc,' Thomas pressed, desperation edging his voice.

Arthur's expression didn't change.

'It is not our concern, Thomas. You must learn to let it go.'

Rage simmered beneath Thomas' skin, threatening to explode at Arthur's nonchalance. He hated resorting to this, but he knew it was the only way to break through that stoic exterior of his.

'Emilia's brother is going to *die*, and it will be your fault,' Thomas snarled. 'When that happens, you'll be the one who stood in our way, the one who let the people responsible walk free.'

Emilia went pale at Thomas' dire proclamation. Arthur's composure cracked as he clenched and unclenched his hands, the conflict written plainly in the movement.

'They might not go after your brother,' Arthur said at last, addressing Emilia directly. His voice, though controlled, lacked its usual confidence. 'You cannot be sure.'

'But they might, Arthur,' Emilia said. 'You cannot be certain of that. And I wouldn't be able to forgive myself if I let this go and they end up killing him.'

The unspoken accusation was loud between them: *I would not be able to forgive you either.*

Something unfamiliar tightened in Arthur's chest. The thought of Emilia's anger unsettled him, leaving a faint nausea twisting in his stomach. For the first time in years, his conviction wavered.

'It is not safe,' he said, his tone unusually imploring. 'Even if I were to turn a blind eye and grant you the permission you seek, it is not safe. That alone is reason enough to deny your request.'

He paused, choosing his next words with care.

'I truly am sorry, but I cannot, in good conscience, allow either of you to continue this investigation.'

The sincerity in his voice only deepened Emilia's irritation.

'You're not sorry,' she said bitterly.

'I am,' Arthur insisted.

'You're not.'

'Emilia—' he began, but she turned away, not wanting to listen to anything more he had to say to her.

'You're not going to change your mind?' Thomas asked.

Arthur shook his head.

'No. My decision is final.'

Thomas expected it, yet anger still tightened his jaw.

'Come on,' he said, turning to Emilia. 'Let's go.'

He reached for her hand, intent on leading her out of the office, but Arthur's sharp voice stopped them in their tracks.

'Where do you think you're going?'

Thomas turned back, defiance plain on his face.

'We don't have to stand here and listen to you. We can carry on with our investigation without your permission. You don't have the authority to stop us.'

Arthur's gaze hardened, a chill creeping into his tone.

'In case you've forgotten, you are still employed by the Agency. I do have authority over you. *Both* of you,' he said. 'And let me remind you, in case you haven't read your Spirit Manual in full: spirits who wish to remain in the Spirit World are required to maintain employment. Without it, you will be sent for judgment.'

Thomas stared at him, stunned, as Arthur said, 'That's what you were about to say, wasn't it? That you intend to quit the Agency?'

Emilia clenched her fists, resisting the urge to wipe the smug look off his face. His usual stoicism was irritating enough, but this . . . this air of self-satisfaction was unbearable.

'You can quit if you insist,' Arthur went on, 'but understand this: you will not have time to pursue your investigation. I was lenient enough to grant you permission to look into your deaths. No one else will be so accommodating.'

'You aren't being accommodating now, are you?' Thomas muttered.

But he knew Arthur was right. Thomas hadn't read the Spirit Manual cover to cover, but he didn't doubt the truth of Arthur's words. If they left the Agency without securing another position, they'd lose their place in the Spirit World. And if that happened, their chances of taking down J.Tech would vanish entirely.

Thomas tightened his grip on Emilia's hand and resumed pulling her towards the door. He needed space to think and privacy with Emilia to figure out their next move. But Arthur misread the movement.

'*Stop*.'

The command froze them in place. The tension in the room grew heavier, pressing down on them like a physical weight.

Emilia felt a sudden tug on her arm, a force pulling her back. She glanced down, and to her horror, black smoke was spilling out from the gemstone set into the bracelet Arthur had given her. The smoke stretched and twisted like a living rope, its other end coiling around Arthur's forearm. His fingers gripped it tightly, his knuckles white.

'I am not letting you leave,' he said, his voice low and iron-hard.

Emilia stopped moving. Not because the smoke was restraining her, but because of the sheer force of Arthur's rage. She had never seen him like this before.

His face was a portrait of controlled fury. His normally emotionless eyes were dark and stormy, blazing with an intensity that rooted her in place. His jaw was clenched so tightly that the muscles in his face twitched, his brows drawn together in a fierce line. Every detail of his expression radiated a ferocity that she hadn't known he was capable of. And the way his gaze locked onto her, unwavering and almost accusatory, made her feel like she was the only other person in the room.

Instinct kicked in, and she tried to pull free from the smoky tether. When that failed, she fumbled with the bracelet, clawing at it in a desperate attempt to remove it. But it wouldn't budge. The metal clung to her wrist like it had been fused there, seamless and immovable.

'Arthur, let go,' she demanded, her voice shaking.

Her struggle only seemed to fuel his anger. He wound the smoky rope tighter around his arm, shortening it and drawing her closer inch by inch. His movements were slow but deliberate, a quiet assertion of power that made her pulse quicken.

Thomas, still gripping her other hand, dug in his heels, trying to keep her from being dragged away. But Arthur's strength was undeniable, and the pull of the smoke was relentless. Despite Thomas' efforts, Emilia found herself being hauled forward like deadweight caught between them.

When she was close enough, Arthur grabbed her wrist, firm and unyielding. His touch was cold like steel, and she realized with growing dread that there was no way to fight him off. Thomas' hand slipped from hers, and she felt the loss acutely, the absence of his grounding presence leaving her feeling untethered.

And then, everything disappeared. The room, the air, the faint hum of tension. All of it dissolved into a sea of darkness. The smoke enveloped her completely, swallowing her whole. She had been pulled into a chasm, the world vanishing in an instant.

Emilia gasped, but no sound escaped her. There was nothing to see, nothing to hear, only the crushing void closing in from all sides. Panic surged through her as she tried to make sense of what had happened, but the answer eluded her. She was alone, adrift in the darkness, with no idea of what awaited her next.

22

Emilia stumbled as the world around her shifted abruptly, Arthur's office dissolving into a void of pitch black. Her breath hitched, and she instinctively reached out, but her hands met nothing but empty air. She blinked rapidly, trying to adjust to the darkness, but it was impenetrable, a suffocating shroud that swallowed all light.

Her heart pounded in her chest, each beat echoing loudly in her ears. She could hear her own breathing too, quick and shallow, the sound unnervingly loud. She turned in place, searching for any point of reference, but the darkness was absolute, stretching endlessly in all directions. She felt for the bracelet around her wrist. It was still there, but she couldn't sense the smoke tugging on it any longer.

'Arthur?'

She'd said it softly, but it sounded unnaturally loud in this space of nothingness, the sound swallowed almost immediately by the surrounding darkness. Panic began to claw at the edges of her mind. She had never experienced anything like this—a complete and utter absence of light and sound. Her eyes were open, but she could not see a thing, not even her hands right in front of her. It was unnerving.

She could feel her skin prickling, as if the darkness itself were a living entity, brushing against her with cold, invisible fingers. She took a tentative step forward, her footfall eerily silent on an unseen surface. The ground beneath her was solid, but it offered no comfort.

'Arthur?' she called again, louder this time, desperation creeping into her voice.

She strained her ears for any response, but the silence was absolute. Her mind raced with questions and fears. Where was she? Why was Arthur so angry, and why had he brought her here?

Just as her composure began slipping, a faint, almost imperceptible light flickered in the distance. It was a pinprick of white in the vast expanse of black, wavering like a distant star. Emilia's heart leapt with hope and apprehension. She took another step towards it, then another, her movements cautious and hesitant.

As she moved closer, the light grew brighter, revealing a shadowy silhouette within its glow. Arthur stood there, his figure sharp and defined against the encroaching darkness. He looked eerily calm amid the chaos raging in her mind. She must've looked scared and frazzled, yet he appeared pristine and unbothered, his hands in his pockets as he watched her. His eyes, usually so emotionless, now gleamed with a ferocity that sent a shiver down her spine. His anger had yet to abate.

'Arthur?' Emilia's voice was a whisper, carried away by the emptiness around them. 'Where am I? What is this place?'

'A separate domain under my control,' he replied, his voice low and resonant.

His words were as calm as his bearing, but there was an unmistakable edge to them.

'Why did you bring me here?' she asked.

Arthur's gaze faltered, his anger ebbing as he advanced towards her, the darkness around them seeming to pulse with his movement.

'Because we need to talk, and this is the only place where we won't be interrupted,' he said quietly before narrowing his eyes at her. 'Nor will you be able to run away.'

The shadows seemed to press in closer, their presence tangible. The oppressive darkness felt almost alive, surrounding her like a sentient force. It took all her willpower to keep her fear in check. She nodded slowly, her gaze darting back to Arthur, who seemed utterly at ease in the unsettling void. The faint glow around him offered the only semblance of light, a fragile island in the consuming black.

Her voice wavered as she spoke.

'Arthur . . . ' she gestured to the darkness enveloping them. 'Spirits can't do this. This'—she glanced at the bracelet on her wrist—'this isn't normal. What are you?'

Her words hung in the air, laced with suspicion and unease.

'You're not a spirit.'

Arthur's face remained impassive, though his eyes darkened. He took a slow, deliberate breath, as if bracing himself. The shadows around them seemed to ripple in response to his exhale.

'I'm a Grim Reaper,' he said. It was the first time he had ever admitted the truth aloud, and the admission felt heavy in the space between them. Yet, there was no hesitation because *she* was the one asking. He had chosen to tell her and no one else.

Emilia's stomach dropped. Her blood turned cold, and she took a step back, staring at him with wide eyes. The myths, the stories of Grim Reapers—beings who wielded immense power, who shepherded souls to their final destination—flooded her mind. She had always thought they were mere folklore, twisted embellishments of the truth. But now, standing before one? It was too much to process.

'You're a Grim Reaper?' she echoed. Her thoughts raced, tripping over themselves as fear and disbelief warred within her. 'How? Why?'

Arthur's features softened, a faint trace of sorrow flickering in his eyes. The anger that had dominated his expression moments earlier had dissipated, replaced by something more complex.

'I didn't choose this,' he said, his voice quieter now, almost resigned. 'It's what I am, *who* I am. My ability to share my energy with others, and this domain . . .' He made a sweeping motion with his arm at the endless void around them. 'It all comes with it.'

He paused, letting his words settle over her. 'But I didn't bring you here to explain what I am. I brought you here because there's something you need to know. Something that concerns your . . . venture with Thomas.'

At the mention of Thomas, a new wave of anxiety gripped her.

'He's fine,' Arthur interrupted, his tone leaving no room for doubt. 'He's outside the domain. But he is fine.'

She swallowed hard, gathering her courage for the conversation ahead.

'What is it you need to tell me?'

Arthur ran a hand through his hair, dishevelling it in a rare show of frustration. For the first time, he looked less composed, the cracks in his calm exterior showing.

'I need to apologize for what happened earlier. For losing control.' He paused. 'For using my energy on you like that. It was . . . unforgivable.'

Emilia frowned, her gaze dropping to the bracelet still encircling her wrist. The gemstone glinted faintly in the dim light, its presence a reminder of everything that had just happened.

'Did you give me this so you could control me?' she asked, her tone sharper than she intended.

'*No*,' Arthur said quickly. His expression shifted to one of alarm, almost as if the suggestion itself had wounded him. 'Never. I would never do that to you.'

He stepped closer.

'That bracelet was meant to protect you. I told you that when I gave it to you, and I meant it. What I did out there . . . that wasn't planned. I wasn't thinking. I let my emotions get the better of me, and for that, I'm sorry.'

They stood in silence after his apology, the shadows around them shifting uneasily, mirroring the tension between them.

'I'm not against you investigating your death, but I cannot allow you to get involved with the Living in the way that you intend to. Bringing down an entire organization for its misdeeds . . . It's not what we do. We're *dead*, Emilia. There are boundaries we do not cross.'

'You already said all that,' she mumbled, her voice laced with frustration.

'And you're not listening,' he said wearily.

'You're my boss, not my keeper. I want to help Thomas. My brother is involved. I'm not going to stand by and do nothing. I don't want him ending up here, like me.'

A flicker of something vulnerable crossed Arthur's face, and for a moment, the darkness seemed to falter.

'I don't want you getting involved with the Living to such an extent,' he said softly. 'It's dangerous. More dangerous than you realize.' He drew in a breath.

'I cannot bear the thought of something horrible happening to you outside the Spirit World.'

Emilia stared at him, stunned. The words were filled with an emotion she couldn't quite name. Her mind raced, trying to reconcile the stoic, detached Arthur she knew with the one standing before her now, his usual calm cracking under his emotions.

She shook her head, her defiance rekindling.

'You don't get to make that call,' she said. 'I have a right to make my own choices. You can't control everything and expect me to just go along with it.'

Arthur's expression tightened, his conflict evident. He took another step closer to her, the shadows pulling back as if giving them space. His voice, when he spoke, was earnest.

'I know. And I'm sorry for how I've behaved. But . . . I *care* about you more than you realize. My actions were wrong, but my intentions were honest. I only want to protect you.'

'I can take care of myself,' she said, though the uncertainty in her voice betrayed her lack of confidence.

'What's going on, Arthur? You're saying weird things and acting even weirder. I don't understand what's happening, and you're not making it any easier.' She gestured around them. 'All of this just because you needed to talk to me?'

'And the things you're telling me . . .' she hesitated. 'You care about me? You want to protect me? To keep me safe? What are you talking about, Arthur?'

His shoulders tensed. The shadows around them shifted again, restless and uneasy.

'I haven't been entirely honest with you,' he said. 'I . . . I knew you before. When you were alive. We were friends. At least, I'd like to think we were.'

Emilia's breath caught in her throat, her mind reeling. Before? When she was alive? She searched his face for answers, but he continued before she could speak.

'And since then,' he added, 'I've become . . . fond of you. Quite fond, in fact. More than I should be.'

The admission, raw and vulnerable, left Emilia at a loss for words. She stared at him, her emotions a chaotic tangle of confusion, anger, and something else she couldn't yet define. For the first time, she saw Arthur not as the enigmatic figure of authority she had always known, but as something more.

Something achingly human.

23

The hospital corridors were dimly lit, the harsh fluorescents casting a sterile, cold glow on the white-tiled floors. Arthur moved through them, unseen by the Living, his presence a shadow among shadows. As a Grim Reaper, he was accustomed to the solemn silence of hospital rooms, the soft beeping of machines, and the faint scent of antiseptic. Tonight, he was here for another soul, a terminally ill patient in room 314.

As he neared the room, the door creaked open. A young woman stepped inside, carrying a small bouquet of daisies. Arthur paused, his interest piqued. She wasn't there for the man he was going to reap. Quietly, he followed her inside, his form blending seamlessly into the shadows.

The woman scanned the room, her gaze landing on an elderly man sharing the space. She approached his bedside with a gentle smile.

'Good evening, Mr Emerson,' she said softly, placing the flowers on the small table beside him.

'The nurses told me you like daisies, so I thought I'd bring some for you.'

Arthur lingered near the doorway, watching as she pulled up a chair and sat down. She spoke to the unconscious man as though he could hear her, her voice warm and soothing. She talked about the weather, her brother's slow recovery, and little details about her day. There was no response from the man, but she didn't seem to mind. She brushed a strand of hair from her face, her expression serene and unguarded.

Arthur couldn't look away. Her presence was a stark contrast to the task he was there to perform. She brought a sense of life to the sterile, sombre room, and for the first time in centuries, he felt a flicker of something unfamiliar. It was faint, almost imperceptible, but it stirred in his chest all the same.

Over the next few days, Arthur saw her again and again. Each time he visited the hospital, she was there, speaking to different patients with that same gentleness. He learned that her name was Emilia and that she came to the hospital every day to visit her comatose younger brother. Her dedication and kindness drew him in, though he didn't fully understand why. She was like a beacon of light in the otherwise grim environment. A warmth he could not ignore.

Finally, on a quiet afternoon, he decided to make himself known to her. He wasn't sure what compelled him to do it, only that the pull was too strong to resist.

He found her in the hospital cafeteria, her nose buried in a book as she sipped on a cup of tea. Taking a deep breath, he cloaked himself in the guise of a living man—an ordinary visitor—and approached her table.

'Hi,' he said, sliding into the seat across from her. 'Mind if I join you?'

She looked up, startled. Her eyes, a soft shade of brown, met his, and for a moment, she said nothing. Time seemed to stretch, the bustling cafeteria fading into the background. Arthur gave her a small, hesitant smile, which Emilia reciprocated warmly. She closed her book.

'Not at all. Are you here visiting someone?' she asked, her voice carrying the gentle kindness he had come to associate with her.

Arthur nodded, slipping into his carefully constructed role as a concerned relative.

'Yes, my . . . uncle. He's not doing too well.'

Her expression softened, and her eyes reflected genuine sympathy.

'I'm sorry to hear that. Hospitals can be tough places. I do hope things get better for him.'

'Thank you,' Arthur murmured, finding himself momentarily caught off guard by her sincerity.

They talked for a while, the conversation starting with polite pleasantries before delving into more personal anecdotes. Arthur was fascinated by her outlook on life. Despite the obvious pain she carried, Emilia's kindness was unwavering, her spirit resilient. She had an uncanny ability to find light in the darkest corners, and he found himself drawn to her in a way that unsettled him.

Over the next few weeks, their encounters became routine, almost like an unspoken ritual. Whenever Arthur was sent to the hospital, he would seek her out. They'd sit together in the cafeteria or talk in the hallways, their conversations ranging from mundane topics like favourite books to fleeting glimpses of her struggles. Emilia, unaware of his true nature, spoke freely, and Arthur, though careful with his words, found solace in her presence.

With each interaction, the strange warmth in his chest grew, a sensation that both intrigued and confused him. Grim Reapers were not meant to feel, and yet, here he was, anticipating their conversations, seeking her out without reason, pulled by a force he couldn't explain.

Then came the day that shattered the fragile balance he had built.

Arthur had been sent to the hospital for another reaping. The destination was listed as the parking lot, which struck him as unusual but not unheard of. Focused on his task, he didn't dwell on the details, suppressing the faint hope that he might see Emilia again once his duty was complete.

But when he arrived, the sight before him made his heart stop. The only person there was Emilia.

She stood by her car, oblivious to his presence as she rummaged through her bag. The realization hit him then.

She was the soul he had been sent to reap.

Arthur froze, a crack splitting through the calm detachment he had cultivated over centuries. In that moment, every rule, every duty that had governed his existence as a Grim Reaper felt like a cruel joke. For the first time, he loathed what he was.

He couldn't move, couldn't summon the will to approach her. The thought of taking her soul, of extinguishing the light she carried, was unbearable. And yet, he knew there was nothing he could do to stop it. His role was not to intervene, only to guide. But as he watched her, unaware of the fate about to befall her, Arthur felt a deep, wrenching anguish that he couldn't ignore.

In that moment, he understood the depth of what he had come to feel for her.

And it terrified him.

His heart clenched with a pain he didn't know he could feel as the speeding jeep struck her. The sickening sound of the impact echoed in his mind, and he watched helplessly as her life ebbed away before him. He stood there, paralysed, as the world around him seemed to crumble.

She was gone. The one human who had sparked something within him, something he couldn't even name, was now beyond his reach. He knew that once she passed into the Spirit World, she wouldn't remember him. Only memories of the Living remained intact, and he, who had never truly lived, would fade completely from her thoughts.

Never before, in his millennia as a Grim Reaper, had Arthur felt that a life had been so unfairly cut short. Emilia's time had been stolen, her moments with him cruelly severed before they had truly begun. He told himself he was being selfish, but a part of him didn't care. He couldn't let her go. Not like this.

When her soul crossed into the Spirit World, Arthur was there, watching from the sides as she began to adapt to her new reality. To his surprise and unease, she joined the Agency, a decision that set her on a path far removed from the peaceful afterlife most souls chose. Unable to bear the thought of being separated from her, Arthur used his connections to secure a position as the head of the Agency. He justified it as a way to oversee her safety, but deep down, he knew it was his selfishness that drove his decisions.

However, proximity came with a price. Arthur's attempts to remain detached created a chasm between them. He kept his distance, never revealing their prior acquaintance, afraid of confusing or unsettling her. Yet his silence and the stern facade he adopted as her superior only served to alienate her further. Emilia's aversion gnawed at him in ways he couldn't articulate, a constant reminder of his inability to express the emotions swirling inside him.

Still, he continued to watch over her. He followed her progress, silently proud of her resilience and strength. But his resolve began to fracture when Thomas joined the Agency. Arthur couldn't ignore the reckless influence Thomas seemed to have on her. Emilia, once careful and measured, began throwing herself into danger without hesitation. It was as though she were trying to prove something—to herself, to Thomas, to the world. Arthur's unease grew the more time she spent with Thomas.

When Emilia insisted on investigating her death, Arthur begrudgingly allowed it, knowing he couldn't deny her. But the investigation led her to uncover more than just the circumstances of her demise. It revealed a corrupt corporation that had played a role in her death and that of countless others. And when that led to more dangerous ventures—her insistence on taking down the company involved in her death—he knew he had to put his foot down.

Watching her put herself at risk again and again went against every instinct he had. He had failed to protect her in life, but he refused to make the same mistake twice. He couldn't save her then, but he would do everything in his power to keep her safe now.

Even if it meant having to stand in her way.

24

Emilia reeled at Arthur's revelation. Shock gave way to anger, then to something raw and harder to name. They had known each other before her death. Not only had he known her, but he'd also known that she had been murdered. He had *watched* it happen. And all this time, he had said nothing.

The realization hit her hard. The memory of his impassive reaction when she'd first told him about her death surfaced with painful clarity, the way he hadn't even bothered to feign surprise. After all, it hadn't been anything new to him. And now, she'd learned that he had taken on the role as the Agency's head simply to stay by her side while she remained oblivious. He had been content to watch her stumble, ignorant and lost, as she tried to navigate the Spirit World. It stung in a way she couldn't quite articulate, leaving a burning bitterness in her mouth.

'Why didn't you tell me any of this before?' she demanded.

Arthur looked pained, his usual stoicism cracking under her gaze.

'I meant no harm by it; you must believe me. I didn't want to overwhelm you. I thought it would be easier for you to start fresh, without the burden of knowing.'

'Then you shouldn't have said anything at all. If you wanted to spare me, you should have stayed silent.'

'I know,' Arthur admitted. 'You're right. But I had to say something because you're letting Thomas sway you, and I can't let you interfere with things in the Living World.' He paused, his frustration bleeding through as the shadows around them seemed to shift. 'This isn't just about you, Emilia. It's about the balance of life and death. Grim Reapers like me exist to maintain that balance. If you interfere too much, it could lead to catastrophic consequences. I'm trying to prevent that.'

'And I've told you time and time again that my brother's life hangs in the balance. How can you expect me to stand by and do nothing? He might die!'

'The dead should not concern themselves with the Living,' he said. 'I've told you this many times before. I don't expect you to accept it right away, but you must understand. You're not just risking your own peace. You're risking *everything*. We were friends once, Emilia, and I care about you deeply. I cannot stand by and watch you make choices that could unravel things we cannot control.'

Emilia's jaw tightened, her emotions warring within her. She wanted to scream, to demand that he tell her why he hadn't trusted her with the truth earlier. But beneath the anger, there was a flicker of doubt, a seed of something she wasn't ready to confront.

'Friends?' The word tasted bitter. 'Friends don't decide what's best for each other without even talking about it.'

'*This isn't just about you*,' he repeated. 'This goes beyond us. The Living World is dangerous for those who interfere too much. There are forces that will stop at nothing to maintain balance. I do not wish for you to disappear because of it.'

'Disappear? What are you talking about?' she asked.

'Spirits who meddle beyond what is expected of them will cease to exist. They will not return to the Spirit World, they will not be granted reincarnation, and they will not face judgment. They will simply . . . *disappear*.'

Emilia felt it in her chest, the quiet terror beneath her anger as the gravity of his words took hold.

'I am trying to prevent that from happening to you,' he said, no less resolute.

'Why do you care so much?' Her voice cut through the silence. 'You're a Grim Reaper. It shouldn't matter to you what happens to me.'

'I care about you, not out of affection . . . At least, I don't think so.' He faltered, searching for clarity in emotions he barely understood. 'We were friends. I *am* your friend, and I cannot ignore the bond we share. I cannot ignore *you*.'

Emilia drew in a deep breath, her anger shifting into something more fragile, though her resolve held firm.

'If we were friends,' she began, her voice steadier now, 'then you must know how much my brother means to me. Everything I'm doing is for him. What's the point of reincarnation if I have to watch him stay in danger? Just as you vow to protect me, I have to protect him. J.Tech will not stop unless someone stops them. If my brother comes out of his coma, they'll hurt him again.'

'The Living World is no longer for the likes of us,' he said.

'I know! I know,' Emilia said. 'But I *cannot* stand by while my brother is in danger. He's the only family I have left.'

Arthur ran a frustrated hand through his hair. His teeth clenched as he fought the rising tide of anxiety that threatened to overwhelm him. The thought of Emilia putting herself in harm's way was unbearable.

'Emilia,' he began, his voice strained, 'if you interfere too much, you could be destroyed.'

'I know the risks,' she interrupted. 'But I have to do this.'

Arthur closed his eyes, struggling to quiet the storm of conflicting thoughts swirling in his mind. He understood her desperation all too well, her need to do everything she could for her brother. And that understanding had him cornered, leaving him acutely aware of the dangers she faced. As the head of the

Agency and a Grim Reaper, his purpose had always been to maintain the balance between life and death, not to interfere with it.

He wanted to protect her, to shield her from the perils that awaited her in the Living World. But he couldn't ignore the resolve in her eyes, a resolve born from the same fierce determination that had always defined her. Their bond, one forged long before her death and still unbroken, left him with no choice. The decision had already been made, yet it pressed heavily on him.

He sighed, the sound carrying both his resignation and his weariness.

'I can't stop you, can I?' he asked in a quiet, subdued voice. 'You're going to do this no matter what I say.'

'I have to.'

He took a deep breath.

'All right.' He held up a hand before she could react. 'On one condition: you let me come with you. I will help you and Thomas get this done.'

Emilia stiffened, mistrust flickering across her expression. It wasn't that she didn't value his offer, but trust did not come easily any more, not after everything he had withheld. Still, she couldn't afford to refuse. Convincing him to let her confront J.Tech had been an uphill battle and she wasn't going to risk losing his support now.

'You'll need my help if you want to get anywhere with your plan,' Arthur said, recognizing the conflict in her expression. When she furrowed her brow in confusion, he elaborated, 'You're dealing with the Living, people who are alive. Neither you nor Thomas can interact with them directly. You'll hit walls you can't break without someone like me.'

Emilia frowned, the truth of his words sinking in. She hadn't considered the practical challenges they might face once they started the investigation proper and despite her feelings on the matter, she knew he was right. Reluctantly, she yielded.

'Fine. You can come with us.'

'Good,' he said simply, though he appeared to relax a little. 'Then let's get started. We have a lot of work to do.'

The shadows around them shifted, unseen energy rippling through the space. Emilia tensed, bracing herself instinctively as the darkness began to pulse. Without warning, the shadows exploded outward in a burst of light, nearly blinding her. She raised a hand to shield her eyes, her senses reeling from the sudden shift. After a few disorienting seconds, the light receded, and when her vision cleared, she realized they were back in his office. The darkness of his domain was gone, replaced by the muted, sterile lighting of the Agency headquarters. It was as if they had never left.

25

When the curtain of darkness lifted, Emilia found herself back in Arthur's office. Her attention immediately drawn to the hallway beyond the open door, where Thomas was locked in a heated exchange with the office administrator.

'Uhh . . .' Emilia muttered, glancing at Arthur. He made a small, impatient motion, clearly indicating she should deal with it before the situation worsened.

Emilia moved quickly. She caught Thomas by the elbow and steered him away, offering rushed apologies to the furious administrator as they retreated. The woman scowled at Thomas as she smoothed down her blouse, her manner suggesting she would have slapped him if it weren't against protocol.

'What were you doing?' Emilia hissed as soon as they were out of earshot.

Thomas opened his mouth to answer, then stopped short, taken aback by her sudden reappearance. The shock barely had time to settle before the questions came tumbling out.

'What happened? Where did he take you? Are you okay? Did he do something to you?'

'I'm fine, Thomas,' she said, placing a hand on his shoulder to steady him. His frazzled state eased slightly, though worry still lingered in his eyes.

He looked genuinely scared, and she couldn't blame him. If their roles had been reversed and he had disappeared like that, she'd have been terrified too. She owed him an explanation, and it would be better to catch him up on everything before they faced Arthur again.

They found a quieter stretch of hallway, and Emilia filled him in on what had happened: Arthur's revelations, his warnings, and his eventual offer to help. She omitted certain details, like the bond they'd shared before her death, and the unease his conflicted concern had stirred. Those knots were hers to untangle.

When she finished, Thomas' expression darkened.

'He wants to help?' Scepticism sharpened his words. 'I don't trust him. Not after what he did earlier. He was dead set on keeping us from getting involved, and now he suddenly wants to help? I'm not buying it.'

Emilia understood his doubts. Arthur's earlier actions had been questionable at best, and Thomas had every right to be wary. But she couldn't let his misgivings derail their progress. She repeated the same argument that had convinced her to accept Arthur's help.

'He has a point,' she said, her tone measured. 'It's not like either of us can interact with the Living at will. We're still learning, and he'd be a big help.'

Thomas mulled that over, irritation clear in the set of his jaw. Deep down he knew she was right, but that didn't make swallowing his pride any easier. Arthur's earlier stunt had left a bitter taste in his mouth, and he couldn't shake the feeling that trusting him was a mistake.

'Thomas?' Emilia prompted gently. 'Are we good on this?'

A beat passed. Then, reluctantly, he grumbled, 'Yeah, fine.'

'Good,' she said, relieved. 'We should probably go speak to Arthur.'

Back in the office, Arthur had resumed his position behind his desk, already absorbed in a stack of documents. He looked up as they entered, his face a mask of calm indifference. His attention passed over Thomas, who trailed in after Emilia, a glower on his face.

They took their seats opposite him, the air between them heavy with unresolved tension.

'Let's decide what we should do next,' Emilia said, glancing between them, though her focus lingered on Thomas. 'Any ideas?'

Despite his animosity towards Arthur and his reluctance to accept his involvement, Thomas wasn't one to let pettiness cloud his judgement. He exhaled loudly, leaning forward in his seat.

'The Aspen Hollow PD is definitely involved in this somehow, particularly those two: Blake and Marcel. And we also know your brother, Eldon, is tied up in this as well,' he began, his focus solely on Emilia, pointedly excluding Arthur. 'The problem is we have no clue how those two officers are connected, and we don't know exactly what Eldon was working on, or rather, what he uncovered that got him targeted in the first place. I suppose those are good places to start.'

'We should work on—'

'Let's split up,' Thomas cut in.

'Um, okay?' She tilted her head. 'How do you want to do this, then?'

'I've gotten my memories back, and I know those two at the PD. I've got more intel on that front, and I'd be better suited for that.' Confidence edged his tone. 'Likewise, you know your brother better than any of us. I suggest splitting the work to cover more ground. I'll tackle Blake and Marcel, find out how they're tied to all this. You can dig into what your brother was working on. He would've stored his investigation somewhere—a computer, an external hard drive. If you can find that, it'll be a huge step forward.'

Emilia was impressed. Since regaining his memories, Thomas had seemed more assured, almost perfectly embodying the role of a detective. His plan was methodical, and it was clear he had thought it through. She hadn't expected anything less, but the certainty with which he laid out his plans made her regard him with new appreciation. It must have shown on her face, too, because he cleared his throat, his gaze shifting away as a faint blush crept up his neck.

'What? If you've got a better idea, say it,' he muttered, his tone defensive.

'I don't,' Emilia said. 'I think your plan is brilliant.'

Arthur, who had been silent up until this point, finally spoke, 'And my role? What should I do?'

'Do whatever you want,' Thomas spat without looking in Arthur's direction, his irritation surfacing once more.

Emilia tried to salvage the situation. But Arthur didn't flinch at Thomas' harsh tone, remaining unmoved. Emilia couldn't tell if his lack of reaction was a result of patience or sheer indifference, but with Arthur, either seemed plausible.

'In that case, I shall accompany you,' he said, directing his attention to Emilia.

Of course he would choose to go with me, she thought, but she kept the remark to herself. Instead, she reached for the master skeleton key resting against her chest and held it out to Thomas.

'If you're going off on your own, you should take this,' she said. 'Remember to focus on where you want to go before using it.'

He accepted the key after a brief pause, his fingers brushing hers as he gave her a small nod.

'Thanks. Let's meet back here when we're done.'

Then, in a quieter voice meant only for her, he added, 'Be cautious around him. And be careful.'

'You too,' she replied. 'If anything feels wrong, come straight back. Arthur's right about meddling being dangerous. I don't want anything happening to you.'

Thomas gave her a quick, reassuring hug. Even in that moment, his stubbornness persisted, and he refused to acknowledge Arthur, not sparing him so much as a glance. Gripping the master skeleton key tightly, he slid it into the lock on the office door and twisted. The door opened, revealing a swirling void of darkness beyond. Emilia caught a fleeting glimpse of nothingness before Thomas stepped through without looking back. The door closed behind him, leaving only silence in his wake.

26

'He despises me,' was the first thing Arthur said the moment Thomas left.

Emilia looked towards the office door, then back at him. She couldn't deny it, not when Thomas had made it abundantly clear.

'Right now, yes,' she admitted. 'He's still angry about what happened earlier. Give him time. I'm sure he'll be fine once he's had space to cool off.'

Arthur's gaze lingered on the door a moment longer, wondering if she was right about Thomas. Despite how it may seem, he did not enjoy being on bad terms with those under his charge.

'Now then,' he said, 'What shall we do regarding this matter of your brother's investigation? What do you know about it so far?'

'Very little, only that it has deep ties to J.Tech. He mentioned it to me once before, but I can't remember what he said exactly.'

'Did he leave anything with you?'

She shook her head and repeated what she'd already told Thomas: Eldon had visited her a few days before his incident, they'd talked briefly about the new article on J.Tech he was working on, then left without sharing specifics.

'He didn't bring anything with him or say anything strange?' Arthur pressed.

Emilia searched her memory for details that might have been important, but nothing stood out. Once again, she shook her head.

'If he came to my place empty-handed, then he must have left his work somewhere else. We should search his apartment first,' she suggested.

Arthur nodded and extended his hand towards her. When she glanced at it in confusion, he said, 'You gave the master skeleton key to Thomas, remember? We have to travel between the realms my way now.'

'Right . . .' she mumbled, taking his hand. In the blink of an eye, they materialized in front of her brother's apartment. She frowned and tugged gently at their still-clasped hands.

'How do you know Eldon's address?'

He shrugged nonchalantly.

'I know most things. A lot of things, actually.'

She eyed him sceptically, unconvinced. Then, she tugged on their intertwined hands again until he released his hold. She had suggested going to Eldon's place in the hope of finding something—what exactly, she didn't know—that might point them towards his investigation into J.Tech. She had expected it to be challenging, but she hadn't been prepared for the sight that greeted them when they stepped through the front door: complete and utter *chaos*.

Furniture was overturned; drawers had been pulled out, their contents scattered across the floor. Papers were everywhere, some torn and others crumpled as if discarded in a hurry. The living room, once neat and orderly, now looked as though a storm had swept through it. Cushions were ripped open, their stuffing spilling out like entrails. Books lay strewn across the ground, spines broken and pages torn. The coffee table had been upended, one leg snapped, and the glass top shattered, its shards glittering dangerously in the dim light.

'What the hell happened here?' she murmured.

Her brother's usually tidy home was a wreck. Every corner of the apartment bore marks of a thorough and violent ransacking. The kitchen was no better—cabinets had been thrown open, with pots, pans, and broken dishes scattered across the counters and floor.

She wandered into the bedroom, where the bed had been stripped of its sheets and the mattress tossed to one side. Clothes had been flung out of the closet, forming a chaotic pile on the floor. The bedside table lay upturned, a lamp shattered beside it.

It was clear that whoever was responsible had acted in desperation, tearing through the apartment with no regard for the destruction left behind.

'They were here,' Emilia said, horror creeping into her voice as Arthur stepped past her, his eyes scanning the wreckage with detached calmness.

The mess and the violence with which this chaos had been wrought only cemented her resolve to see the investigation through to its end. She had been right: whoever was behind this was still after her brother and his work. Eldon wouldn't be safe as long as they remained in pursuit.

Arthur's presence kept her grounded, and she found some comfort in his unshaken manner.

'They were looking for his work too,' she said.

He nodded, impassive as he surveyed the damage.

'It appears so,' he replied.

'Do you think they found it?'

He gave the room a once-over.

'I doubt it,' he said. 'They wouldn't have been this thorough otherwise. Desperation like this suggests they didn't find what they were looking for.'

Despite the chaos, they decided to search the apartment themselves. Though they didn't know exactly what they were looking for, it was better to leave no stone unturned. Emilia started her search in the bedroom but found nothing out of the ordinary. She moved on to Eldon's study, where the disorder was equally severe.

The desk drawers had been pulled out and emptied, their contents strewn across the floor among scattered books. A chair had been knocked over, and the computer monitor was cracked, hanging precariously off the edge of the desk.

She carefully stepped through the debris, crouching to sift through papers. Her hands still struggled with handling physical objects, but the energy from the bracelet Arthur had given her proved useful. She found she could manipulate it to shift things around with surprising ease. The energy seemed almost intuitive, responding to her intentions.

She was so engrossed in experimenting with the bracelet that she didn't notice Arthur approaching.

'Having fun?' he mused, a rare trace of mirth in his tone.

She startled, nearly falling over, and spun around to glare at him. Her irritation faded quickly, though, when she realized he was smiling. No, not just smiling—he was *laughing.*

She stared at him, wide-eyed and speechless. Never in her life, or rather her death, had she imagined she'd see Arthur laugh. The sound unsettled her more than the ransacked apartment and yet, to her immense horror and confusion, she found she liked the sound of it.

Clearing her throat and gesturing at the bracelet, Emilia mumbled, 'It's like it knows what I want it to do.'

Arthur, who had moved closer to her, followed her gaze to the soft glow emanating from around her wrist.

'Energy is easier to control when you have it in abundance,' he explained. 'You've struggled since becoming an agent because your own reserves are limited. But I imbued the bracelet with a fraction of my energy, so it should be easier for you now.'

He reached out and clasped his hand over the bracelet, his fingers brushing against her wrist. Warmth spread from his touch, and the opal in the bracelet glowed brighter.

'You were using too much,' he said. 'I replenished it so you can continue having fun.'

Emilia frowned, feeling a spark of annoyance.

'I was working,' she protested. 'I wasn't having *fun*.'

Arthur offered no response, but there was a faint hint of fondness in his expression that made her stomach twist uncomfortably.

'Did you find anything?' he asked. She didn't bother asking him the same question. If he'd found anything from his search, she would've been the first to know.

'I was just about to start looking,' she said.

'Together, then,' he replied.

Emilia began her search and moments later, something caught her attention. It was a photograph, or rather, half of a torn photograph. Lifting it carefully, she realized it was an old picture of her and Eldon. She was a teenager then, her arm draped around her brother's shoulders as they laughed, sunburned and carefree during a road trip.

Flipping it over, she found a note scrawled in Eldon's familiar handwriting: '... hidden in plain sight.'

She remembered gifting this photo to Eldon when he'd graduated. The message must have been added later. It could mean nothing, but the unfinished sentence nagged at her. Setting the torn photo down, she began searching for the missing piece.

It took some time, but she finally spotted the other half buried beneath a pile of papers in the corner. She tugged it free and knelt to place the two pieces together, her heart heavy with both relief and sorrow.

The brother she loved was still out of reach, present only through these fragmented clues.

She turned the photo over and read the full message:

The key to everything lies close to my heart, hidden in plain sight.

Her fingers traced the words, a strange unease settling in her chest.

'The key to everything lies close to my heart . . .' she murmured.

'You found something?' Arthur asked when he saw her kneeling by the photograph. He moved towards her, his expression sharpening with interest.

His voice sounded distant as Emilia's mind raced to decipher the meaning behind her brother's cryptic message. If Eldon had taken the time to write something on the back of a photograph of the two of them, it had to mean *something*.

'The key to everything lies close to my heart,' she repeated. 'The key . . .'

She flipped both halves of the photo again, this time scrutinizing the image itself. Her gaze locked onto Eldon's grinning face. Around his neck was a silver necklace, a keepsake he almost never took off. She had seen it countless times, yet she had never given it much thought until now.

Her pulse surged. The *key* close to his *heart*, hidden in plain sight.

The necklace! It had to be.

'I know where we have to go,' she said, her voice filled with urgency as she looked at Arthur.

'Where?'

'Hope Spring Memorial,' she replied. 'We have to get to where my brother is.'

Arthur lifted his hand without question. She moved to take it, then paused, looking back at the torn photograph on the floor. The risk of it being found was too great.

'Can you destroy that before we leave?' she asked.

They weren't supposed to interfere with the Living World, let alone destroy objects that belonged to the Living. But he couldn't refuse her. There was something about being with her like this that stirred a long-forgotten familiarity in his chest. Besides, he suspected they were about to meddle even more significantly anyway.

With a flick of his wrist, the two halves of the photograph disintegrated into fine dust, scattering to the floor. She watched it disappear, then turned back to him.

'Let's go.'

Without another word, she placed her hand in his, and the world around them shifted once more.

27

The sun was dipping below the horizon when Thomas made his unceremonious landing in front of the Aspen Hollow PD building. He avoided looking at himself, aware that the fading light would make him appear eerily translucent, and kept his gaze fixed elsewhere. Looping the master skeleton key around his neck, he slipped it beneath his shirt for safekeeping. If he lost it now, he'd have no way back and would truly be on his own.

Thinking of his isolation pulled his mind towards Emilia, and naturally, to Arthur. Irritation stirred, familiar and unwelcome, but he forced it down. He was still agitated about earlier and couldn't understand why Emilia was so forgiving of Arthur's transgressions. It grated on him, but he knew it wasn't his place to interfere, no matter how much he cared for his friend.

He pushed the feeling aside. There was work to be done: find Blake and Marcel, and uncover their involvement in the case to see how deeply they were tangled in this mess.

He passed through the empty lobby and peered into the bustling workspace beyond. The floor was as busy as the first time he'd been there, but neither Marcel nor Blake were at their desks. Wandering aimlessly through the space, he carefully avoided the throngs of people and somehow found himself in the evidence locker room.

The room was dimly lit, the only source of light coming from the emergency exit sign. As his eyes adjusted to the darkness, he found that he could see surprisingly well. He walked down the cramped rows of shelves, taking note of the stacked boxes that contained evidence from cases spanning years.

Turning the corner, Thomas stopped short. The shelf where Emilia's box should have been was empty. A perfect rectangle of dust marked where it had once rested.

Disappointment tightened his chest. He had hoped to comb through the evidence to jog his fractured memory about the case. Now, even that faint hope was dashed.

Nonplussed, he left the evidence locker and returned to the chaotic workspace. Hovering near Marcel's desk, he scanned the clutter of paperwork scattered across its surface. He tried several times to reach for something, but his hands passed straight through them. The frustration was immediate and biting. He now understood Emilia's struggles with interacting with the physical world. His success with the occult kid, Dean, must have been beginner's luck after all.

Curiously, he discovered that waving his hand through Marcel's computer caused the screen to flicker. His interference seemed to disrupt the signals, a small, strange power he hadn't realized spirits possessed. Filing the observation away for later, he straightened and looked around once more. Where in the world was Marcel? His absence didn't seem to bother anyone else; the other officers remained deeply engrossed in their own work.

On a whim, Thomas stepped outside. Circling the building, he searched the area and finally spotted Marcel by the back entrance. The man was crouched against the wall, his hand quivering as he held a lit cigarette.

The last time Thomas had been at the precinct with Emilia, he recalled catching a faint whiff of cigarette smoke wafting from Marcel as they had passed the stairwell. Now, as he lingered outside the building, the memory clicked into place. If Marcel wasn't at his desk or anywhere inside, he had likely gone for a smoke break.

Thomas stayed in the shadows, taking the opportunity to watch Marcel. He'd known both of them in passing during his life. They were colleagues within the same department and their alleged involvement with J.Tech had come as a complete shock.

Marcel looked worse for wear. Even under the harsh orange glow of the back entrance lamp, Thomas could see the man's pale, haggard features. Dark circles ringed his eyes, and his movements were jittery, his fingers trembling as he brought the cigarette to his lips. He stared straight ahead, lost in thought, his posture radiating unease. Whatever was eating at Marcel had clearly driven him to the edge.

Distracted as they were, neither Marcel nor Thomas realized that they were no longer alone. The soft click of the back door opening and closing had gone completely unnoticed. But Thomas felt it—an unnatural prickle at the back of his neck, a warning that sent a ripple of dread through his spectral form.

He turned, and what he saw nearly unravelled him.

Blake stood there, barely contained fury rolling off him in suffocating waves. Even as a spirit, untouched by the Living, Thomas felt a deep, instinctive chill. This was a rage so potent, so harshly restrained, that it seemed to vibrate in the air—thick and volatile. Blake's eyes were locked onto Marcel with a murderous intensity, and Thomas, for all his ethereal existence, wanted nothing more than to step out of the way.

Blake moved, no, *stormed* forward with a force so intense it seemed to swallow all the sound around him. Before Thomas could retreat, the man walked straight through him, his fury searing like an open flame. Thomas reeled, disoriented, his very essence scattered for an uncomfortable moment before he was pulled back together. Blake's focus was singular, with the kind of unwavering rage that promised violence.

But even in his fury, he retained enough control to act with purpose. His hand shot out, grabbing Marcel by the collar and yanking him forward with brutal efficiency.

Instead of lashing out immediately, Blake dragged Marcel through the narrow alleyway behind the precinct. Marcel's cigarette slipped from his grasp, tumbling to the uneven ground in a scatter of glowing embers. Blake shoved him against the brick wall past a rusted dumpster. His iron grip tightened as he moved, swift and unrelenting. Here, shrouded in darkness, there would be no interruptions. Whatever was coming, it would not have an audience.

None that were living, at least.

'B-Blake,' Marcel stammered.

'What the hell did you do?' Blake snarled, his face inches from Marcel's.

'Nothing, I—' Marcel began, but Blake wasn't having it. He cut him off with a venomous growl.

'The captain just reopened the case Alexander was working on before he died. That doesn't happen unless something big gets flagged. It wasn't me, and it sure as hell wasn't anyone else at the precinct. So, I'll ask you again: *What the hell did you do*?'

Marcel's already pale face turned ashen. He fumbled for words, but no coherent explanation emerged. His silence only fuelled Blake's anger. With a sharp shove, he slammed Marcel harder into the brick wall, his grip tightening around Marcel's collar.

Finally, Marcel managed to sputter, 'I . . . I took something from the evidence.'

Blake's expression darkened, his temper snapping.

'You blithering idiot!' he bellowed, throwing a punch that caught Marcel squarely in the jaw. He crumpled to the ground, clutching his face as blood trickled from his nose.

'I *told* you to leave it alone! I told you tampering would only make things worse! Why the hell didn't you listen?'

Marcel stayed on the ground, his free hand pressed against his bloody nose, unable or unwilling to meet Blake's glare. His silence only seemed to enrage Blake further.

'What did you take?' Blake demanded, his voice sharp and unforgiving.

Marcel faltered, cold sweat beading along his hairline as he stubbornly kept his silence, refusing to answer Blake's question. He avoided looking at the other man, even as Blake loomed over him, his glare cutting like a knife.

The seconds stretched into agonizing minutes, broken only by Blake's sudden, bitter laughter.

'I see,' Blake said, realization flickering in his eyes as he took Marcel's refusal for confirmation. 'You took the documents that could have tied you to the case, didn't you? Cleared any shred of evidence that might have implicated you, and let everyone else burn.'

Marcel's fists clenched tightly at his sides, his teeth grinding audibly.

'I had more to lose than you!' he shot back. 'There was nothing there that would've pointed to you. If they dug any deeper, they'd have known I was involved. I had to do something.'

Blake's expression twisted into a sneer.

'You jeopardized everything when I told you to leave it alone. The case was *closed.* No one was poking around, at least until the documents turned up missing. Now they're tearing it apart.'

Marcel lowered his gaze, his defiance waning under Blake's relentless glare. He didn't regret stealing the documents. If anything, he still believed it had been necessary; it was a move to protect himself if the case ever resurfaced. After all, there was no incriminating evidence against Blake in those files.

'J.Tech wouldn't have done a thing,' he muttered. 'It was up to me to cover my own back.'

Blake scoffed, the sound dripping with contempt.

'Do you really think that was the only copy?'

Marcel stiffened, his eyes finally shifting to meet Blake's. The cold knot of dread in his stomach tightened.

'You really are stupid, Marcel,' Blake spat. 'Alexander didn't find the originals. He found a *copy*. J.Tech's lawyers keep *everything*. Every document, every file, locked away somewhere only they know. So, congratulations, genius, you risked everything for nothing.'

Marcel's mouth opened, but no sound came out. It felt like a bucket of ice water had been dumped over his head.

Blake leaned closer, his voice dropping to a low, menacing whisper.

'You haven't forgotten what they did to that girl and her brother, have you? Do you really want to end up like them? If you're even thinking of leaving J.Tech, think again. They'll destroy you. Hell, they'll destroy everyone you've ever cared about.'

Marcel's face paled even further, his defiance shattered in the face of the truth. He nodded weakly, whatever fight he had left completely drained away.

'Good,' Blake said. Straightening, he glanced towards the precinct's back entrance. 'Now, get back to work. Clean up the mess you made before it gets any worse.'

Marcel dragged himself to his feet, his hands still trembling. He didn't respond, didn't look back, as he shuffled towards the precinct doors. Thomas, who had been silently observing the entire exchange, felt his unease deepen. Whatever secrets these two were guarding, they weren't just dangerous. They were lethal.

28

The blithe way Blake had spoken about Emilia's death and her brother's accident filled Thomas with a senseless rage. He couldn't fathom how anyone could be so indifferent to something so devastating. It was ironic, considering how, as a detective in life, he'd always emphasized the importance of maintaining an emotional distance from cases. He'd preached detachment as a necessity, a shield to protect judgement from being clouded. But now, seeing that very detachment felt disorienting, even hypocritical.

In life, he'd believed that cold objectivity was vital, a means to ensure justice was served without bias. But as a spirit, that perspective felt hollow, even cruel. Blake's casual dismissal of Emilia's death, someone Thomas considered a good friend, stirred something raw and unrelenting inside him. He wondered if this was what death did to the soul: stripped away the pretence, the rules, leaving behind only unfiltered emotion. His anger was now cold and sharp, like a blade forged from contempt.

As much as Thomas wanted to confront Blake for his indifference, he forced himself to stay on task. There were pressing matters to address. Marcel's stolen documents—those that had gone missing from the evidence locker—seemed pivotal to uncovering J.Tech's web of treachery. They contained information that could tie Marcel to J.Tech and, by extension, to the case surrounding Emilia and her brother. Blake's revelation that J.Tech's lawyers maintained original copies of every document added a new layer of intrigue. It was a lead Thomas couldn't ignore.

If he and Emilia had any hope of exposing J.Tech's secrets, they'd need those original documents. Blake's threats, his derision, and Marcel's shattered bearing painted a picture of a man backed into a corner. J.Tech had a stranglehold on its operatives, controlling and lording over them through fear.

To bring J.Tech down from beyond the grave would require more than just haunting those involved. They needed evidence—incontrovertible proof that could expose the company's corruption. And that meant finding the lawyers Blake had mentioned.

Thomas' anger began simmering again as he moved away from the precinct, taking a silent vow. He couldn't change what had already happened, but he could still fight for justice. Not just for himself, but for Emilia and her brother, and for every life J.Tech had ruined.

Marcel was exhausted. He was mentally and physically drained. When had he last had a proper rest? When had he last gone through a day without constantly looking over his shoulder? When had he last felt safe?

It was hard to remember. The days blurred together in a relentless cycle of dread and vigilance. Every creak of a floorboard, every shadow out of place, sent his nerves alight. His body ached from tension, his mind foggy from lack of sleep. Guilt clung to him like a second skin, weighing him down. No matter how hard he tried, he couldn't shake it off.

He longed for a moment of peace, a time when he didn't have to second-guess every glance from a stranger, when the voices in his head didn't insist that every unfamiliar face belonged to a hitman sent by J.Tech to end him. He couldn't even recall the last time he'd slept without nightmares chasing him into the dark.

He stepped into his apartment, closing the door behind him. The lights were off, but he couldn't muster the energy to turn them on. Sluggish and worn, he leaned against the door, closing his eyes and exhaling a shaky breath. It felt like he'd been running on fumes for months, surviving on nothing but paranoia and fear. He opened his eyes and stared at a spot on the ceiling, his voice a hoarse whisper.

'I don't think I can do this much longer, Eldon.'

The empty apartment swallowed his words, offering no comfort. How much longer *could* he hold out before his body, or worse, his mind, gave out completely? How much longer could he keep this up?

He pushed away from the door, dragging himself all the way to his room. He fell heavily onto the bed and reached for the bedside drawer. Inside, nestled within a manila envelope, was the very document he'd stolen from the precinct.

Blake was right. He *was* stupid. Foolish to believe this was the only copy of the document. Foolish to think J.Tech would be careless enough to let such a vital piece of evidence slip through their fingers. He'd been naïve, certain that once he had his hands on it, he'd be free from the organization's clutches. But Blake's reminder that J.Tech had original copies safely locked away, had destroyed that illusion entirely.

Marcel stared at the envelope, his fingers trembling. He'd risked everything for this . . . for nothing. And now, he had no clear way out. The realization was like a vice tightening around his chest, constricting his breath.

He couldn't stop replaying Blake's words in his mind, each one cutting deeper into his resolve. J.Tech had original copies of everything. The stolen document he'd pinned his fragile hope on was meaningless. His entire gamble had been for naught, leaving him worse off than before. Trapped. Cornered. His every move watched by unseen eyes, and his every thought tangled in regret.

Closing his eyes, he collapsed back onto the bed. The springs groaned under his weight, much like his spirit groaned beneath the crushing despair. The ceiling above him was nothing more than an expanse of cracked plaster, but his gaze bore into it as though the answer to his predicament might materialize if he stared long enough.

How had it come to this? How had he allowed himself to sink so deeply into this abyss?

Marcel had once believed he could outsmart J.Tech. He'd told himself that survival was a matter of strategy, of playing their game long enough to find an escape. But now he saw the truth. They weren't just holding the cards; they were the ones who had built the table. Every avenue of escape had been blocked before he'd even thought to look for it.

Exhaustion gnawed at him from every angle, its teeth sharper now that the adrenaline of survival had waned. His mind raced, yet every thought spiralled into the same grim conclusion: there was no way out.

He hadn't intended for things to turn out the way they had. Eldon was his friend. They shared a love for investigations, but where Marcel had taken the path to being a police detective, Eldon had gone into investigative journalism. They'd traded intel with each other multiple times on low-level cases, and on that fated day, Marcel had assumed the case Eldon was working on was not as high stakes. Oh, how wrong he was.

Eldon had caught wind of a big corporation being involved in large scale privacy violations and illegal surveillance. It was a case Marcel had heard of before. The Aspen Hollow PD had worked on several claims concerning J.Tech, but it had always amounted to nothing. Somehow or other, the claims would be proven false, or they would be dropped.

Marcel didn't understand it, but he didn't care enough to dig deeper. Eldon, however, would not give up. He kept at it, until he found something of interest: someone within the precinct was working for J.Tech and was involved in obstructing and misleading any investigation into the corporation.

Eldon had begged and begged him to help. Pleading for Marcel to look into this for him. He couldn't say no. The mole he had found was Blake, and that discovery had been what started their downward spiral into chaos.

First came Eldon's accident. Marcel had thought nothing of it, until he received an anonymous email.

> *We have proof of your involvement in our dealings. Communication logs, falsifying reports to mislead investigations, and proof of illicit payments.*

It wasn't true, of course. None of it was true. But J.Tech was more than capable of fabricating whatever they needed to sully his name. It wasn't until later that he found out they had planted false evidence of his involvement and eradicated any proof of the real mole. He was a scapegoat. But as long as he did what they wanted him to, he was safe.

But the threat was clear.

If we go down, you're going down with us.

Somewhere, a clock ticked softly, counting seconds he could never reclaim. Each movement of the second hand felt louder, mocking him with its steadiness while his life crumbled around him. For the first time in what felt like years, he didn't have the strength to fight—not the fear, not the guilt, not the suffocating despair. He hadn't just failed himself. He'd failed everyone who might have been counting on him. And worst of all, he'd failed to protect the only thing he'd sought to salvage: a future free from J.Tech's clutches.

29

Emilia felt an uncomfortable sense of foreboding as she materialized in a cramped, dimly lit space—a janitor's closet. The antiseptic sting in the air was strong enough to make her nose wrinkle. Shelves lined with cleaning supplies and bottles of disinfectant crowded the walls.

'Sorry,' Arthur said, releasing her hand and awkwardly shuffling backward. He tried to give her some space, but the confines of the room had their limitations. 'This is where I usually appear when I come to Hope Spring. Habit, I suppose. I forgot it would be a bit . . . tight with two people.'

Emilia shrugged, brushing off his apology, and walked through the door, seamlessly passing into the hallway beyond.

'Do you come here often, then?' Considering who he was, the answer seemed obvious, but she asked anyway.

'I used to. Not so much since I took charge of the Agency.'

She nodded thoughtfully, her gaze shifting to the busy hallway. The scent of antiseptic was less overwhelming here, though it still clung stubbornly to the air. Nurses bustled past with quick, purposeful steps, their faces a mixture of focus and exhaustion. The sterile environment seemed to amplify the weight of unspoken worries that lingered in the corners.

As they moved down the corridor, Emilia couldn't help but notice how the Living seemed to subtly divert around Arthur.

'That's convenient,' she said, her voice carrying a faint edge of jealousy she hadn't intended. The constant effort to dodge and avoid collision with the Living was exhausting. It was a small, nagging reminder of her current state.

Arthur smiled, his expression disarmingly warm. She still wasn't used to seeing him like this, though this version of him had been appearing more frequently as he grew comfortable around her.

'They sense me,' he said. 'Even if they can't see me, the Living have an instinct when it comes to death. A kind of sixth sense, I suppose.'

They stopped outside Eldon's hospital room, and immediately, an overwhelming tightness bloomed in her chest.

'We're here,' Emilia said. The words came out strained as she fought the knot forming in her throat. She swallowed hard, trying to keep her emotions in check.

Arthur watched her for a moment, studying the rapid flicker of emotions that crossed her face.

'You don't have to go in if you don't want to. I can look for the necklace, and you can wait out here.'

His voice was steady, but his eyes betrayed his concern. It was clear he could see how affected she was just by being there.

'No, I—' she faltered, swallowing again before finding her words. 'I want to go in. I need to see him.'

'Are you sure?' he asked.

She nodded.

'I haven't seen him since . . .' She paused, steadying herself. 'Since my death.'

The admission hung in the air between them, feeling strange even after months of her being dead.

'You don't have to,' Arthur said. 'Not if it'll make this harder for you.'

Emilia didn't answer. She turned and passed through the door without looking back. She knew she didn't have to do this, but a deep, stubborn part of her insisted she *must*. She needed to see her brother, to reassure herself he was still there. A dull ache of guilt pulled at her, gnawing away at her resolve. She had been his older sister, his protector. And yet she'd left him—alone, vulnerable, fending for himself after her untimely death. It was a failure she couldn't forgive herself for.

She needed to confront the guilt that had been eating away at her since that fateful day. It wasn't her fault. And the sooner she accepted it, the sooner she would come to terms with it.

The muted beeping of medical monitors that she'd heard faintly from the hallway grew louder as she entered the room. Her eyes landed on the figure lying in the hospital bed, and she froze. It felt like an eternity since she'd been this close to him.

Her brother looked the same as she remembered, his face relaxed and peaceful in a way that almost fooled her into believing he was simply asleep. She stepped closer, her hand hovering over his for a moment before pulling back. A pang of frustration and sadness twisted in her chest as Arthur joined her quietly. He stood behind her, careful not to intrude.

'Are you all right?' he asked.

She nodded stiffly as she said, 'We should look for the necklace.'

Gesturing towards Eldon, she added, 'Would you . . .? I'm still not that good at interacting with objects. It'll be much faster if you do it.'

Arthur adjusted the collar of Eldon's hospital-issued gown, feeling underneath it. Then he turned and shook his head, his expression apologetic. No necklace.

'I was certain he would have it on him,' she said.

The door creaked open, and a nurse entered. Emilia instinctively moved aside but drifted too close to the heart monitor. Its beeping turned erratic, filling the room with sharp, alarming sounds. The nurse frowned and rushed to check Eldon's vitals, her movements brisk and precise. Arthur gently tugged Emilia away from the machine, guiding her to a safer distance. The moment she stepped away, the monitor's beeping slowed to its regular, steady rhythm.

'We interfere with electronic signals,' he whispered, leaning close to her. It was a moot gesture since the Living couldn't hear him, but it still felt natural. 'Best not to linger too close.'

The nurse, who looked puzzled at the disturbance, scribbled a few notes on her clipboard and double-checked the monitor's wiring. Once she was satisfied it had been a fluke, she left the room.

Arthur waited for the door to close before speaking again.

'Have you seen your brother wearing the necklace since his hospitalization?' he asked. 'They might have removed his personal items and stored them elsewhere.'

'I can't remember,' she admitted, a flush of embarrassment creeping over her.

Arthur didn't press her.

'No matter. It's worth checking. Come on.'

He led her out of the room and down the hallway to a storage area near the nurses' station. One wall was lined with cubby holes, each labelled with patient names and room numbers. He scanned the labels quickly, zeroing in on *E. Elliot*.

'Here,' he said, pulling the basket free. Inside were only a few items: a wristwatch, a cardholder, and some loose change. But no necklace.

He replaced the basket and turned to Emilia. The question in his expression was clear: *Are you sure the necklace exists?*

Emilia's shoulders tensed.

'He never takes it off,' she said, defensive, though she couldn't hide the doubt that laced her tone. 'He was wearing it the last time I saw him. I'm sure of it.'

Arthur's silence wasn't judgemental, but it seemed to deepen her frustration. The necklace had to exist. It had to be here. But it wasn't. And with each passing second, the sinking realization grew harder to ignore: the necklace was nowhere to be found.

30

'Yo,' Thomas said, peering over the divider at the petite girl sitting behind the desk.

He had spent the better part of the day mulling over the discussion he'd overheard—concerning the missing documents and the lawyers—but no matter how much he thought about it, he couldn't settle on the best way forward. In the end, he decided to return to the Agency. As he arrived, it occurred to him that there was someone who might be able to help.

Sadie looked up from her computer screen, startled to see Thomas leaning casually against the divider. Her attention flicked past him once before settling back on him.

'No Emilia?' she asked.

'Nah, she's with Arthur. They had some things to take care of.'

'The two of them? Together?' Sadie's eyebrows rose, her tone matching the surprise on her face.

Thomas shrugged. He wasn't about to get into that.

'I need your help,' he said instead, moving around the desk and dragging a chair over to sit beside her.

She gestured towards a stack of folders on her desk.

'These are some targets that were recently approved—'

'No, no,' he interrupted impatiently with a dismissive hand. 'Not that. I'm not here for work. I'm here for you.'

Sadie blinked, taken aback.

'Me?'

'I heard you're the best researcher in the department,' he said. 'And there's something I need you to find for me.'

Before she could point out that her role didn't extend beyond researching potential targets, Thomas launched into an explanation. His words tumbled over one another as he recounted the events that had unfolded in the Living World, carefully skimming over details that were not necessary to share. Sadie might have been a friend, but even he knew better than to reveal too much to someone who wasn't directly involved in their affairs.

By the time he finished, Sadie was leaning back in her chair, her lips pressed into a thin line. A flicker of irritation crossed her face, her effort to maintain composure doing little to mask the obvious annoyance reflected in her eyes.

'Arthur gave you *lessons*?'

It wasn't the question itself that caught him off guard, but her tone. She sounded agitated, and it unsettled him. He rubbed the back of his neck before mumbling, 'He had his reasons.'

'Arthur doesn't typically take risks, nor does he get personally involved in training potential agents,' she countered, her voice clipped.

'It wasn't just me. Emilia was there too,' Thomas said.

Something shifted in Sadie's expression then, her irritation momentarily giving way to realization.

'Emilia,' she echoed. 'Of course.'

She studied him in silence, her attention dropping briefly to the inked number on his wrist before returning to his face.

'Well, at least you have some experience scaring the Living now,' she said dryly in a weak attempt to sound nonchalant. 'Anyway, who are these lawyers you're looking for?'

Thomas had expected the question and readily explained his involvement in the investigation into Emilia's death. Sadie drew in a slow breath and had to turn away, hardly able to control her countenance. When she looked at him again, her perfectly calm mask revealed nothing of what she felt, leaving Thomas all the more puzzled.

'*Arthur* permitted the two of you to look into Emilia's death?' she asked, her voice strained.

Thomas hesitated at the sudden change in her demeanour.

'Are you all right?' he asked.

'I'm fine. Answer the question,' she said. 'Please.'

He eyed her warily, but said, 'He gave us permission, yeah.'

Another measured breath, and she forced a smile, her tone lightening as she said, 'It shouldn't be too difficult to track down those lawyers.'

'Really?' he asked, surprised.

Sadie nodded.

'The difficulty comes after.'

'What do you mean?'

She folded her arms, tilting her head slightly as she regarded him.

'What I mean is: how are you planning to get the documents once I figure out who has them?'

Thomas paused, the flaw in his plan glaringly obvious. He hadn't thought that far ahead. It was a good question, one he didn't have an immediate answer to.

Sadie tapped her finger against the desk, thinking. Then, without another word, she turned to her computer and began typing. Her focus was sharp, her fingers flying across the keys as she navigated through files and databases. Occasionally, she scribbled a note or adjusted a search parameter. Thomas watched in silence, his curiosity growing with each passing moment. At last, she leaned back, studying the open document on the screen.

'Well,' she said, swivelling her chair to face him. 'I know the identity of the person you're looking for.'

He'd known Sadie had a reputation for being one of the best researchers in the department, but he hadn't expected results this quickly. He leaned forward to read over her shoulder.

The name 'Lucas Caldwell' was written in bold at the top of the file. Beneath it was a detailed profile: a renowned lawyer employed by one of the firms contracted by J.Tech. By process of elimination, Sadie had identified him as the individual most likely to be in possession of the incriminating documents; he was the key to exposing corruption within both the company and Aspen Hollow PD. One detail, in particular, caught his attention.

'This looks like a target's file,' he said, noting the scare compatibility percentage listed at the bottom. He looked at her questioningly. 'Why?'

Sadie's grin was almost mischievous.

'Why do you think?' she asked.

'I . . . don't know,' he admitted, his confusion mounting. Her expression didn't help either. She looked far too pleased with herself.

'Because he *is* a target,' she said, her tone light but deliberate. '*Our* target. And we're going to scare him.'

Thomas went still. Then understanding set in and the implications of her words made him cringe.

'You're serious?' he asked.

Sadie nodded, her enthusiasm infectious.

'*Dead* serious.'

The clock on Lucas Caldwell's office wall ticked rhythmically, a steady reminder of another late night at work. He sat at his mahogany desk, fingers absently tapping the edge of a stack of case files. The dim glow of his desk lamp barely lit the room, leaving shadows to pool in the corners like silent, watchful sentinels. He rubbed his temples, trying to focus on the legal brief in front of him. But something felt off. He frowned and shook his head, brushing it aside as a symptom of fatigue.

A soft *click* echoed through the office. He paused, his pen stilling in his hand, and glanced around. The air shifted subtly, heavy and cool. Then his desk lamp flickered. Annoyance crept into his expression, but it was tinged with unease.

'Great,' he muttered, 'probably the wiring again.'

His voice sounded small in the stillness.

He exhaled, intending to calm himself, but froze as he saw his breath mist in the air. The temperature had dropped sharply, a chill seeping into his bones. His fingers stiffened over the keyboard of his laptop as its quiet hum began to distort, crackling. The screen blinked erratically, windows opening and closing on their own. Then the screen went black. For a moment, everything was silent. Just as Lucas began to reach for the power button, a single word appeared in stark white letters: *LEAVE.*

He jerked his chair back, heart pounding, but before he could fully process what he was seeing, the files on his desk erupted into the air. Pages scattered in a chaotic flurry, circling him like a paper storm. They crashed down all at once, a cacophony of rustling that seemed deafening in the quiet room. Books toppled from shelves, their spines cracking loudly as they hit the floor. He barely managed to dodge a heavy legal tome that came hurtling towards his head.

Lucas scrambled to his feet, his chair clattering to the floor behind him. Shadows began to shift along the walls, twisting and slithering unnaturally. They moved with intent, not like the ordinary play of light and dark. Panic clawed at his chest as he backed away from the desk, his gaze darting wildly around the room.

When he turned towards the large window behind his desk, his breath caught. Reflected in the glass was a figure standing behind him. But not his own. The image was fleeting, a pale, spectral shape draped in shadows, its face obscured. He spun around, fists clenched and ready to throw a punch, but there was nothing there. The office was empty.

And then he heard it.

The voices.

Low and guttural at first, as if spoken from some distant abyss. They grew louder, more insistent, until one voice broke through the racket, right next to his ear: '*Get out of here.. . . .*'

The words were distorted, warped as though dragged through layers of water, but the malice in them was unmistakable. Lucas whipped his head around, his breath coming in shallow gasps. There was no one there. He stumbled towards the door, tripping over the fallen chair in his haste. The voices seemed to follow him, whispering, urging, commanding.

They grew more intense, more venomous, their words merging into an incomprehensible torrent of ramblings. Lucas could feel the icy breath brushing against his skin, colder than the room itself. The logical side of his brain was screaming at him, telling him that he was imagining it all. He staggered backward, his legs hitting the edge of his desk, stopping him. His wide-eyed gaze snapped to the reflection in the window again—but what stared back at him wasn't just his own face. There were others now: twisted, gaunt faces, their hollow eyes staring, mouths moving in unison as if chanting in a chaotic jumble.

The office door, heavy and oak-panelled, slammed shut with a deafening bang. The force reverberated through the room, rattling the walls and shaking the very foundations of the office. Papers scattered across the floor began to rustle again, but this time, they moved deliberately, guided by an unseen hand. Lucas watched in horrified disbelief as the documents aligned themselves into a crooked, uneven formation. The word they spelled turned his blood to ice: *RUN*.

His body locked in place as the shadows along the walls surged. They expanded and stretched, their inky tendrils creeping closer with each flicker of the dying desk lamp. The light buzzed frantically, casting the room in intermittent flashes of distorted shadows and faint illumination. With a final sputtering whine, the lamp sparked and went out, plunging the office into thick, suffocating darkness.

For a moment, silence reigned. The only sound was Lucas' laboured breathing and the rapid pounding of his heart. Then came a loud crash. Something slammed violently into the desk, sending it skidding a few inches across the floor. The sound jolted Lucas into action. He stumbled, nearly losing his footing, and darted towards the door a second time. His hands fumbled desperately for the handle, the cold metal biting into his trembling fingers. At first, it resisted, but with a sharp twist and a surge of adrenaline, he forced it open.

The instant he stepped into the hallway, the oppressive weight lifted, leaving him shaken but free. The whispers ceased as though a switch had been flipped, and the icy chill that had gripped him dissipated. Lucas didn't dare look back. He broke into a run, heading straight for the emergency staircase, bypassing the elevators entirely. His only thought was to get as far away as possible from the nightmare he'd just escaped.

Back in the office, the chaos seemed to fade, the atmosphere retreating into an eerie stillness.

31

Thomas stared at Sadie, his mouth agape, as they stood amid the wreckage of Lucas Caldwell's office. When she had suggested treating the man as their target to get him to leave, this was not what he'd expected. Not for one second had he thought that *Sadie* would have it in her to terrify anyone, let alone cause such complete havoc. Yet here they were, and he had been proven very, very wrong. What Sadie had done was beyond anything he could have imagined, making Arthur's lesson seem mild in comparison.

'What?' Sadie said defensively when she caught the look on his face. 'Just because I'm a researcher doesn't mean I can't also be good at scaring the Living.'

'I can see that,' Thomas murmured, partly in awe and partly in fear. He looked around the room, taking in the mess left in the wake of her destructive methods. Papers were scattered everywhere, books lay sprawled in heaps, and the desk lamp was shattered on the floor. 'But was all this really necessary?'

Sadie was hopping across the scattered papers like a child avoiding stepping on cracks in the pavement.

She paused mid-step and glanced back at him, an expression of disgust crossing her face.

'What?' he asked.

'Did you even read the document I put together on this guy?' she asked.

Thomas shrugged.

'I skimmed through it.'

Her exasperation was immediate.

'This is why none of you appreciate the effort I put into research. If you actually read what I wrote, you'd understand why this was necessary.'

'All right, fine. Why don't you enlighten me?' Thomas said.

'Lucas Caldwell is a workaholic,' she explained, gesturing around the room. 'He never leaves this office unless he has a meeting, and he even sleeps on the sofa in the next room. If we wanted to get those documents, we had to get him out of here. And what's the best way to make the Living run for the hills?'

'By scaring them,' Thomas admitted grudgingly.

'Exactly.' Sadie nodded, a smug look on her face. 'And now, we have free rein over his office. He's not coming back any time soon. Not until the sun's up, at least.'

Thomas rubbed the back of his neck, finally understanding her reasoning. Sadie hadn't just gone to extremes for the fun of it, though she clearly enjoyed herself. She'd wanted to ensure that Caldwell wouldn't even consider returning until the terror subsided. Still, her approach left him feeling aghast.

Sadie stood in the middle of the room, surveying the chaos with her hands on her hips.

'I probably should have thought twice about sending all his papers and case files flying,' she said. 'Finding the documents we need is going to take some work.'

Turning to Thomas with a gleam in her eye, she said, 'Arthur's taught you how to interact with objects, right?'

Thomas stared at his hands.

'I . . . sort of have some experience,' he muttered, but even to his own ears, it sounded unconvincing.

Sadie didn't seem too bothered.

'Just do your best,' she said breezily before moving to the other side of the room. She wasn't expecting much from him, which was precisely why she'd decided to come along. If she counted on him, they'd never get anything done.

The two settled into a comfortable silence, each taking one side of the room. Papers rustled underfoot as they sifted through the wreckage Sadie had caused. The minutes dragged on, before finally, Thomas broke the quiet.

'How are you so good at haunting?' he asked, casting a look her way. 'I don't think I could ever get on your level.'

Sadie held a page up to the light before tossing it aside.

'No special reason,' she said. 'I used to watch a lot of horror movies before I died. Plus, I've got an insane amount of stored energy. Comes in handy.' She flashed him a quick grin. 'You'll get there soon enough.'

'If you're so good at it, why are you a researcher? You'd rake in loads of points scaring people the way you do.'

Sadie's tone turned bored, her movements languid as she sifted through the scattered papers.

'This kind of thing is tedious for me,' she said. 'I don't have the same motivation as you or Emilia when it comes to points. I'm just doing what fits my fancy. Right now, that's researching. Sitting in a comfortable chair and digging into my current project beats running around and terrifying people any day.'

Thomas abandoned his futile attempts to move anything in the room. It was taking all his concentration just to see in the dim light, let alone focus enough to interact with objects. Sadie, as expected, was making steady progress, even while muttering about how much harder she'd made things by sending the papers flying. It had been excellent theatrics for scaring Lucas, but not so great for efficiency.

Thomas wandered over to a tall bookshelf, squinting at the spines of the books that hadn't been knocked over. He wasn't paying much attention but he caught a glimpse of something that made him stop short. A face stared back at him from the shadows. He startled, taking a step back, his heart racing. It took him a moment to realize it wasn't Lucas, but rather an oil painting of the man. The dim light and his distracted state had made it seem almost lifelike.

Shaking his head, he stepped closer, examining the portrait. On impulse, he leaned in and poked his head through the canvas. He pulled back almost at once, his eyes wide.

'Sadie!' he called, his voice echoing in the quiet room. 'I found it! I think.'

Sadie came over to him, a sceptical look on her face.

'You think?'

Thomas pointed at the painting.

'There's a safe behind it. It's got a bunch of case files and some cash.'

She grabbed the edge of the portrait and swung it aside with ease. Behind the canvas was a sleek electronic safe embedded in the wall. Safes were always a gamble; sometimes, the energy imprints of the Living clung to them like a faint whisper, and other times, they were as sterile as if untouched by human hands.

She knelt in front of the keypad.

'Let's see what we're working with,' she muttered. She leaned closer to scrutinize the numbers. Faint traces of residual energy shimmered in the air, just enough for her to pick up the patterns.

'Seven, two, eight, and zero,' she said aloud.

'You know the code?' he asked, impressed.

'I know the *numbers*,' she corrected. 'The Living sometimes leave traces of energy on things they touch frequently. Seven, two, eight and zero have been pressed the most. But I can't tell the sequence.'

Thomas pondered this, then turned back to the painting. A thought struck him, and he stepped back to inspect the canvas more closely. Then, to Sadie's bemusement, he leaned through it, poking his head out the other side with a triumphant grin.

'I've got it,' he said. 'It's eight-two-zero-seven.'

She regarded him.

'How do you know that?'

'I thought I recognized the art style,' he explained, pointing at the signature hidden in the corner. 'He's known for hiding numbers in his work. Lucas probably commissioned this piece and used the hidden numbers as his safe code so he wouldn't forget.'

Sadie was impressed despite herself.

'All right, let's give it a shot.'

Hovering her fingers above the keypad, she carefully pressed the sequence: 8-2-0-7.

The safe emitted a soft beep, followed by a heavy clunk as the lock disengaged. The door swung open to reveal a neat stack of files, some with edges yellowed with age. Sadie rifled through them quickly, her hands pausing when she reached a folder labelled 'J.T.'.

'See?' Thomas said, tapping the side of his head with a proud smile. 'I *contributed*.'

She scoffed, but the corner of her mouth twitched in an almost reluctant grin. She grabbed the folder and tucked it under her arm.

'Let's get out of here,' she said. 'Before Lucas gets brave enough to come back.'

32

Sadie and Thomas left Lucas Caldwell's office and materialized in an abandoned movie theatre, her choice of location. Thomas found the decision surprising and couldn't help but feel intrigued.

Without hesitation, he drifted away from her, moving down the cracked aisle between rows of dusty, moth-eaten seats. The scent of mildew hung in the air, and a pervasive chill seemed to settle over the place. Faded movie posters clung stubbornly to peeling walls, their titles smudged and illegible as though time had blurred even the stories they'd once told.

Sadie lingered near the entrance, watching as Thomas made his way to the front of the theatre. The old projector loomed high in the rafters, silent and rusted, awaiting a film that would never roll again. He stopped beneath the enormous screen, its yellowed canvas stretched taut across the far wall and tilted his head as if expecting something to flicker to life on its surface.

'You used to come here a lot?' he asked over his shoulder, curiosity colouring his tone.

She shrugged as she joined him at the front.

'Like I said, I watched a lot of horror movies, and this place was a treasure trove for them. They had everything, from the classics to the obscure.'

Her gaze swept across the empty theatre, nostalgia softening her voice as she continued, almost to herself.

'It used to be packed in here. Every weekend, every holiday, there'd be a line out the door.' She sighed, her shoulders sagging slightly. 'Now it's empty. Forgotten.'

Thomas followed her line of sight to the remnants of the concession stand at the back of the room. The shattered display was littered with splinters of glass and candy wrappers from a lifetime ago.

'Yeah,' he murmured, her words settling over him.

A moment of silence passed between them before he changed the subject, asking, 'Why'd you pick this place, anyway? Shouldn't we be heading back to the Agency? I need to keep Arthur in the loop about things.'

Sadie dropped onto the velvet carpet flooring, sitting cross-legged.

'That's the problem. We *can't* go back.'

He frowned, 'Why not?'

She took out the folder tucked under her arm.

'Because of this. We can't bring things from the Living World back to the Spirit World. We have to stash it somewhere safe first.'

'And this is your "safe place"?'

Sadie shrugged.

'It could be. I thought of it on a whim. It's abandoned, and no one comes here. Seems as good a spot aş any.'

'Wait,' he said, something having occurred to him just then. 'If we can't bring things into the Spirit World, what about those sweets we used to bribe the Nameless Spirit? Aren't those from the Living World?'

Sadie laughed, the sound ricocheting in the empty theatre.

'I was wondering when you'd pick up on that,' she said before explaining, 'We can't bring *things*, objects, into the Spirit World. Food is an exception.'

'Seems a bit redundant, don't you think? It's not like we can consume them.'

She shrugged.

'The Spirit World isn't just for us. There are many whose culture includes food offerings for the dead. The Postal Service is also responsible for deliveries outside the cemeteries, especially where food is concerned. Spirits can't eat the food, but it's nice to know that our loved ones are thinking of us.'

'Of course, smuggling sweets is *my* speciality.' She winked.

Thomas surveyed the room and moved towards a random seat in the middle row. He gripped the worn cushion, and with a burst of energy, managed to rip it away from its plastic base. Beneath the cushion was a narrow, hollow space. He grinned, pleased with himself.

'Here,' he said, pointing at the cavity. 'Perfect hiding spot.'

'Are you sure about this?'

He nodded. Convinced by his certainty, she slid the file into the gap.

'All right. Your call.'

He replaced the cushion, patting it down until it looked undisturbed. He pointed at the small metal plate affixed to the seat's rim.

'F-20,' he said. 'Don't forget.'

Sadie gave him a smile.

'F-20.'

When they returned to the Agency, Sadie headed straight for her desk to finish her paperwork, leaving Thomas to go to Arthur's office alone. He had half-expected the room to be empty, but he walked in just as Arthur and Emilia materialized. Even now, he wasn't entirely accustomed to how casually they moved between realms.

'Thomas!' Emilia exclaimed, relief brightening her expression. 'I'm so glad you're all right. Did everything go okay?'

Seeing her unharmed eased some of his own worries. He nodded, and the three of them settled around Arthur's desk, sharing their respective accounts. Thomas dove into his story, describing Marcel, the trip to Lucas Caldwell's office, and the elaborate haunting Sadie had pulled off. He added that even though he'd been in on the plan, her theatrics had been terrifyingly effective and far beyond what he'd anticipated.

While Emilia struggled to wrap her head around the idea of Sadie's prowess in haunting the Living, Arthur didn't look remotely surprised. A shadow crossed his expression, a flicker of concern tightening the corners of his mouth. The reaction was subtle, but enough for Emilia to notice.

When she looked to him, he shook his head imperceptibly and dismissed her worries with a small smile that did little to ease the tension in his posture.

Arthur had known that Sadie's involvement was inevitable, but he had expected her to be a passive observer, not an active participant. The fact that she had willingly inserted herself into the investigation at Thomas' behest, and used her abilities so openly, set him on edge.

One look at Emilia—watching her chatter excitedly to Thomas about having another strong and reliable ally—was enough for him to force his concerns aside. He would deal with whatever complications arose when the time came. For now, this would have to suffice.

'She has always had a remarkably high energy level,' he said, rejoining their conversation.

'And she's really good at researching,' Thomas added, explaining how they'd found the file hidden in Lucas' safe and the reason they'd had to stash it in the abandoned movie theatre. 'Sadie mentioned we couldn't bring the documents back here. Something about them disintegrating if they crossed into the Spirit World.'

'She's right,' Arthur said. 'Objects from the Living World brought to the Spirit World would be destroyed. If that file were lost, all your efforts would have been for nothing. Hiding it was the right call.'

'So, what do we do now?' Emilia asked.

'Our priority hasn't changed. We need to locate your brother's necklace. The information in those documents could be vital, but the necklace, whatever it contains, may be even more critical to our investigation.'

'Necklace?' Thomas asked. 'What necklace?'

It was Emilia's turn to explain: the complications surrounding their investigation, the importance of the necklace, and how its disappearance was impeding their progress. As she spoke, something about the necklace's description tugged at Thomas' memory. A nagging thought itched at the edge of his mind, growing stronger the more he tried to place it.

Then it clicked.

He grabbed a pen from Arthur's desk and a blank sheet of paper, sketching out a quick drawing. When he finished, he turned it towards them.

'Is this the necklace you're looking for?'

Emilia's eyes widened in shock as she stared at a rough sketch of Eldon's necklace.

'How . . .' she started, her voice trailing off.

'I have it,' Thomas said. 'I know where it is.'

33

Emilia hadn't expected to find herself here again, yet here she was. The corridor looked just as she remembered: flickering overhead lights, eerie silence, and shuttered units lining both sides. They were back where it had all begun. The storage facility.

'This place gives me bad vibes,' Emilia muttered under her breath, shuddering as she stared at the lights. The building's neglected state made it clear that upkeep wasn't a priority.

Thomas glanced over his shoulder at her, raising an eyebrow.

'You're *dead*, and this gives you the heebie-jeebies?'

After sketching the necklace earlier, Thomas had explained its importance. The piece was central to his investigation, tying Emilia's death to her brother's incident. He had taken the necklace from the hospital and hidden it in the unit he'd rented here. Distrustful of the precinct's integrity, he'd concealed it even within the supposed security of the storage unit. Following his death, the unit had been cleared, but, fortunately, the necklace had remained undiscovered.

'Good thing, too,' he'd remarked. 'The rats back at the precinct would've destroyed it.'

Its existence had slipped his mind until Emilia had mentioned it, jogging his memory.

They passed through the shutters of the unit at the end of the corridor.

'At least it's still untouched,' she said. Dust blanketed the corners, speaking to the months that had passed since it was last used.

Thomas, however, was studying the ceiling. Following his line of sight, Emilia noticed the opening to a ventilation shaft.

'I stuffed it up there,' he said, pointing.

'Where, exactly?' she asked.

'Partway down the shaft.' His gesture was vague at best.

When she gave him a pointed look, he shrugged, saying, 'I know, I know. I was really paranoid about someone finding it.'

'How'd you even get it up there?'

'Swing and toss,' he said matter-of-factly.

Emilia pressed her fingers to her temples.

'Great, you genius. And how are we supposed to get it out now? We can't just pull it through the shaft. We'll have to retrieve it the same way you tossed it in.'

Thomas didn't argue, looking sheepish as he said, 'I kind of knew that, but I figured it'd be future-me's problem.'

'Well, future-you, what *are* we going to do now?'

They stood in silence, staring at the ventilation shaft. Neither of them had any immediate ideas. Thomas, for all his growing ability to interact with objects in the Living World, couldn't do much if he couldn't reach the necklace.

Then his attention caught on Emilia's wrist. More specifically, the bracelet she wore. He looked between the braided metal band and the shaft, a plan forming in his mind.

'I think you can get it,' he said.

Emilia snorted, 'If you can't, I obviously can't.'

'On your own, maybe not,' he said, nodding towards her bracelet. 'But with that, I think you can.'

Her gaze dropped to the bracelet, to the intricately woven band of metal that pulsed faintly with an ethereal glow. The gem at its centre swirled with a kaleidoscope of colours, unmistakably imbued with Arthur's energy. Thomas had a point. She'd used the bracelet before back at her brother's apartment and it made harnessing energy far easier than relying on her own reserves.

'That day in Arthur's office,' Thomas continued, a trace of bitterness in his tone as his expression soured at the memory, 'he used his energy to pull you towards him. Maybe you can do something similar.'

She doubted she could replicate Arthur's precision, but she might manage something.

'Where exactly is the necklace?' she asked.

Thomas pointed to a spot partway down the shaft.

'I heard a *thunk* around there when it landed.'

Emilia drew a steadying breath and concentrated. She focused on pulling energy from the bracelet to her palm, picturing the power accumulating there. When she felt a tingling warmth in her hand, she aimed the invisible force upward at the shaft.

Nothing happened.

Then a loud crack reverberated through the unit as the metal shaft split at the point of impact. The material shuddered and warped, bending outwards like peeled bark. A glint of silver caught her eye as the necklace dangled by its chain.

'Nice,' Thomas said, reaching out to grab it before it could fall. He held it up triumphantly.

Emilia allowed herself a small smile. The success felt monumental, a rare moment of competence. With the necklace secured, they left the storage facility and headed to their agreed-upon meeting point. When they arrived at the abandoned movie theatre, they were surprised to find not just Arthur waiting for them, but Sadie as well.

She sat slouched in one of the front-row seats, looking unimpressed, while Arthur was perched with his usual composure in seat F-20, one leg crossed over the other and the case file resting on his lap. He gestured for them to settle down as they approached, his expression calm but expectant.

'He dragged me here,' Sadie grumbled, shooting a glare at Arthur. Then she leaned closer to Thomas, hissing, 'Did you tell him I was the one who scared that lawyer?'

'What? Did you really think he'd believe *I* did it?' Thomas shot back, his voice equally low. 'On *that* scale? No way.'

Arthur's attention flicked their way, faint amusement surfacing before he spoke.

'Quiet, you two,' he said. 'We have much to discuss.'

Thomas and Emilia took the seats in front of them. As they settled, Arthur's focus shifted to Emilia, his sharp eyes landing on the bracelet adorning her wrist.

'Did you run into trouble?' he asked, his head tilted towards her.

'Trouble?' Emilia repeated, confused.

He nodded at the bracelet and said, 'You used my energy.'

'Oh.'

Emilia recounted how they'd retrieved the necklace from the ventilation shaft. When she finished, Arthur's lips quirked into a faint smile.

'Did you have fun?' he asked.

She gave a half-shrug, about to respond, when Sadie loudly cleared her throat.

'Some of us have actual work to get back to. So, let's hurry and get this over with.' She added under her breath, 'What am I even doing here?'

'Thomas,' Arthur said, lifting his voice just enough to be heard, 'the necklace?'

Thomas shot Emilia a look before pulling the necklace from his coat pocket and passing it over. Arthur examined the piece briefly, his fingers deftly twisting the top until it popped off, revealing a small thumb drive nestled inside. He scrutinized the drive, then sealed the necklace again.

'Have you reviewed the contents?' he asked, looking at Thomas.

'It's a complete archive of everything Eldon compiled on J.Tech. In the right hands, it could destroy the company,' Thomas said.

'In the right hands,' Arthur echoed, closing his eyes and pinching the bridge of his nose. 'We need someone in the Living World who can use this evidence. Keeping it here is pointless. We can't act directly, and we can't interfere beyond this.'

The silence stretched until Sadie broke it.

'Okay, so again, why am *I* here? This has nothing to do with me. I helped you once. That's it.'

Arthur's eyes locked on hers.

'You're here because I need you to find the person best suited to handle this evidence. Someone we can trust to finish what we cannot.'

Sadie opened her mouth to protest, but Arthur continued before she could.

'I need your research skills,' he said.

She sank back in her seat, defeated.

'Fine,' she grumbled, shooting a glare at the others. 'But only because I was already planning to get back to my research.'

34

Back at the Agency, Sadie wasted no time burying herself in her research. She had muttered something about 'getting it over with' as she disappeared into her workspace. Emilia, on the other hand, meandered back to her desk, her steps slower than usual. Thomas followed close behind, watching her with a wary eye. There was a distracted air about her that he couldn't ignore.

'You good?' he asked, dragging a chair next to her desk and sitting down.

Her fingers brushed against the edge of the bracelet on her wrist. Finally, she looked at him, her expression troubled.

'Do you really remember everything that's on that drive?'

Thomas folded his arms as he considered her question.

'Vaguely, yeah,' he admitted. 'But not the fine details. I know it's a complete archive of Eldon's research. All the evidence needed to back every claim he planned to expose in his article. It was thorough, impressive even. That's why I hid it somewhere hard to reach, even in the storage unit.'

A crease formed between his brows. Though most of his memories had returned since his death, some remained hazy. This particular detail—why he'd gone to such lengths to conceal the drive—was one of them.

'My brother . . . He wasn't involved with J.Tech, was he?' Emilia asked. 'I mean other than investigating them for his article.'

The question caught Thomas off guard. Her face was calm, but her eyes betrayed the storm of thoughts brewing behind them. She didn't look away, waiting for his answer.

'As far as I know, no,' he said carefully. 'Eldon was digging into their operations, but only as a journalist. He was good at his job. Too good, even. That's what got him into trouble, not any deeper involvement.'

Emilia knew her brother well. Eldon had always been willing to take risks for the sake of a story, chasing leads no matter how dangerous they were. She trusted his integrity, but J.Tech's influence was insidious, their reach extending far beyond what anyone realized. She'd seen it firsthand—how they manipulated systems, silenced dissent, and controlled the narrative. If Eldon had underestimated them . . . Her fingers curled into a fist as she took a steadying breath. She wasn't sure what she'd been hoping to hear from Thomas, but the nagging doubt in her mind refused to be quieted. She needed to believe in her brother, but she also needed answers and reassurance.

‘He wasn’t involved in the way you’re thinking,’ Thomas finally said. ‘If Eldon was involved with J.Tech at all, it would’ve been to expose them, not to work with them. If they’d managed to buy him off, they wouldn’t have had a reason to hurt him.’

Emilia nodded. She needed to hear that.

‘Thanks, Thomas.’

Thomas watched her for a beat before asking rather suddenly, ‘Is there something going on between you and Arthur?’

The unexpected question made her flinch.

‘What?’ she blurted.

‘I mean,’ he continued, a little more cautiously, ‘he seemed pretty chummy with you earlier . . .’

Emilia’s gaze dropped to the desk; heat crept into her face in a way she found thoroughly unpleasant.

‘It’s nothing,’ she said hastily. ‘We were just talking. I used his energy from the bracelet, and he wanted to know what I did with it. That’s all.’

Thomas didn’t look convinced but, to her relief, didn’t press the matter. She took the chance then, seizing on the first thing that came to mind to change the subject.

‘Why didn’t Arthur look through the thumb drive himself instead of asking you about its contents? You said yourself that you couldn’t recall all the specifics.’

Thomas shrugged.

‘I suppose it’s because we aren’t allowed to interfere. But really, I’m not sure.’

‘Not so much as that,’ Sadie’s voice chimed in from behind them, startling them both. She approached with a folder in her hand. 'We're natural enemies of Living World tech. Sure, we can manipulate it for hauntings, but interacting with computers or other systems? Forget it. I'm sure you've noticed how often it backfires.'

Emilia recalled what Arthur had said back at the hospital when she had unintentionally disrupted the monitors in Eldon's room.

'But if that's true,' she said slowly, 'then . . . what exactly is Arthur doing with the thumb drive and file?'

'Let's not get ahead of ourselves,' Sadie said, her tone dismissive but not unkind. 'Arthur knows what he's doing. Besides, leaving the thumb drive and file unattended was a bigger risk. Handling it himself was probably for the best.'

She brushed off further discussion with a wave of her hand.

'Anyway, I'm done with my research.' She held up the folder, then unceremoniously dropped it onto Emilia's desk. 'Took me a while, but I think this is the best option.'

Thomas reached for the folder.

'Took you a while? That barely took any time at all.'

Sadie grinned.

'That's all from me for now,' she said, already turning to head back to her desk. She paused mid-step and added, somewhat reluctantly, 'Let me know if you need help with anything else.'

Thomas opened the folder once she had left. A photograph lay clipped inside.

'*Him?*'

35

Arthur sat on the bench; his gaze was fixed on the vast nothingness stretching out before him. The world around him resembled charcoal sketched on a faded canvas, stripped of colour or life. Only he and the folder of documents beside him appeared vivid, as if untouched by the bleak surroundings. The Void he occupied resembled a distorted echo of the park near Hope Spring Memorial—familiar, yet hauntingly *off*.

In the Living World, the real park buzzed with life: children's laughter, families picnicking, and dogs chasing squirrels. Here, the imitation held none of that vibrancy. No sound. No movement. Just a hollow, desolate replica.

But Arthur wasn't here for nostalgia. If he wanted to experience the world as it was, he could have easily gone to the Living World. No, his purpose here was far more deliberate.

He sat with his arms crossed, his fingers tapping rhythmically against his bicep, his expression stoic as he stared into the distance.

Tap . . . Tap . . . Tap . . .

He had nearly counted to a hundred when a shadow emerged in the distance. The figure approached slowly, its form sharpening into the shape of a boy dressed entirely in white, his eyes empty of pupils. The Nameless Spirit radiated irritation as he drew closer, though Arthur remained seated, unmoved by the boy's arrival.

'Took you long enough,' Arthur said flatly.

'You are insufferable,' the Nameless Spirit shot back, his voice laced with disdain. He climbed onto the bench without invitation, glaring at Arthur with an intensity that felt palpable despite his featureless eyes. 'What do you want?'

Arthur turned his head slightly to regard him. The Nameless Spirit's perpetual scorn was a personality trait that had been a constant thorn in Arthur's side, but he had long since stopped letting it bother him.

'I needed to see you,' he said.

The Nameless Spirit scoffed.

'If that's all, you could've summoned me from the fourth floor. Why drag me out here?'

Arthur's gaze shifted back to the Void.

'I didn't come here to argue with you.'

The boy's scowl deepened. When he didn't respond, Arthur continued.

'I need a favour,' he began.

'No,' the Nameless Spirit interrupted before Arthur could elaborate.

'You *owe* me, Spirit,' Arthur said, his voice carried a warning edge, his patience clearly fraying. The

Nameless Spirit, unbothered, leaned back on the bench, defiance written in every line of his posture.

'Do I need to remind you that it was *you* who tipped Emilia and Thomas off about the master skeleton key?' Arthur said. He'd readied the threat in anticipation of the boy's usual resistance.

The boy flinched, his bravado faltering, allowing Arthur a moment to bask in satisfaction.

'You didn't think they'd actually manage to get it, did you?' Arthur continued. 'But they did. And now we're dealing with the consequences of that and cleaning up the mess.'

The Nameless Spirit huffed in agitation, but relented, saying, 'Fine, *fine*. What do you need?'

Arthur tapped the folder next to him twice with deliberate precision. Then, from the inside pocket of his jacket, he withdrew the thumb drive and placed it on top of the folder.

'I need you to hide these,' he said.

The Nameless Spirit blinked, his pale, empty eyes flickering between the items. His nose wrinkled in clear distaste.

'Things from the Living World?' he asked. 'I can't do that.'

'You can.'

The boy's frown deepened, and he crossed his arms as if warding off the very idea.

'Things from the Living World belong in the Living World,' he countered firmly. 'They don't belong in the Spirit World. An esteemed Grim Reaper such as yourself should know better.'

Arthur's silence was daunting, his gaze still fixed on the infinite expanse before them. When he finally spoke, his voice was quiet.

'This isn't the Spirit World, though, is it?'

The Nameless Spirit flinched, the words lodging themselves uncomfortably in his throat. A prickling unease began to creep over him, something he rarely experienced and hardly knew how to process. He shifted, fidgeting slightly as his spine tingled with the first whispers of dread.

'No,' the boy admitted reluctantly. 'It isn't.'

Arthur turned to face him fully now.

'Then this shouldn't be a problem,' he said simply.

The Nameless Spirit stared at him, the emptiness of his gaze masking the turmoil stirring within. He shifted on the bench, his usual scorn giving way to something more defensive.

'Would it help if I said I don't want to keep those things here, instead of saying that I couldn't?' he tried.

'No.'

The boy glared at the white sky above. He released a frustrated sigh that sounded more like a petulant groan.

'You're so aggravating,' he muttered, his boyish voice slipping into a whine.

'The Void is your domain,' Arthur said. 'This shouldn't be much of an issue for you. If I left these things here, they'd be problematic. But if *you* handled them, it'd be fine. Wouldn't it?'

The Nameless Spirit glowered at him; his sharp features twisted into a pout that might have been amusing under different circumstances. After a long moment, he exhaled sharply, his resistance crumbling.

'Fine,' he said at last, resigned. 'But if this comes back to bite me—'

'It won't,' Arthur assured him.

The boy huffed, snatching the thumb drive and folder with a speed that belied his irritation.

'You owe *me* after this,' he grumbled, hopping off the bench with exaggerated flair. 'And don't think I'll let you forget it.'

The Nameless Spirit found it both irritating and disconcerting how Arthur always seemed to know too much. But then again, what didn't he know? The boy raised his hand, moving with the fluidity of someone performing a ritual they'd mastered long ago. His fingers curled as if gripping something tangible, though the air was empty. With a deft motion, he appeared to pull the very fabric of the Void over the folder and flash drive, draping them in invisibility. The bench, now smooth and unremarkable, gave no indication that the items had ever been there.

As the gatekeeper of realms, the Nameless Spirit's responsibilities extended far beyond guarding thresholds. The Void, a liminal space between worlds, was under his stewardship. It served as a holding ground for spirits transitioning elsewhere, a nexus where the boundaries of existence blurred. Nothing entered or exited the Void without his knowledge. And yet, Arthur was the exception, the singular entity who could traverse this space unbidden. It grated on the boy more than he cared to admit.

Arthur adjusted his tie, preparing to leave now that his business was concluded. But the Nameless Spirit's voice stopped him, sharper and more serious than before.

'I do not care about you or your little schemes, but you shouldn't meddle in the Living World,' the boy said, his pale eyes narrowing. 'This isn't something I have to tell you of all people.'

Arthur paused.

'You're blaming me for meddling?' he asked. 'You're the one who told them about the master skeleton key. Don't pin this on me.'

'You're getting too involved with her,' the Nameless Spirit said. There was a knowing edge to his words; he knew more than he let on.

Arthur turned his head slightly, just enough to glance over his shoulder. He didn't need clarification. He knew well enough the person who was the topic of their conversation.

'She's a friend. I'm helping her. That's all.'

The boy's laughter was soft but biting.

'A friend? You do not have *friends*, Grim Reaper.'

'She's a friend,' Arthur repeated, his voice leaving no room for argument.

The Nameless Spirit's lips curved into a sly smirk.

'Let's put that to the test, shall we?'

He snapped his fingers, the sound echoing faintly in the endless expanse. At first, nothing happened. Arthur remained unfazed, his manner unshaken.

'That won't work on me,' he said. 'I'm not a lost spirit. I'm a Grim Reaper.'

The boy's expression didn't change. Moments later, a figure began to materialize in the Void. At first, it was indistinct, a hazy silhouette without form or substance. But as it moved closer, its shape grew sharper, details emerging until it stood fully formed before them.

Arthur's entire body tensed, his jaw clenching as recognition dawned.

'*Well*,' the Nameless Spirit said. 'What do we have here?'

It was Emilia.

Not the real Emilia, of course. Spirits couldn't enter the Void unless summoned. But this was no ordinary projection; it was a manifestation of Arthur's subconscious, brought to life by the Nameless Spirit's meddling.

The boy's smirk widened as he observed Arthur's reaction.

'You know,' he began, his voice light but edged with mischief, 'a person's subconscious in the Void always takes the form of someone they cherish. Someone who brings them the most comfort.'

Arthur said nothing, his gaze locked on the apparition before him. His silence spoke volumes, though he refused to let the boy's words provoke him. Grim Reapers did not usually have subconscious representations in the Void, and he did not have one either. Until now. The projection of Emilia standing before them was proof that the real her was beginning to affect him in ways he could not comprehend.

It reflected his growing awareness of the flurry of emotions that had started to swell within him.

'Do you still think she's just a friend?' the Nameless Spirit pressed, words dripping with mockery. 'Your subconscious seems to disagree.'

Arthur remained silent, his eyes hard and his posture rigid. The Nameless Spirit's smugness only grew.

'That girl isn't just your friend, Grim Reaper. You're lying to yourself if you think otherwise.'

36

'Of all people . . .' Thomas muttered irritably under his breath as they sat in Arthur's office, the file Sadie had given them now open on the desk between them.

'You do not agree with Sadie's suggestion?' Arthur asked, deliberately avoiding Emilia's gaze.

Though he'd done his best to dismiss the Nameless Spirit's accusation, it lingered, gnawing at him. Every time he glanced at Emilia, the thought surfaced—his subconscious had taken *her* form. That had to mean something, even if he refused to admit it.

'It's not that I disagree with her,' Thomas said, frustrated. 'It's just . . . I don't think he's the right person for the job we need him to do.'

'What's wrong with him?' Arthur asked, frowning at Thomas' evident irritation.

'For starters, it's *him*!' Thomas replied with exasperation, waving a hand at the file as if that alone should suffice. When Arthur's confusion persisted, Thomas heaved a sigh and elaborated.

'Marcel is one of the guys involved with J.Tech. I don't trust him one bit, and I have no idea why Sadie would suggest he's the perfect person to help us bring down the very company he's working for.'

Arthur's eyes returned to the file. As expected, Sadie had been thorough. Her reasoning was laid out clearly, supported by various, and very valid, points. One of the key arguments she had presented was Marcel's existing connection to J.Tech. While Thomas viewed this as a liability, Sadie had framed it as an advantage. According to her, Marcel's involvement with the company would mitigate suspicion if he suddenly acquired the file and thumb drive. Authorities would naturally conclude that his insider status gave him access to the information. His decision to turn against J.Tech could then be interpreted as an act of redemption, a plausible narrative that might even garner public sympathy.

Arthur found no immediate flaws in Sadie's logic. Her analysis was sound. However, Thomas was not so easily swayed and continued to voice his objections with vigour.

'He knows Eldon,' Thomas said, his tone sharp with emphasis. 'Don't you think that's weird? Don't you think it's *suspicious*?'

Arthur finally looked at Emilia, gauging her reaction. He wasn't certain how he felt about Marcel's connection to Eldon, and for reasons he did not examine too closely, he found himself looking to her for direction. But Emilia seemed unbothered. When their eyes met, she offered a faint, awkward smile and shrugged. Clearly, she wasn't as concerned as Thomas was.

'Sadie has already addressed that point,' Arthur said.

Sadie's file detailed Marcel's acquaintance with Eldon, acknowledging the connection but downplaying its significance. In fact, she had outlined several ways they could leverage this connection to their advantage, chief among them being emotional manipulation. Her plan involved exploiting Marcel's soft spot for his friend, a strategy that was hardly ethical but undeniably effective, especially if the situation escalated. Her meticulous approach had covered every angle, and even Arthur struggled to find fault with her reasoning. She'd noted that while the relationship was worth monitoring, it wasn't an inherent disqualifier altogether.

Thomas, however, was far from convinced.

'I still don't like it,' he muttered.

'Your concerns are noted,' Arthur said at last. His tone firm but not dismissive as he drummed his fingers lightly against the desk. 'But unless you have a better alternative, we'll proceed with Sadie's recommendation.'

Thomas looked ready to argue, but Emilia cut in first.

'Maybe we should trust Sadie on this. She's never steered us wrong before.'

He scowled but said nothing more, clearly unhappy but unwilling to push back against Emilia's measured reasoning. Arthur, meanwhile, allowed himself another glance at her. Her calmness was a stark contrast to the unease he'd been battling since the Nameless Spirit's remarks. She didn't seem to realize how her presence affected him, and he wasn't sure whether that made things better or worse.

Defeated, Thomas slumped back in his chair, irritated.

'Fine,' he said at last. 'What's next?'

'Do we have any ideas on how to bring Marcel over to our side?' Arthur asked.

'Why don't you ask Sadie since she knows everything?' Thomas mumbled begrudgingly.

To his dismay, Emilia chimed in, 'That's actually a good idea.'

Arthur summoned Sadie to his office without delay. Thomas wore his annoyance openly at first, but it faded as their discussion unfolded. Sadie's expertise on the matter was undeniable, and her thorough research left no room for doubt. She seemed to know almost everything there was to know about Marcel. Even Thomas, begrudging as he was, couldn't help but acknowledge that.

As the conversation progressed, Sadie suddenly said, 'No matter how we approach this, it has to look like a haunting. That's the only way we'll get away with it.'

Arthur agreed, but Emilia and Thomas exchanged puzzled looks.

'What do you mean?' Emilia asked.

'Remember what I said about not interfering directly in the Living World? If we overstep, there are consequences. One way to avoid that is to disguise our actions as hauntings. Or rather, to actually haunt them.'

'Wait,' Thomas said, sitting upright and turning to Sadie. 'Was that why you created a target file for that lawyer?'

'Exactly,' Sadie replied, as though her meticulous foresight was nothing extraordinary. Addressing the group, she continued, 'As I was saying, we need to approach Marcel in a way that seems otherworldly. We could frighten him into compliance or simply use the scare as a guise. Either way, his connection to Eldon is our way in. It's his weak spot, at least from what I've gathered.'

Emilia frowned slightly. 'You really think exploiting his friendship with Eldon will work?'

'Absolutely,' Sadie said with certainty. 'Marcel's loyalty to Eldon can be a powerful motivator. Whether it's guilt, fear, or some lingering sense of responsibility, we can use it to nudge him in the right direction. He doesn't have to know the whole truth; he just needs to believe that helping us is the right choice.'

'Then we proceed with caution. If we're going to use fear, it needs to be controlled. A means to an end, not chaos for its own sake,' Arthur said.

Time dragged on as they hashed out the details, debating various angles until, at last, a plan began to take shape. It wasn't a solid plan since most of it hinged on Marcel's reaction, but it was *something*, and something was always better than nothing.

Sadie rose to her feet as she said, 'That's all from me. I'm not carrying out another scare, so you lot will have to take it from here. My advice? Get on with it. No time like the present and all that.'

'Right,' Thomas muttered. He stretched, then turned to Emilia and Arthur. 'You coming?'

Emilia trailed after him but stopped when Arthur's hand closed around her arm. She looked over her shoulder at him, tilting her head quizzically, and silently asking, '*What?*'

Arthur shook his head: '*Nothing.*'

He shifted his grip to her wrist, fingers closing around the bracelet. A faint hum vibrated through it as it pulsed with a new influx of energy, flowing steadily from his hand into hers. Emilia watched the wisp of glowing energy coil and settle within the band. She glanced at him, only to find he was already looking at her. He smiled.

'Just in case you needed more,' he said.

She willed herself to ignore the warmth rising to her face, and the way her pulse quickened. Why in the world was she reacting like this? He'd shared his energy with her countless times before. This was nothing new. And yet, something about the way he smiled at her now felt different, disarming.

What was wrong with her?

No—what was wrong with *him*? Why was he smiling at her like that?

37

Marcel's footsteps echoed softly through the late-night hospital corridor. Despite knowing it was pointless, a part of him always hoped that on one of his many visits to Hope Spring Memorial, he'd open the door to find Eldon sitting up and grinning at him, just like he used to whenever he dropped by the precinct. Today wasn't that day either.

His head throbbed with the headache that had been plaguing him since yesterday, and his shoulders sagged under a burden that was more than fatigue. It was the dull, ceaseless weight of guilt—a heavy, insidious thing that pressed down on him a little more with each visit. He paused in front of the elevator, pressing his thumb and forefinger against his temples and closing his eyes, hoping to ease the ache.

A faint rustling noise stirred behind him. He ignored it. Marcel didn't scare easily, and his logical mind quickly reasoned that the sound could've been anything: the soft shift of a patient turning in their bed, perhaps. But then he felt it. A chill that slid up his spine and pooled into a tingling sensation at the nape of his neck.

The fine hairs on his arms prickled.

He turned sharply, scanning the corridor.

Nothing.

The hallway was empty.

He let out a shaky breath he hadn't realized he'd been holding and shook his head. The lights overhead hummed steadily, but the space around him felt darker somehow, as though the shadows had grown thicker and were inching closer. He gritted his teeth, trying to shake off this feeling.

He didn't scare easily.

Turning back to the elevator, he jabbed the call button repeatedly, his eyes fixed on the digital display above the doors.

Come on . . . Come on . . .

The rustling noise came again, this time louder, closer. He clenched his jaw and kept his focus on the elevator, determined to ignore it. The button's dull glow offered a small anchor, though it did little to calm his nerves.

Then he heard something else. Footsteps. Light, almost playful, like a child skipping down the corridor. His stomach tightened. The hallways were supposed to be empty. There were no other visitors this late at night and especially not children. He was certain of that. At least, he *had* been certain.

Swallowing hard, he hesitated before glancing over his shoulder. He didn't know what he expected to see, but the relief that washed over him when he saw nothing there was almost dizzying. The hallway remained as deserted as before. Yet . . . something caught his attention. He squinted, his gaze narrowing on a door about twenty paces away.

It was slightly ajar. Normally, it wouldn't mean much. But this door . . .

It was Eldon's.

He knew he had closed it when he left. He always did. Why was it open now? Who had opened it? It couldn't have been the nurses; they wouldn't leave a door ajar. The rational voice in his head screamed at him to ignore it, to get away while he still could, but his gaze kept drifting back to it.

The elevator's digital display flickered, the arrow hovering on the second floor as if it had stalled there. The elevator itself showed no signs of ascending to the sixth floor. Again, a vague discomfort pressed at the edges of his mind. Something wasn't right.

The open door to Eldon's room seemed to draw him in, beckoning, tugging at him with quiet insistence. But he resisted the urge, taking several steps back to put distance between them. Turning away, he headed towards the stairwell. Six flights of stairs weren't insurmountable, and at this point, it seemed the better option.

The hallway was unnervingly quiet. Even the nurses' station was vacant. He tried not to dwell on the strangeness of it, focusing instead on reaching the stairwell. When he arrived, he grasped the handle and pushed.

It didn't budge.

Frowning, he tried again, throwing his weight into it, but the door remained stubbornly locked. He rattled the handle a few more times, frustration mounting. Then, reluctantly, he glanced back down the corridor.

Eldon's door was still open, the only one in the hallway. He swallowed hard. It felt like the hospital itself was pushing him in that direction, leaving him with no alternatives. His pulse thrummed in his ears as he retraced his steps, each one heavier than the last.

When he reached Eldon's room, he hesitated at the threshold, his breath shallow. He peered inside. Eldon lay motionless in his bed, his face peaceful, the sharp lines of his features softened in his deep, unbroken sleep. Marcel stepped inside cautiously, scanning it more out of habit than reason. It was empty. And yet, the sensation of not being alone—of being watched—pressed down on him.

The air felt colder here, denser. A faint shiver ran up his arm. The door had clicked shut behind him, even though he hadn't touched it. The sound echoed in the silent room, sharp and absolute. Every instinct screamed at him to leave, but something rooted him in place.

Then he heard a mechanical click. His eyes darted to the cabinet across the room, just as the door swung open with a low creak. Something inside caught the fluorescent light and gleamed. Marcel approached it against his better judgement, and the air seemed to thicken with each step he took.

He reached the cabinet, his hand hovered over the edge of the door before he pulled it wider. The hinges groaned in protest, the sound grating in the silence. Inside, was a glossy photograph: a picture of him and Eldon. One he recognized instantly.

Marcel's stomach churned. He wouldn't have thought much of it, would have chalked it up to some coincidence or even a mistake. But he knew this photograph. He *knew* it.

It was the very same one from his apartment.

How the hell had it ended up here?

By the time Marcel burst out into the hallway, his sense of reality had begun to fray. He nearly collided with the night nurse as he fled, and somehow made it all the way to his car without stopping. The elevator, he later learned, had not been malfunctioning, something the night nurse had confirmed with visible confusion, and the stairwell door had been unlocked the entire time.

He was certain of what he'd seen and experienced, yet it felt unreal. The pounding in his head only grew worse as he drove back to his apartment, a relentless thrum that seemed to echo his unease. He checked the rearview mirror repeatedly, searching the empty backseat for reassurance. Still, the feeling of being watched lingered. It was irrational, he told himself. Exhaustion, stress, and a warped imagination. But deep down, he knew the truth was far stranger.

The moment he reached his apartment he slammed the door shut behind him and twisted the lock into place. His breath came in short gasps as he moved to the living room, heading straight for the frame that housed the photograph of him and Eldon.

The frame was there.

The photograph was not.

The realization sent a chill creeping down his spine and raised the hairs on his arms.

His hands trembled as he reached for the light switch. He flipped it on. Nothing. He flipped it again. The bulb sputtered weakly, casting flickering shadows that seemed to stretch and twist unnaturally before plunging the room back into darkness. He stood frozen, his pulse hammering in his ears. Then he moved quickly, trying the other switches in the apartment. None of them worked. The entire place was cloaked in gloom.

His nerves were completely frayed by the time he stumbled into his bedroom. With every movement he made, the shadows around him seemed to expand and contract, shifting as though they had a will of their own. His breathing grew erratic, each shallow inhale only heightening his awareness of the suffocating atmosphere. Despite his pounding heart and the tightness in his chest, he tried to rationalize what he was feeling.

It's exhaustion, he told himself. *I'm just tired. That's all this is.*

But . . . it wasn't just his imagination. He could *feel* it. The walls seemed closer, and the darkness thicker, as though it had substance.

He shook his head violently, trying to dispel the growing dread.

'No,' he muttered, 'no, I'm overthinking this.'

All he needed was sleep. Tomorrow, he'd call an electrician to fix the faulty wiring. Everything would be fine. It had to be fine. But in the back of his mind, he knew the night was far from over. It was only just beginning.

A soft scraping sound pulled Marcel from his thoughts, like nails dragging over wood. The noise had come from behind him. His wardrobe. A chill swept through the room, settling over him like an icy shroud. He was used to this by now, though he wished he wasn't. The sensation ran along his skin, a dread he couldn't shake off. Slowly, he glanced over his shoulder, half-expecting to see the wardrobe door creak open. But there was nothing. The sound stopped.

But the silence didn't last.

A breath brushed against his ear.

A hollow whisper slipped into the air, trailing through the room like a tendril. Someone was definitely there with him. He straightened, his eyes darting around the darkness, heart hammering in his chest. It was too dim to make out much beyond the faint shapes illuminated by the moonlight streaming through the window. He shivered as an icy feeling clawed at his gut. His gaze fell on the mirror across the room, and he startled, only to exhale in relief when he realized it was just his reflection staring back at him.

But then he noticed something he hadn't before.

He could see himself clearly, but everything else in the mirror looked . . . *wrong*.

The room in the reflection wasn't his.

Curiosity warred with fear, but something urged him forward. His trembling steps carried him closer to the mirror. In the reflection, he could make out faint, shifting shadows, outlines that almost resembled people. His mind resisted shaping them into anything concrete. He leaned in, squinting, trying to decipher the scene. What was he looking at?

Rows of chairs stretched out around his mirrored self, their shapes shadowy and distorted. They became clearer in time, and he began to recognize the familiar features of a lone figure standing in what appeared to be an abandoned theatre. But the person staring back at him wasn't just anyone.

'Eldon . . .' he murmured, leaning in closer. But no, this wasn't his friend. The eyes were familiar but . . . different.

It was a girl.

Eldon's sister.

He blinked, his mind struggling to process what he was seeing. It couldn't be her. She was *dead*. But there she was, staring back at him from the mirror's surface with an intensity that pinned him in place.

Marcel stumbled back, his heel catching on something in the darkness. He tried to steady himself, but the moment overwhelmed him. He fell, the world tilting around him as darkness rushed in. The last thing he saw before losing consciousness was her reflection, her piercing gaze watching him as he slipped into the darkness.

38

Thomas loomed over Marcel's unconscious body, hands planted on his hips, an exasperated sigh caught on his lips. The room was brightly lit now, everything restored to its original state. He shook his head and cast a pointed look at Emilia, his expression hovering between amusement and disbelief.

'Do you make it a habit of doing this to every guy you meet?' he asked.

'I'm sorry,' Emilia said, throwing her hands up in frustration. 'How was I supposed to know he'd trip and pass out like that?'

Thomas pulled a face, equal parts scepticism and mild reproach, before turning to Arthur. By any measure, their haunting had been a flop. Marcel had not been scared into compliance, and the results fell far short of Sadie's ruthless success with Lucas Caldwell.

'At least he didn't die,' Emilia muttered.

Thomas raised an eyebrow, *Really? That's your defence?*

Emilia shrugged, out of better arguments. Unconsciousness *was* preferable to death.

Their plan, devised back at the Agency, had started in the hospital. Among Sadie's extensive notes on Marcel was his meticulously predictable routine. He visited Eldon once or twice a week, usually on Fridays or weekends. This consistency worked in their favour; it confirmed that Marcel still cared about his friend, a connection they needed to exploit.

Arthur had assigned the task to Emilia and Thomas, choosing to observe rather than intervene unless absolutely necessary. That decision accounted for the mediocrity of the haunt. Thomas, with more energy to spare than Emilia, had carried the bulk of the effort, though his inexperience limited him. Still, the scare had yielded something.

Thomas discovered he had a knack for mimicking sounds—footsteps, whispers, faint echoes—and he exploited that talent to its fullest. While the noises hadn't terrified Marcel outright, they contributed to his mounting sense of dread. Emilia, meanwhile, focused on manipulating the room's temperature, sending icy chills rippling through the space. The combination, while far from flawless, was enough to unnerve someone already on the edge of paranoia.

The photograph had been Arthur's idea.

'Humans are sentimental creatures,' he'd said. Something that invoked Marcel's bond with Eldon would stir the guilt they needed to use as leverage. And it had worked. At least partially. Marcel had recognized the picture and reacted to it. That was a start.

The dread that had begun to build from Marcel's experience in the hospital and his tense drive home was carefully cultivated. Emilia and Thomas worked in tandem, gradually nudging him closer to the brink. Their plan centred on the mirror in his bedroom, which they manipulated to reflect the abandoned movie theatre. That was where they planned to leave the evidence for him to find.

Revealing herself to Marcel had been Emilia's idea. It was a risk, only made possible by Arthur's energy stored in the bracelet she wore. She'd thought showing him her face, imploring him for help, would bridge the gap between fear and understanding. After all, he needed to know what had been done to both Eldon and her, the horrors that tied them all together. But the execution hadn't gone as planned.

'It was a good try,' Arthur reassured them. 'A great one, in fact. Both of you have come a long way.'

Emilia looked at her wrist, where the inked numbers marking her points had changed. She now had 180 points.

'I didn't know I could still earn points for scaring people,' she said. She was a researcher now, not an active agent.

'A scare is a scare,' Arthur replied.

Thomas, grinning broadly, held up his own wrist to show her the number 100 etched onto his skin. His excitement was infectious, and even Emilia couldn't help but smile at his enthusiasm.

Their attention returned to Marcel, still unconscious on the floor. His chest rose and fell steadily, the only sign of life in the room.

'What now?' Thomas asked.

'Technically, we haven't achieved what we set out to do,' Emilia said, looking nervously at Arthur. The obvious solution—scare Marcel again—sat poorly with her.

'I don't think we should try scaring him again,' Arthur said. 'He was already rattled after the mirror incident.'

'Isn't that the point?' Thomas asked.

'Usually, yes. But if we push too hard, he might do something reckless.'

Marcel was impulsive, and given his current state of mind, anything was possible. And while demons weren't exactly chasing him, the trio's presence was enough to make him believe otherwise.

The absurdity of it all struck Emilia. Three of them, standing over an unconscious man, debating the ethics and effectiveness of their haunting methods. Her thoughts drifted as she watched Marcel. She had grown accustomed to moments like this—pauses between their chaotic attempts to manoeuvre the Living World. But this one felt different. It was quieter, more reflective, and much more unsettling in its own way.

She caught herself thinking about Arthur. When had his opinions begun to matter so much? When had she started thinking of him as a friend? Or maybe even something more? Things between them had undeniably changed, and it left her more confused than ever. Still, she was relieved to see that the tension between Arthur and Thomas had eased. Thomas had returned to his usual self, at least where Arthur was concerned and the animosity between them seemed to have dissipated. For that, she was grateful.

'Emilia?'

She blinked, realizing she'd been staring off into space.

'I'm sorry, what?' she asked, glancing between Thomas and Arthur, who both looked at her with concern.

'You drifted off. Are you all right?' Arthur asked.

'Yes, sorry. I was just lost in thought,' she said with an embarrassed smile.

Arthur studied her a moment longer before saying, 'Right. Well, we've decided to wait.'

He motioned to Thomas.

'It's not ideal, but we're going to keep an eye on Marcel. Track his movements. If we push him too far, he'll bolt. I'm convinced of it.' Thomas scowled at Marcel, sprawled on the floor. 'Coward.'

'There's no point in rushing this if it risks ruining everything. We need Marcel, and we can't afford to lose him.'

'I *am* sorry about the mirror. I didn't expect him to pass out like that,' Emilia said, remorse tugging at her.

'It wasn't your fault,' Arthur said. He pointed at the culprit: a cable stretched haphazardly across the room, plugged into a corner socket. 'He tripped over that and knocked himself out. No one could've predicted that.'

'Besides,' he continued, a faint smile on his lips, 'it was a clever trick to make yourself appear in the reflection. Incredibly well done. Don't beat yourself up over it.'

Thomas, who'd been glowering at Marcel, brightened at Arthur's words. He flashed Emilia a thumbs up, his grin returning in full force.

Despite the mishap, a quiet sense of accomplishment settled over them. The haunt had worked, at least in part, and now all that remained was to wait. For what, exactly, Emilia wasn't entirely sure.

39

Thomas, Emilia, and Arthur had agreed to take turns watching over Marcel, holding off on any further action until he had calmed down. For now, he was far too shaken, and any attempt to approach or frighten him again would likely prove useless. Unfortunately for them, the haunting had affected Marcel far more deeply than they had expected.

Not only had his paranoia worsened, he was now thoroughly convinced that the apparition he had seen in the mirror was Eldon's dead sister, come to exact revenge for his supposed involvement in her death and her brother's accident.

'That wasn't my intention!' Emilia shouted at him as she watched him stagger across the room, muttering under his breath. She knew it was pointless to yell. He couldn't hear her. But the sheer depth of his misunderstanding was infuriating, especially as it chipped away at his sanity little by little.

'You're so stupid,' she muttered, slumping back against the headboard.

She burned with annoyance as she watched him bite his fingernails, pacing the short length of the room like a caged animal. The curtains were drawn tight, and the sliver of moonlight visible through the small gap fell across the carpet in a pale stripe. The mirror she had used as a conduit to appear before him was gone. Earlier, she had wandered the apartment and found it shattered in the cramped storage room. Every other mirror in the apartment had towels over them, held in place by multiple rounds of duct tape. They would never get away with using the same trick twice.

'How long has he been like this?' Thomas asked from the doorway, his head poking into the room before stepping inside. He dropped onto the bed beside her, looking every bit as exhausted as she felt.

'It feels like forever,' she muttered.

Thomas gave a low whistle. 'I didn't think he'd be this much of a handful.'

'None of us did,' she replied, rubbing at her temples.

A week had passed since the initial haunting, and in that time, Marcel had only deteriorated. He had done little else but prowl the apartment, muttering to himself in weak attempts to reaffirm his sanity. But even that, she realized, was troubling. His behaviour bordered on obsession, a desperation to piece together a reality that now felt fragmented and hostile to him.

'How are we supposed to work with someone who's lost his damn mind?'

'I don't know,' Emilia admitted. She rested her elbows on her knees, burying her face in her hands. 'This wasn't how it was supposed to go.'

'It's not your fault,' he said. 'The guy's just . . . a mess. Always has been, probably.'

'You're not helping.'

He shrugged.

'What do you want me to say? He'll snap out of it?' He nodded towards Marcel, who was now mumbling something incoherent. 'Because I'm not sure he will.'

Emilia watched Marcel pace the room. The plan had seemed so simple when they'd discussed it: scare him, push him towards action, and use his guilt to their advantage. But watching him unravel like this made her wonder if they'd miscalculated entirely. Marcel wasn't just scared, he seemed broken. And a broken man couldn't help anyone, least of all them.

'I don't think this is going to work,' she finally admitted. Thomas agreed.

'Arthur might have put a little too much faith in Sadie's choice because *this*'—he gestured broadly at Marcel—'is not the kind of guy who's going to stand up to a multimillion-dollar company like J.Tech.'

Emilia winced, unable to argue with his assessment. Marcel looked unkempt beyond recognition. His hair stuck out in wild tufts, dark circles sagged beneath his eyes, and his clothes were rumpled and stained, the same ones he'd been wearing since the day of the haunting. He had not changed, shaved, or showered, and his erratic behaviour only added to the image of someone barely holding it together.

'I'm sure Sadie had her reasons,' she said. 'Marcel will pull through. He has to.' She frowned, watching him stop mid-step, wringing his hands together. 'I think.'

Thomas snorted, pushing himself to his feet.

'Well, I'm going to that one room at the back to practise using my energy. This guy doesn't go back there, does he? If he sees me moving stuff, he'll freak out even more.'

'He usually stays holed up in here,' Emilia said. 'Go ahead. I'll stay and keep an eye on him.'

'Shout if you need me,' he said before disappearing through the wall, leaving her alone with Marcel once more.

Unlike Marcel, who was stuck in a loop of paranoia, Thomas had spent the past week honing his abilities. The haunting had motivated him, especially after the significant number of points he'd earned. Emilia admired his resolve, even if it was hard to share it while watching Marcel deteriorate before her eyes.

Time passed slowly, the silence broken only by Marcel's incessant mutterings. Then, without warning, a thunderous knocking shattered the quiet, rattling the front door on its hinges. Marcel's entire body went rigid with fear. His wide eyes locked on the door, but he made no move to answer it. The knocking grew louder, more insistent, until it suddenly stopped, leaving an eerie stillness in its wake.

Marcel exhaled shakily and turned to retreat into his room, but he didn't make it far before the door exploded with a deafening crash. Splinters of wood flew across the hallway as the door slammed to the ground, revealing a figure framed in the jagged opening.

'*Marcel*,' a voice snarled, low and furious. 'Where the hell have you been?'

Blake stepped over the wreckage, his face contorted with rage. He crossed the room in quick, aggressive strides and grabbed Marcel by the collar, yanking him forward with such force that the smaller man stumbled.

Marcel's prolonged absence from work had caused problems, and Blake, with his notoriously short temper, had assumed the worst. Marcel's refusal to answer his calls or respond to his messages had only added to his growing fury.

'Do you have any idea what you've done? The mess you've left me to clean up?' Blake bellowed. 'I had to cover for you, you selfish bastard! You don't get to just disappear and leave me to deal with the fallout!'

Marcel tried to stammer a response, but Blake cut him off with a sharp shove that sent him sprawling. Emilia, though invisible to them, flinched at the impact.

Blake lost what little control he had left as he unleashed a flurry of punches, each blow punctuated by rage and shouted accusations.

'You think you can just walk away? That you're the only one who's struggling?' he yelled, his blows landing without restraint. 'Grow up, Marcel! You're pathetic!'

Emilia panicked. She didn't know what to do. Arthur had given them strict orders not to interfere, but Marcel was already on the verge of unconsciousness. If this continued, he would die.

A deafening, guttural roar tore through the apartment just then, a chorus of furious voices rising as one. The sound wasn't human; it reverberated through the walls. Emilia turned to see Thomas standing there, fuming, his gazed locked on Blake. This . . . this was a *haunting*.

'Thomas—' she murmured, moving towards him, but he cut her off, his voice calm and controlled, a stark contrast to the chaos unfurling around them.

'Leave this to me. I'll deal with him.'

The sudden disturbance had pulled Thomas from the back room. But when he entered the foyer and saw Blake relentlessly beating Marcel, his worry transformed into seething anger. Not at the sight of Marcel, whom he cared little about, but at the man towering over him. Blake's presence reignited a fury Thomas thought he had buried long ago.

Seeing Blake again dragged Thomas back to the day he'd overheard Blake speak about Emilia's death with cold indifference. No remorse. No humanity. Just indifference, as though her murder was an inconvenience rather than a tragedy. That memory had festered, an open wound in Thomas' soul. Now, with Blake standing right before him, the anger surged anew, fierce and unrelenting.

Energy buzzed through him, electrifying and potent, feeding off his rage. He had never felt this powerful in death. Every ounce of his remaining essence had been set ablaze. He raised a hand, and in an instant, every lightbulb in the room shattered, plunging the space into darkness. Sparks flew, their flashes illuminating Blake's terrified face. The temperature dropped sharply, frost forming on the walls and windows as a thick fog swirled up from the ground.

Blake released Marcel and staggered backward, his legs shaking as the fog curled around his ankles like ghostly hands. Shadows deeper than night stretched along the walls, clawing their way towards him, writhing as though alive.

Thomas advanced, his arm outstretched, and a wave of unseen force erupted from him, slamming Blake against the wall. The man gasped, pinned in place as though an invisible hand clutched his chest, crushing the air from his lungs. The room quaked in response to Thomas' wrath. Furniture trembled, then levitated, before smashing into walls and splintering into jagged shards. Books flew from shelves, ripped apart midair as unseen claws shredded them into confetti, the paper fragments swirling in a violent storm.

Blake collapsed to the floor, scrambling to crawl away, his movements sluggish as if the very ground beneath him had turned to quicksand. His shaking hands fumbled for his phone. He managed to pull it from his pocket, his breath coming in panicked gasps. He didn't know who to call; he just knew he needed help.

Before he could press a single button, the phone exploded in his hand. Blake yelped, clutching his injured hand to his chest, his eyes darting around wildly. Terror consumed him. He tried to speak, to scream, but no sound escaped his lips.

Then, just as suddenly as it had begun, the chaos ceased. The fog evaporated, and the shadows retreated to the corners of the room. The air was still. Silent. If not for the shattered furniture, scattered papers, and shards of glass littering the floor, Blake might have convinced himself it had all been a nightmare. But the destruction spoke otherwise.

His ragged breaths echoed in the ruined room as he sank to his knees. Overwhelmed by the ordeal, his vision blurred, as the world spun around him. His body gave out, and he collapsed into unconsciousness.

40

Emilia's mind reeled as she took in the devastation around her. The apartment had been reduced to a disaster zone, fragments of broken furniture and shattered glass strewn across the floor. She hadn't realized Thomas was capable of such ferocity. This hadn't been just a scare; it was total destruction. Blake lay unconscious on the ground, his body limp and his breathing shallow. Nearby, Marcel cowered against the wall, his knees drawn to his chest, whimpering softly with his head buried in his hands as though trying to block out the world.

Emilia's attention shifted to Thomas. He stood rigid with his back to her, staring at Blake's prone form. Something about his stillness unnerved her.

'Thomas?' she called, her voice barely above a whisper. She took a cautious step towards him, then another.

When she reached out to touch his shoulder, his body seemed to lose all strength. He crumpled to his knees, his head drooping as though the energy sustaining him had been completely drained. Emilia rushed forward instinctively, her panic surging.

'Thomas?' she repeated, kneeling beside him. Her hands hovered uselessly as frustration and fear bubbled inside her. She hadn't known spirits could collapse like this, and the realization left her feeling unmoored.

She forced herself to stay calm and take stock of the situation. Blake was out cold. Marcel was a trembling mess, barely holding himself together. The apartment was in a shambles. And Thomas . . .

She steadied herself. Thomas couldn't die again, that much she knew. Still, the suddenness of his collapse rattled her. She closed her eyes briefly, drawing in a measured breath. If he'd exhausted his energy, she might be able to restore it—and by extension, revive him—by channelling energy into him.

A faint tingling spread through her as she summoned the familiar hum of power, letting it flow from her hands and into him.

'Thomas?' she whispered again, giving him a gentle shake.

He did not stir.

Emilia's heart sank as her eyes roamed over him. He didn't look injured, if spirits could even sustain physical injuries, but something was very wrong. Gently, she lifted his hand, turning it over to examine his wrist. Her breath caught when she saw the inked number. The last time he'd shown it to her, it had read 100. Now, the number sat well past 500.

She lowered his hand and settled beside him, legs folding beneath her. She considered her options. She could use the master skeleton key to return to the Spirit World and find Arthur, but leaving Thomas and Marcel here alone didn't feel right. Her thoughts turned to the bracelet at her wrist. Arthur had always been able to sense when she drew on its energy.

Perhaps . . . there was another way to get his attention.

Wrapping her hand around the bracelet, Emilia urged the energy stored within to expand, willing it to flow outward. If she drained the bracelet completely, there was a chance Arthur would notice. He'd warned her before about overusing its power, but this was an emergency.

'Come on,' she muttered under her breath, squeezing her eyes shut as she pushed harder. The familiar vibration of the bracelet's energy coursed through her, building steadily as she pushed it outward.

She had no idea if it would work, but she had to try.

A soft pulse spread through the room, the gem glowing faintly at first before intensifying. The energy rippled out in waves, vibrating the air around her. A faint hum filled the room, the dust stirred, swirling low to the ground, as nearby objects quivered. With one final pulsating wave, the energy drained completely. Emilia watched as the colourful swirls within the inlaid gem dulled and faded.

A beat of silence passed.

'What happened?'

She spun around, startled by the familiar voice, even as a wave of relief and comfort washed over her. Arthur stood behind her, his expression caught between worry and irritation as he took in the state of the room: the shattered furniture, the overturned objects, the debris scattered across the floor. Finally, his eyes settled on her.

'What happened?' he repeated, his voice tight with tension. His eyes shifted to Thomas lying motionless on the floor.

'Blake . . .' Emilia said, gesturing towards the unconscious man sprawled nearby. 'He broke down the front door, showed up out of nowhere, and went wild. He started beating the hell out of Marcel. I didn't know what to do, and you told me not to interfere, but Thomas.. . . .' She hesitated, the memory of the haunting still vivid. 'He lost it when he saw Blake. I don't know what happened. I don't know why he reacted like that.'

'*Thomas* did all this?' Arthur asked in disbelief.

Emilia nodded. Arthur exhaled a slow, controlled breath. When he spoke again, he appeared calmer, almost gentle.

'Are you all right? This must have been quite a shock.'

'I'm fine, but Thomas . . .' Her gaze drifted back to Thomas lying prone on the floor.

'Leave him. He'll recover,' Arthur said, stepping closer. 'He must have burned through his energy to do all this.' He motioned to the wreckage surrounding them. 'He's not accustomed to expending so much energy so quickly. He'll wake once he's regained some of it.'

She'd suspected as much. But why had Thomas pushed himself this far just to scare Blake? She didn't understand the depth of his anger, but for him to exhaust himself like this . . . Blake must have done something terrible to provoke such a reaction.

'I tried to channel energy into him,' she mumbled distractedly.

'It doesn't work like that. Spirits cannot share energy between them,' Arthur said. An amused smile graced his features when he added, 'It was nice of you to try.'

'But you . . .' she stopped, her words trailing off when she realized her mistake. Arthur, seemingly having read her mind, reminded her gently, 'I'm not a spirit. As you well know.'

'Right. Grim Reaper,' she said, wincing at her foolishness. Of course Grim Reapers were different. Of course they had an inexhaustible reserve of energy that they could channel into objects or share with other beings. Of course spirits didn't have the same freedom.

Her attention returned to Blake. 'Will he be all right?'

Arthur stood over him, observing him in silence for a moment.

'He'll be fine. There hasn't been a reaping notice for him. At least, none that I'm aware of.'

He had a contemplative expression on his face as though sorting through the tangled threads in his mind. Satisfied with whatever conclusion he'd drawn, he crossed the wreckage to crouch beside her, his movements precise and deliberate. To her surprise, he took her hand with unexpected gentleness.

'Are you truly all right?' he asked again. 'When I felt the energy in your bracelet drain so rapidly, it alarmed me. I wasn't prepared for it to deplete at such a rate.'

'I'm sorry,' she said. 'I didn't know any other way to reach you.'

Arthur's hand over hers kept her grounded, his concern tangible enough to seep through the cracks in her composure.

He inclined his head in acknowledgment. Then, with a quiet efficiency, he placed his hand over the bracelet. A faint glow emanated from his touch, and the swirling colours within the inlaid gem slowly returned. The energy pulsed gently once more, reassuring in its rhythm.

'I must ask you to refrain from summoning me that way in the future,' he said, though his tone held no real reprimand. 'Unless, of course, your intention is to frighten me half to death.'

It was a rare attempt at humour, and she realized belatedly that he was teasing her. Before she could stammer an apology or explain that she hadn't caught the joke, he spoke again, giving her no time to respond.

'Don't worry,' he continued. 'I won't make the same mistake of leaving your side again. If I remain with you, there will be no need to summon me at all.'

His words settled something within her, a reassurance that spread warmth through her chest despite the bleak surroundings. Arthur rose and scanned the room once more. The air around them was now charged with a different energy.

'Now then,' he began, his gaze sharp and purposeful. 'Did Marcel leave before or after this ruckus?'

Emilia blinked, confused.

'What?'

'When did Marcel leave?' he repeated, his tone remained even. 'Was it after Thomas began scaring Blake or during?'

Her stomach dropped as realization hit. She'd been so focused on Thomas and Blake that she hadn't thought to check on Marcel. Panic flared as she looked around the room, her heart pounding.

'*What?*' she nearly shrieked, the word tearing out of her. She twisted to scan every corner of the destroyed apartment. She noticed then what she should have noticed before.

Marcel was nowhere to be seen.

41

Arthur and Emilia stood on either side of Marcel's bed, staring down at him. The events of the past day had left him utterly shaken. Seeing Blake being flung around had been the final straw; traumatized and thoroughly convinced his apartment was haunted, Marcel had used the last of his strength to flee to a nearby motel. Neither Arthur nor Emilia would have known this if it hadn't been for Sadie.

Emilia had been too distraught by her mistake to focus on much else, apologizing repeatedly for her lapse in attention. Arthur's calm reassurances that he wasn't upset did little to ease her. She had been tasked with watching over Marcel, but her attention had been entirely on the unconscious Thomas. She hadn't even noticed when Marcel had slipped away. The mistake gnawed at her, each apology spilling out as a futile attempt to repair the situation.

Arthur, sensing her need to unburden herself, let her speak without interruption. Meanwhile, he'd silently lifted Thomas onto his back, intending to carry him safely to the Spirit World before addressing the matter of Marcel's disappearance.

They were in Arthur's office, with Thomas resting on the couch, when Sadie arrived. She'd heard of their return and had come seeking news about their attempt to get Marcel to concede. She showed no surprised at Thomas' condition, nor did she pry into the details of what had transpired. It was one of her peculiarities: she always seemed to know more than she let on, and little ever appeared to catch her off guard.

After hearing what had happened, Sadie offered to help track Marcel down. True to form, she located him with astonishing speed, pinpointing his exact room at the motel. How she managed this was anyone's guess, and as always, Sadie showed no inclination to reveal her methods.

'We can't scare him any more,' Arthur said, looking at Marcel's sleeping form. 'If we push him too far, we might tip the balance of his mind. The consequences of that would be irreversible.'

Emilia stayed quiet. After her earlier mistake, she felt she had no right to weigh in on the situation. She glanced at Arthur, catching the familiar look of deep concentration on his face. The ticking of the wall clock grew louder in the stillness, filling the space as they both mulled over what to do next.

Finally, he spoke.

'You must handle the next part yourself.'

'Handle what . . .?' she asked, hesitant.

'He has seen your reflection in the mirror,' Arthur explained. 'Naturally, he'll assume you're the one haunting him, trying to communicate. We can use that. You will enter his dreams and speak to him there.'

The idea left her momentarily speechless. She hadn't even known such a thing was possible, let alone how to do it.

'In his dreams, you will explain our intentions,' Arthur continued. 'If necessary, appeal to his guilt, as Sadie suggested.'

The very thought of intruding on Marcel's dreams left her feeling apprehensive, even as something in it tugged at her curiosity. She wasn't sure she was ready for such a task, but Arthur's certainty left little room for doubt.

'We'll need help,' he added after a pause. 'I know I promised not to leave your side, but I cannot take you to the place you'll need to go for this to work. Stay here. I'll bring him. I won't be long.'

Before she could ask who he meant, Arthur had vanished, leaving her alone with Marcel. She barely had a minute to process his departure when he reappeared, the Nameless Spirit in tow. The Spirit's displeasure was immediate, his scowl deepening as his gaze landed on Marcel.

'You're crazy,' the Nameless Spirit said to Arthur. 'What happened to not interfering—'

He stopped short when he noticed Emilia. His words faltered, and his sharp eyes flickered between the two of them. After a beat, he released a heavy breath, as if arriving at an unspoken conclusion.

'Oh,' he said flatly, his irritation melting into a tone of boredom. Any remaining interest he had drained away as he fixed his attention pointedly on Emilia.

'Well?' He extended his hand towards her, palm up, as if expecting her to take it. 'Let's get this over with before he wakes.'

Emilia looked at Arthur, who gave her a quick, reassuring nod. Sensing her reluctance, the Nameless Spirit's expression turned impatient. He grabbed her hand, his grip firm but not harsh.

'Come,' he said tersely.

He lifted his other hand and sliced through the empty air. At first, she thought he was merely gesturing at something until she saw the space before them ripple and then tear open. It was as though he had peeled back the fabric of reality to reveal a shimmering void, fluid and reflective like an oil-slicked mirror.

'What . . .?' she began, but he was already stepping through it, pulling her along behind him.

The other side—for she could think of no other way to describe it—was a corridor, unnaturally long and shrouded in dim, shifting light. The walls appeared to undulate like liquid shadows, alive and restless. Flecks of dull, silvery light floated in the air, suspended like dust motes, their faint glow casting warped shadows across their faces. The corridor seemed both endless and claustrophobic, stretching into infinity while pressing down on her from all sides.

It reminded her vaguely of the space Arthur had once created with his energy, but this was stranger and imbued with a disturbing sense of sentience.

'What is this place?' she asked. Her voice echoed, amplifying in the silence until it seemed to come from all directions at once.

'Nowhere,' the Nameless Spirit replied. 'It doesn't have a name. It's a bridge, a passage that links one realm to another. It's taking us from the Living World to the Hollow.'

'The *what*?' she asked, her discomfort growing as she searched for the corridor's end but finding none within sight.

'The Hollow,' he repeated, lacking any inclination to elaborate. 'It's an in-between space, like the Void, except it's for the Living. A temporary place, what the Living might call "dreams". It changes with each person's mind, a constantly shifting plane shaped by their memories, fears, and desires. I'm taking you to that man's Hollow.'

Emilia's grip tightened around his hand.

'And what happens there?'

'You'll see,' he said. 'Just keep moving and don't wander. The Hollow doesn't take kindly to trespassers.'

As they walked, a faint, low hum filled the air, growing louder and more insistent with every step. The sound was soon joined by whispers, drifting in from all directions—indistinct and eerie, carrying tones that stirred a sense of foreboding deep in her gut. The floor beneath her feet was slick, a mix of smooth stone and a softer, clay-like texture that gave slightly with each step.

'How do you know where to go?' she asked.

'I'm the gatekeeper,' the Nameless Spirit said, his tone dismissive. 'All gateways between realms are my responsibility, not just those between the Living and Spirit World.'

Ahead, the corridor narrowed, funnelling them towards an arched opening that pulsed with an otherworldly light. Beyond it lay the gateway to Marcel's Hollow.

The Hollow unfolded as a fractured landscape, a surreal maze stitched together from fragments of Marcel's life. Broken rooms jutted out at impossible angles, some tilting sideways or floating in midair. Familiar objects—picture frames, furniture, and other personal belongings—hung suspended in a thick, grey fog that clung to the air like smoke. At first glance, these objects seemed ordinary, but as Emilia looked closer, she noticed the subtle ways they were warped: chairs with too many legs, mirrors that cracked and bled a viscous black substance, photographs of people whose faces were scratched or blurred beyond recognition.

Overhead, distorted memories flickered like flashes of lightning, streaking across the grey expanse. Faces she didn't recognize twisted into monstrous shapes before vanishing into nothingness. The entire space seemed to pulse with a restless energy, a manifestation of Marcel's inner turmoil.

'The man is full of regrets,' the Nameless Spirit said. 'His Hollow is a reflection of the guilt that consumes him. Even here, he cannot find peace.'

Emilia shivered. Marcel's Hollow was a place of endless unrest, blending the familiar with the nightmarish. It was a portrayal of his fractured soul, laid bare in all its fragility and despair.

In the distance, faint pathways formed and vanished, twisting and winding into the depths of the Hollow. Only one remained steady amid the chaos. The Nameless Spirit pointed at it.

'The man you seek is up that path.'

Emilia paused, eyes fixed on the shifting fog ahead. 'Aren't you coming with me?'

The Nameless Spirit didn't move.

'This is as far as I go. Stay on the path, and you'll be fine. Stray from it, and . . .' He trailed off, leaving the rest unsaid as he shrugged.

The path ahead twisted into the unknown, her fear tangled with disbelief, but there was no turning back now.

'Go,' the Nameless Spirit urged. 'You must hurry before he wakes.'

With one last look at him, Emilia stepped onto the path, the soft hum of the Hollow growing louder as she ventured deeper into Marcel's fractured mind.

42

The path led Emilia deeper into Marcel's Hollow, narrowing as it went until it dissolved into a dense, forested area. Thick trees crowded on either side, their gnarled branches reaching out like skeletal fingers, obstructing her progress and forcing her to slow down. She pushed forwards with growing frustration, swatting at the branches and snapping twigs that tangled in her hair and snagged on her clothes.

After breaking through the last stubborn branch, she stumbled onto an unexpected clearing. And the world changed. Gone were the twisted trees, replaced by the sterile stillness of a hospital room. The contrast was jarring. This part of the Hollow was serene and eerily calm, bathed in a soft, muted light that filtered in from no discernible source. The silence was so profound it bordered on unnatural.

Though disoriented, Emilia knew she was still in Marcel's Hollow, just a different part of it. The room was bare and unremarkable, with an empty bed and a few chairs scattered around, their long shadows stretched darkly across the tiled floor.

Marcel sat in the centre of the room, slouched forward, his hands resting loosely in his lap as he stared blankly at the floor. He looked lost, as though the world around him had faded and left him stranded inside his own thoughts, isolated from everything else. His voice, low and edged, stopped her just inside the doorway.

'What are you doing here?'

He hadn't looked up, still staring at the floor, yet somehow, he knew she was there.

'I came to see you,' she said.

'This isn't real,' he replied. '*You're* not real.'

He turned to look at her. His eyes burned with an emotion she couldn't immediately name. It might have been anger, but it felt misplaced, dulled by the weariness in his posture.

Emilia moved closer, careful with each step as she said, 'I'm real. And so is this place.'

'Is this a dream?' he muttered, almost to himself. 'I remember leaving the house, going to a motel . . .' He trailed off. 'I saw you, didn't I? In the mirror.'

She nodded.

'I've been trying to reach out to speak with you, but . . . things didn't go exactly as planned.'

Marcel's expression tightened, his brows knitting together.

'All those things that happened . . . at the hospital, at the house . . . Was that you?'

She paused, weighing the cost of honesty.

'Some of it, yes,' she admitted. 'Most of it, no.'

His jaw clenched.

'Not Blake?'

'That would be Thomas,' she clarified. 'Thomas Alexander. I think you know him.'

'Detective Alexander?' Marcel's voice softened, registering the familiar name. 'He was there with you? He's part of this too?'

Emilia stayed silent for a long while before saying, 'I think you already know what all this is about, Marcel. I think you've known for quite some time why I've been trying so hard to reach you.'

He lowered his gaze again, staring at his hands as if they held the answers he sought.

'It's about J.Tech, isn't it?'

Emilia chose her next words carefully, hoping to pierce through the layers of remorse in Marcel's eyes, the regret that kept him anchored to his despair.

'We need your help,' she said, watching as his hands curled into fists in his lap, his gaze fixed anywhere but on her.

'You know they won't stop, Marcel. How long will you let them ruin your life? And other people's lives too?' she asked, a note of pleading in her voice. 'They've already taken so much. Don't you think it's enough?' She wavered, but pressed on. 'My life was destroyed because of them, and my brother's life hangs by a thread. If you let them keep going, if you do nothing, how many more lives will they destroy? How many more families will be left broken?'

'They're not . . . murderers,' he muttered quietly. 'Eldon shouldn't have started that investigation.

He was getting too close to exposing them. They had to act. And you . . . you were just . . . unlucky.'

'Is that really what you believe?' she snapped, struggling to keep her composure. She took a calming breath and tried again. 'You know that's not true. They're destroying lives with their unethical practices.'

She barely knew what J.Tech's crimes were, but at this moment, she was willing to say anything to make him reconsider. Even if her accusations were speculative, they seemed to resonate all the same.

Marcel's face twisted with inner conflict. Emilia could sense the crack forming in his defences, the faintest sign that her words were reaching him. Lowering her voice, she softened her tone, attempting to coax him further out of the fortress he'd built around himself.

'Look,' she said gently, 'I know you didn't want this. Not for you, not for Eldon. But the fact is, you're the only one who can stop them. If you feel guilty for what happened, if you feel even a shred of regret, then do something about it. You can't just sit here and let them win. You're Eldon's friend, aren't you? Are you really okay with how things turned out? Does his suffering mean nothing to you?'

Her words pressed between them, the air thick with his turmoil. Emilia could almost hear the battle playing out within him, guilt scraping against resignation. She hated exploiting his emotions, but desperation left her with little choice. This might be the only way to get him to act.

When Marcel finally spoke, his voice was rough and barely audible.

'Maybe . . . maybe it's too late to fix any of this. Too much damage has been done. I don't think I can undo what's happened.'

Emilia stepped closer.

'But you can keep it from happening to anyone else. Do you honestly think there won't be others who'll look into J.Tech? Others who'll get too close to exposing them? And what about Eldon? The only reason J.Tech hasn't gone after him is because he's in a coma. What happens when he wakes up?' she implored. 'How long will you let them hold all this over you? Over everyone? You can make sure no one else has to go through any of this again. Isn't that what matters? Isn't that the only thing that can make any of this right?'

He finally looked at her, and in that moment, she saw the shame and sorrow brimming in the depths of his eyes. He looked exhausted, weighed down by the ghosts of his past decisions. Grief was slow to surface, raw and unguarded, but with it, came something fragile and newly lit.

'They used you, blackmailed you, made you do things you didn't want to do,' she continued, pressing her advantage. 'But you're not that person any more. You can't erase what happened, but you can choose to act differently. You can make them pay, the way they deserve.'

Marcel's breath shuddered, his hands no longer clenched into fists. Emilia stared at him, willing her words, her anger, and her pain to cut through his despair and guilt.

After a long silence, he gave a small, almost imperceptible nod.

'All right,' he whispered. 'I'll do it.'

Relief hit Emilia hard. She was about to speak again when the ground beneath them began to shake. Her eyes widened in alarm as the walls of the room started to crack and crumble. Marcel, however, remained seated, untouched by the chaos. He watched her with a calm detachment as his Hollow came apart and started to disintegrate around them.

The walls collapsed, exposing a void that pulsed and churned with uncontained energy. Emilia struggled to keep her balance on the unstable ground, but Marcel was unaffected, sitting in his chair as if anchored to the collapsing reality. A hand clamped around her forearm.

It was the Nameless Spirit.

'We must go!' he yelled. 'He is waking! We cannot be here when he wakes!'

She twisted back towards Marcel as the Nameless Spirit began dragging her away.

'F-20!' she shouted, her voice rising above the cacophony. 'The abandoned movie theatre!'

The Nameless Spirit tugged her arm with renewed urgency. There was no time to make it back to the corridor. With a swift, forceful motion, he tore a gap in the fabric of space right where they stood. The opening was jagged, raw, and barely stable, but it was big enough for them to escape. He pulled her through just as Marcel's Hollow collapsed entirely, folding into itself and vanishing into nothing.

43

The Nameless Spirit's voice rang through the room.

'I am *never* doing that again! I am *never* taking *any* of you to any realm you don't belong in!'

Instead of the motel, Emilia found herself back in the Spirit World, specifically in Arthur's office. Arthur sat behind his desk, a faint glimmer of amusement flickered in his eyes at the Nameless Spirit's outburst.

Thomas sat nearby, looking shaken but unharmed. Emilia quickly crossed the room to him, elated at seeing him conscious and well again.

'Thomas! Are you okay?' she asked.

He nodded, offering her a small smile.

'I was so angry when I saw Blake,' he admitted, lowering his gaze in embarrassment. 'I didn't even know I had that kind of power.' He gave a faint, uneasy laugh, the uncertainty clear in his voice. 'Arthur explained that strong emotions can sometimes manifest as energy, and I guess . . . I just lost control.'

Understanding softened her features. She could only imagine the depth of his anger, though she decided to let it pass. There would be time for that later.

'I heard I scared Marcel off, too,' he added. 'I'm really sorry about that.'

'It's all right,' she said. 'I should have been watching him more closely. But honestly, I doubt I could've stopped him from running.'

The Nameless Spirit drifted towards the far corner, still muttering to himself, his irritation largely ignored.

'I spoke to Marcel,' Emilia said, drawing their attention. 'He agreed to help us, and I managed to tell him about the abandoned movie theatre.'

'Do you think he got the hint? All of this will be for nothing if he can't find the evidence,' Thomas asked.

Emilia shrugged.

'I think he'll figure it out somehow. He is a detective, after all.'

Arthur rose from his chair. He motioned towards the Nameless Spirit, who was still grumbling under his breath.

'Well done, everyone. The Nameless Spirit and I will retrieve the evidence and place it back in the abandoned movie theatre,' he said, brushing aside the Spirit's muttered complaints. 'It will be some time before we return.'

He turned to Emilia with a pointed look.

'Stay here,' he instructed firmly. 'And do not do anything you're not supposed to.'

To Thomas, he said, 'Work on controlling your energy while I'm gone.'

'How long will it take before you return?' she asked, worried that he might be gone longer than they expected.

Arthur considered this.

'Hard to say. I think I'll stay in the Living World for a while, enough to ensure Marcel follows through on his promise and to monitor the developments that are bound to unfold if he does. With any luck, I will be back soon. Hopefully with good news.'

Arthur left before either of them could say more on the subject, the Nameless Spirit trailing after him, still grousing in discontent.

Arthur had been gone for nearly a month, but Emilia reminded herself that time flowed differently between realms. It was unpredictable, as Arthur had often said. A month in the Spirit World could translate to several months, or even years, in the Living World. In his absence, she had settled back into a routine, almost as if things were finally returning to normal.

Emilia was starting to get the hang of her research work. Sadie had proven to be an excellent mentor, and Emilia had managed to prepare multiple target files that were later approved and chosen by agents in the department. Each successful scare brought a gratifying wave of points, and she was ecstatic to see her total rise to a whopping 485. Putting together a thorough and effective research file was challenging, but the reward of seeing her work pay off—and the steady accumulation of points—made it worthwhile. Although she wouldn't admit it, she was beginning to feel at home in her role as a researcher, and could even imagine herself staying in this role long-term. Maybe.

Thomas, meanwhile, had been honing his skills and was flourishing as an agent. His control over his energy had improved significantly, and his scares grew more consistent over time. Whenever Emilia submitted new targets, Thomas was often the first to claim a file, grinning as he said, 'If I do this right, I'll be helping *both* of us win.' His enthusiasm was contagious, and Emilia found herself rooting for him every time.

Their days were busy with work, but they speculated often about Arthur's time in the Living World. Emilia's curiosity gnawed at her, and she would have jumped at any opportunity to visit the Living World herself if Sadie had not taken the master skeleton key for 'safekeeping'. Neither Arthur nor the Nameless Spirit had forgotten Emilia's tendency to wander and had left strict instructions for Sadie to secure the key. Frustrated, all Emilia could do was wait.

Arthur returned nearly six weeks later.

News of his arrival spread quickly through the Agency, and Emilia found herself racing down the hall, colliding with Thomas as they both sprinted for his office. They burst inside without knocking, their breaths coming in short bursts having run the entire way there. Arthur sat behind his desk, composed as ever, though there was a hint of weariness in his eyes that hadn't been there before.

'What happened?' Emilia asked, jumping straight to the point. 'Did Marcel keep his word? Did he help? Was he able to find the evidence we left him?'

'What about the trial? And J.Tech?' Thomas added, his urgency matching hers.

Arthur regarded them both with a measured expression, a note of quiet amusement in his voice as he said, 'Calm yourselves. There is much to say, but yes, Marcel came through. He found the evidence in the theatre, just as we planned, and it was enough to start an investigation. Things escalated quickly from there.'

Emilia's heart leapt.

'What happened?' she repeated, breathless with anticipation.

Arthur's expression hardened as he continued.

'Apparently, J.Tech wasn't just stealing personal information and manipulating data. There was more to it than we realized. Everything was in Eldon's drive and corroborated by the documents Thomas had stolen.'

'What else were they doing?' Thomas asked, struggling to recall the details even now. Most of the files he'd seen on Eldon's drive had been fragmented or unclear.

'There were schematics, internal memos, and prototype designs that tied J.Tech to an illegal project they were calling the Immersion Initiative. It was a highly classified programme that used experimental virtual reality to create hyper-immersive simulations. Except it wasn't just about creating a new VR experience. They were developing neural implants, devices designed to interface directly with the human brain.'

Emilia felt ill. She had suspected J.Tech of shady dealings, but not this.

'What were they doing with these implants?' she asked, dreading the answer.

'Officially, these implants were part of a cutting-edge entertainment venture, meant to deliver virtual reality so vivid it would feel indistinguishable from real life. But unofficially, they were conducting far more sinister experiments. They used unwitting test subjects to extract and manipulate memories from their brains. Many of these subjects were left in vegetative states. Some didn't survive at all.'

A cold wave of nausea swept over her.

'Eldon?' she whispered, her voice trembling.

Arthur nodded solemnly.

'When they discovered your brother's investigation into the Immersion Initiative and his intent to expose it, they took drastic measures. His coma wasn't caused by the fall as the official story claimed. It was the result of a neural implant they used on him to erase the memories of his findings.'

A part of her had always doubted the story of Eldon's 'accident', but hearing the truth left her reeling. To think that her brother had been subjected to such cruelty . . . it was unbearable.

Thomas gave her hand a gentle, reassuring squeeze, then asked, 'What about the trial? And J.Tech? Did the evidence hold up in court?'

'The trial was brutal. J.Tech's defence team was ruthless. They hired the best lawyers that money could buy, countersued, and tried every possible tactic to dismiss the evidence. They argued the schematics and files were illegally obtained and therefore inadmissible. But the prosecution pushed forward relentlessly. Marcel's testimony was pivotal. He admitted his involvement with the company, and that emboldened others to come forward.'

'Others?'

'Yes,' Arthur said. 'Many individuals stepped up to recount their experiences. Most had signed up for what they believed were harmless VR trials, only to wake up with distorted memories or worse. Their testimonies painted a grim picture.'

'How did J.Tech try to justify that?'

'They claimed the participants had signed waivers and that the risks had been disclosed,' Arthur explained. 'They labelled any adverse outcomes as anomalies beyond their control. But then the prosecution brought in a whistleblower. An engineer who had worked directly on the Immersion Initiative.'

'A whistleblower?'

He nodded.

'The whistleblower confirmed that J.Tech had deliberately bypassed safety protocols and concealed fatal flaws in the implants. They also intentionally targeted vulnerable populations—those they assumed wouldn't be missed—for their experiments.'

'And the verdict?' Emilia asked.

A grim smile touched Arthur's lips.

'Guilty. On all counts. Human rights violations, illegal experimentation, data theft, and corporate fraud. The company's assets are being seized, and several executives, including the CEO, are facing prison sentences. Reparations for the victims are in discussion, though no amount of money can undo the damage caused.'

Swells of emotions threatened to overwhelm Emilia as she said, 'So . . . it's over? J.Tech is finished?'

'For the most part, yes. The company is being dismantled. However, their reach was vast. Some of their technology has already been sold to other entities, and there are whispers of smaller groups attempting to replicate their work. But J.Tech itself is no more.'

Thomas exhaled, a relieved grin spreading across his face.

'Marcel really pulled through, didn't he?'

'He did,' Arthur said. 'He confessed to his role in aiding the company and, in exchange, received a lighter sentence. Blake was also found guilty.'

Looking pointedly at Thomas, he added, 'You'll be pleased to know that you left quite an impression on him. Even without the evidence, he was ready to confess to everything. He's convinced malevolent spirits are after him for his involvement with J.Tech. He's currently serving time in an asylum.'

Thomas grimaced but couldn't hide his glee.

'Yikes. Guess I overdid it, huh?'

44

'Arthur wants to see you.'

Emilia looked up to see one of the other researchers standing in the doorway. The woman smiled and repeated herself, thinking Emilia hadn't heard her the first time.

'I bumped into him in the hallway outside,' the researcher said, pointing over her shoulder. 'He wants to see you in his office whenever you have a moment.'

'Oh,' Emilia replied, rising from her chair and smoothing her jacket. 'Thanks.'

It wasn't unusual for Arthur to call her in, but they hadn't spoken much since his return. When she passed him in the hallways, he was unusually reserved, offering little more than a nod in acknowledgment.

Emilia made her way to his office, her footsteps echoing faintly against the polished floors. Vague guesses about the purpose of the meeting chased one another through her thoughts as she stopped outside his door and raised her hand to knock.

'Come in,' came his muffled voice.

She pushed the door open and stepped inside. Arthur's sharp eyes lifted to meet hers, and for a moment, she thought she saw something in his gaze—something serious, almost contemplative.

'Please, sit,' he said, gesturing to the chair in front of his desk.

Emilia did as instructed, her curiosity growing despite herself. Whatever this was, it felt more significant than his usual check-ins. Arthur wasn't one to summon someone without reason, and his manner suggested he had something important to say.

'Is everything all right?' she asked cautiously.

Arthur leaned back in his chair, his posture noticeably more relaxed than usual. It was a contrast to his typical rigidity, and Emilia couldn't shake the feeling that he was trying too hard to appear at ease.

'Everything's fine,' he said. 'I just wanted to have a bit of a chat with you, that's all. Nothing to worry about.'

'A chat?' she repeated, her stomach twisting at his words.

He nodded.

'How are you holding up after everything that's happened?'

Emilia hesitated, unsure how to answer.

'I'm managing,' she finally said. 'Things feel a little different now, I guess.'

In truth, she felt adrift. She had expected closure once everything was over—relief, maybe even triumph. Instead, things felt strangely anticlimactic. The trial had been a success, her brother was safe, J.Tech had been dismantled, and justice, or at least some semblance of it, had been served. But the sense of purpose that had driven her for so long seemed to have evaporated overnight, leaving behind an emptiness she couldn't fill.

She couldn't explain it, not even to herself. Perhaps it was because the case against J.Tech had consumed her life for so long that its resolution had left a void. Or maybe it was because the ending had come so abruptly that it felt incomplete. She had succeeded, but the clarity or fulfilment she had expected wasn't there. Instead, she found herself grappling with questions she wasn't sure she wanted to face.

With little else to do, she kept herself busy by pouring her time and energy into work, ignoring the persistent ache in her chest. Her brother remained in a coma, trapped in the liminal space between life and death, and she was still here in the Spirit World, working for a system she didn't fully understand.

Arthur reached for a folder from one of the many on his desk. He flipped it open, scanning its contents briefly before speaking, 'I see you've been doing well in the research department.'

'I've been putting in the hours and focusing more on work,' she said. 'Been keeping busy, that's all.'

He closed the folder and rested his elbows on the desk.

'I've been at this job long enough to recognize when someone is throwing themselves into work to avoid something else. It isn't inherently bad, but it isn't sustainable in the long run either.'

'What are you trying to say?'

'I'm worried about you, Emilia,' he said. 'Thomas is turning out to be a fine agent, and he seems to be enjoying himself as well. But you, on the other hand . . .'

He paused, exhaling in a way that felt strange coming from him.

'I just want to make sure you're doing what you want. Not because you think it's the only thing you can or should be doing.'

She considered his words before answering, 'I guess I thought things would feel different after the trial. I'm not sure how, exactly, but this doesn't feel like it. And it's like . . . I don't really know what to do with myself now.'

'That's understandable. You've spent quite a bit of time focused on one goal and reaching it can leave you feeling unmoored. It's something we all deal with at some point. But it's also a chance to figure out what comes next.'

'What comes next . . .' she repeated. The phrase felt formidable, like a door she wasn't sure she wanted to open just yet. 'I suppose I'd keep working. I still have to work towards reincarnation.'

'You're back to where you started, but the circumstances have changed,' he said. 'I hope things so far have gone the way you wanted them to. But if they haven't, you should know it's not too late to choose a different path.'

The way he said it made her chest tighten, and for a moment, she thought there was some deeper meaning behind his words, something personal.

'Arthur, are you okay?' she asked.

He gave her a faint smile that didn't quite reach his eyes.

'We're here to talk about you, not me,' he said. 'You're doing great in the research department, but there's more out there if you're willing to look for it. Just don't lose sight of yourself in the process.'

'Arthur . . . are you sure everything's fine? You're acting a little strange.'

He smiled again, but this time there was something unguarded in the expression, a softness she hadn't seen before.

'You worry too much,' he said. 'But I suppose I can't blame you for that. It's part of who you are.'

'You're being cryptic again. Just say what you mean.'

'What I mean is . . . I'm proud of you.' His gaze lingered on her as though he were seeing her for the first time, or perhaps for the last. 'You've come a long way since the day you first arrived here. You've faced things most spirits never have to, and you've done it with a strength I don't think you even realize you have. To accomplish all that you did, with so little energy . . . You're remarkable.'

Arthur rarely spoke so openly and with such sincerity. Emilia felt a lump form in her throat, her chest tightening at his words.

'What are you saying now?' she asked. 'Why does it sound like you're saying goodbye?'

His smile grew somewhat wistful, a subtle shift that upset her more than she cared to admit.

'Do you remember when I told you that there are consequences for interfering with the Living World?' he asked.

Her heart quickened, dread pooling in the pit of her stomach. A part of her knew where this was going, though she desperately wished she didn't.

'We didn't interfere,' she said, her voice edged with defensiveness. 'All we did was scare the Living.'

He laughed, a sound that felt too light for the weight of the moment.

'And thank goodness for that,' he said. When the laughter ceased, his expression turned serious. 'But I wasn't speaking about *your* interferences. I was speaking about mine.'

'But you didn't—'

'I did, Emilia,' he interrupted gently. 'Multiple times, in fact. Despite all my warnings, all my lectures, I failed to follow my own advice.'

'But you *didn't*,' she repeated, desperate. 'You didn't interfere. I know you didn't.'

'You forget,' he said, his tone calm yet resolute. 'I'm not a spirit like you. My definition of interference is very different from yours.'

Her voice trembled as she asked, 'But . . . what did you do? What's going to happen to you?'

'I'll be fine, Emilia. Nothing for you to worry about.'

Her fear sharpened into anger at the way he dismissed her concerns so easily.

'How can you say that?' she demanded. 'How can you be so calm? And how do they even know you interfered? None of this makes sense!'

He sighed, the sound heavy with a weariness that seemed to settle into his very frame.

'We were being watched the entire time,' he said. 'I was simply too dull to notice.'

The room felt impossibly still in the wake of his words. Emilia's pulse thundered in her ears as she struggled to process what he was saying.

'Watched? By whom?' she asked.

'The overseers,' he replied. 'The ones who maintain the balance between the realms. They assigned someone to monitor me.'

He pinched the bridge of his nose, a small gesture of frustration and regret.

'It was Sadie,' he admitted, the name bitter on his tongue. 'She's one of them. She joined the Agency at the same time you did to keep an eye on me. She knew of our acquaintanceship prior to your death and the fact that I am . . . partial to you.'

Sadie? Of all people? It was almost too much to believe, but she couldn't ignore the signs now that she was seeing them with startling clarity. Sadie's uncanny efficiency, her seemingly endless knowledge, and the way she never used her points—all of it pointed to her being more than a run-of-the-mill spirit.

'You weren't interfering,' Emilia insisted, shaking her head as tears pricked her eyes. 'You were *helping*. You were protecting us.'

'I don't regret any of it, Emilia,' Arthur said warmly. 'Not a single choice I made. But the rules exist for a reason, and I knew what I was risking.'

'You can't just accept this,' she said. 'There has to be something we can do!'

'There's nothing to be done,' he said. 'I called you here to speak to you and make sure you understand that this isn't your fault in any way. None of it is.'

'Arthur . . .' Her voice cracked, his name barely escaping her lips. Her vision blurred with tears that threatened to spill over.

He rose from his seat and walked around the desk, coming to stand before her. For a moment, he simply looked at her, his expression filled with something she could only describe as deep, unspoken fondness.

'You'll be fine, no matter what happens,' he said. 'I need you to believe that.'

It felt like goodbye. He hadn't said the words, but she could feel them in the way he looked at her, the way his voice softened, the way his hand rested on her shoulder. She wanted to demand answers, to argue until he gave her a solution. But the quiet resolve in his eyes told her there was nothing left to say. He'd long accepted that these were consequences he had to face, one way or another.

'You said we were friends. You said you wouldn't leave me,' she cried, her voice breaking as tears streaked down her cheeks. 'I don't want to lose you.'

'I'm sorry, Emilia.'

The words, deceptively simple yet filled with unspoken meaning, weren't just an apology; they were a farewell, an acknowledgment of everything he couldn't say. Her chest tightened as she searched his face, desperate for more, but all she found was the same quiet resolve that both infuriated and reassured her. She nodded, unable to trust her voice, knowing that if she spoke, she might fall apart under the weight of everything he wasn't saying.

45

Emilia left Arthur's office with a storm brewing inside her. His quiet resolve, the way he seemed so at peace with his fate, only made it harder for her to accept the whole situation. She knew he had already made his decision, had come to terms with the consequences of his actions, but she couldn't let it go. Not like this.

As her mind raced, one detail from their conversation surfaced. Arthur had mentioned that Sadie was the one sent to keep an eye on things. Emilia realized with a jolt of surprise that she hadn't seen Sadie in quite some time. She'd naïvely chalked it up to their busy schedules, but now it felt too deliberate to ignore. If Sadie was indeed one of the overseers, then she might know more about Arthur's situation and, more importantly, if anything could still be done to help him.

Determined, Emilia headed back to the research department, but Sadie's desk was empty. She scanned the floor, her eyes darting between spirits engrossed in their work, but there was no sign of her anywhere. Stopping one of the researchers passing by, she asked, 'Excuse me, have you seen Sadie?'

'Not recently,' the researcher replied before hurrying off.

Emilia refused to accept that answer. She asked around some more, collecting vague responses, until someone finally mentioned seeing Sadie near the administration department. She hurried over, her steps quick and purposeful, and after what felt like hours, she spotted Sadie emerging from a corridor near one of the offices. Without hesitation, Emilia rushed to intercept her.

Sadie paused, mild surprise flickering across her face.

'Emilia? What's the matter?'

'I need to talk to you,' Emilia said. 'About Arthur.'

Sadie tilted her head, studying Emilia with a calm, unreadable gaze.

'What about him?'

'You *know* what I'm talking about,' Emilia said, incensed at Sadie's nonchalance.

Sadie didn't respond.

'You're not a researcher,' Emilia pressed. 'You're an overseer sent to keep an eye on us, aren't you?'

The accusation landed, and Emilia saw a flash of something in Sadie's eyes. The other woman stiffened, gritting her teeth before gesturing for Emilia to follow.

'Not here,' she said, leading her to an unoccupied room and closing the door behind them.

Inside, Sadie leaned against the wall, her calm exterior beginning to falter, just enough to reveal a trace of fatigue.

'I should have known he'd tell you.'

Emilia ignored the comment, saying, 'You've been watching us, so you *have* to know he was only trying to help me. He wasn't acting with malicious intent.'

'I know.'

'Then why is this happening?' Emilia demanded. 'Surely you can do something. Make an exception?'

Sadie held her gaze.

'It's not that simple, Emilia. The rules exist for a reason. Arthur understood them when he chose to interfere. Even with good intentions, he knowingly broke those rules.'

'But he did it for the right reasons,' Emilia protested. 'He wasn't acting out of selfishness. None of this would have been possible without him. He was trying to stop something terrible from happening. That has to matter, doesn't it?'

'Intentions do matter. But actions have consequences, regardless of intent. If Arthur's interference had been solely to expose J.Tech, to protect the balance between realms, I might have been able to help him. But that's not what happened.'

'What do you mean? What are you saying?'

Sadie was quiet for a moment.

'Everything Arthur did, he did for *you*,' she said softly. 'His goal from the beginning was to help *you*, not to take down J.Tech. It was *your* goal, and he supported you because of it.'

Arthur's words from earlier replayed in Emilia's mind. He had insisted it wasn't her fault, that he didn't regret his actions. Now she understood why.

He had anticipated this moment, had known Sadie would reveal the truth if Emilia pressed hard enough.

'Arthur told me he interfered in ways that Grim Reapers shouldn't. What exactly did he do?' Emilia asked.

Sadie's restraint fractured. She didn't see the point in keeping things from Emilia any more.

'He did a great deal he shouldn't have,' she said. 'When he discovered your intention to investigate the Living World, he left the master skeleton key on Thomas' desk, ensuring you had access to what you needed. He destroyed objects from the Living World and concealed the evidence in the Void. Not to mention allowing you to investigate your death knowing that you had died under suspicious circumstances.'

Her attention dropped to the bracelet on Emilia's wrist.

'And that. Sharing his energy with you was reckless and unheard of. Unthinkable.'

Emilia's throat tightened. She had known Arthur had bent the rules for them, but she hadn't realized the full extent of his actions. He had risked everything, not for some grand cause, but for her.

'Arthur's actions challenged the very balance we are tasked with maintaining. Because of that, my ability to intervene on his behalf is limited.'

'But he didn't act alone,' Emilia pleaded. 'Thomas and I were part of it too. Surely his punishment could be reduced if it were shared among us?'

Sadie shook her head firmly.

'There is no record of either you or Thomas breaking any rules,' she said. 'Arthur made sure of that. Every action you took was documented as part of Agency work, legitimate hauntings meant to scare the Living. And everything that couldn't be categorized as such . . .' She paused. 'Well, no trace amounts of energy can be found leading back to you or Thomas. I don't mean to speculate, but I am certain Arthur is responsible for erasing any and all traces of your involvement.'

There were no traces of her energy because she hadn't been using her energy, she had been using *his*. He hadn't given her the bracelet because he thought she was weak but because he wanted to shield her from trouble. It was his contingency plan, and it had worked flawlessly.

'But Blake . . .?' she murmured.

'When I compiled Marcel's file for his haunting, I also put together one for Blake,' Sadie admitted. 'Just in case.'

She reached out and took Emilia's hand.

'I don't want you or Thomas to get into trouble, Emilia. Let Arthur handle this alone. He knows what he's doing.'

'But it isn't fair—' Emilia began.

'Listen to me,' Sadie interrupted. 'Don't do anything reckless. Spirits who disrupt the balance between realms risk total obliteration. But Grim Reapers, like Arthur, face different consequences. He understands this, which is why he's taking full responsibility. You must not interfere any further. Leave it alone.'

Emilia's shoulders sagged as helplessness and anger warred within her.

'What's going to happen to him?' she asked.

'Oh, nothing permanent. He'll be sent away for a while, under a sort of suspension and house arrest. I couldn't secure a full pardon for him, but I managed to have his sentence reduced as much as possible.'

'How long will he be gone?'

Sadie's shrug was almost apologetic.

'Unfortunately, I don't have that information. But I suspect it will be some time.'

'I'm sorry it's come to this,' she said, regret replacing her impassive expression. 'But truly, it's for the best that Arthur faces the consequences as intended. This is the only way to ensure the punishment doesn't extend to you or Thomas.'

Emilia accepted it reluctantly. It wasn't the resolution she wanted, but it was better than nothing.

'My assignment here at the Agency is finished,' Sadie said. 'I'll be leaving soon. But before I go, there's something I want you to have.'

Warmth spread from Sadie's hand to Emilia's, travelling up her arm. Emilia looked down as Sadie turned their intertwined hands, revealing the number inked onto Emilia's inner wrist. It was now over 9,000—a total Emilia could hardly fathom.

'Sadie . . .'

'I want you to have my points. Consider it a parting gift. I won't be returning to the Living World, but I hear you still have unfinished business there.'

Emilia was overwhelmed by the gesture.

'I don't know if I can accept this.'

When Sadie saw Emilia being hesitant, she said, 'Points can be shared, and they can also be used to help others.'

'What do you mean?' Emilia asked.

'Points can be used to recall a wandering spirit trapped in their Hollow, for example,' Sadie said, with a knowing smile. She reached into her pocket and retrieved a foil-wrapped candy, placing it gently into Emilia's palm. 'It's my last one. Make good use of it.'

46

The Nameless Spirit stood behind the counter, as motionless and detached as ever. He wasn't in his childlike form today but the taller, more imposing version of himself. He was indifferent as he reviewed files with a kind of practised boredom. His pale, featureless eyes remained fixed on the files, giving no sign he'd noticed her approach.

'Hi,' Emilia said, stopping at the counter.

His attention shifted to meet hers without expression.

'File, please,' he said in a monotone.

'Here,' she replied, but instead of a file, she set the piece of candy Sadie had given her on the counter in front of him.

The Nameless Spirit went still; his white eyes locked onto the wrapped treat. For several seconds, he did not move, as if trying to process this unexpected offering. Then, without a word, he snatched the candy and disappeared behind the counter.

The crinkling of foil reached Emilia's ears, followed by a brief pause. Moments later, the small, childlike version of the Nameless Spirit popped back up. He grinned at her, his sharp teeth and white eyes making the expression a lot more eerie than it would have otherwise been.

Climbing onto the counter with surprising agility, he crossed his legs and perched in front of her, his head tilted in curiosity.

'It's been a while, hasn't it?' he said, resting his chin on his fist as he studied her. His voice was lighter now, carrying the energy of a mischievous child.

'But,' he continued with a smile, 'you're not here just to say hello. You brought me candy as a bribe. Am I right?'

Despite the accusation, there was a teasing lilt to his tone, his grin never wavering. Emilia was surprised. Teasing wasn't something he often indulged in, especially given his usual disdain for anything outside his strict devotion to his role, but she took it as a good sign.

'You seem a lot more approachable now,' she said. 'And a lot friendlier.'

'You brought me candy,' he said simply, shrugging as though that explained everything. Then, with a pointed look, he added, 'And? What do you want?'

'What makes you so sure I'm here for something?'

'Oh, please,' the Nameless Spirit rolled his eyes with exaggerated impatience. 'The last time you gave me candy, you made me tell you about the master skeleton key. You're definitely here for something. So—out with it already. If you keep stalling, I'll start expecting more sweets from you.'

Emilia wasn't entirely sure why she was there. Sadie had given her the candy for a reason, and Emilia had assumed it was to see the Nameless Spirit. After all, who else in the Spirit World had such a notorious sweet tooth? But the purpose of the visit escaped her. Her mind scrambled for answers until a memory surfaced, something Sadie had mentioned in passing at the end of their conversation.

'Tell me about the Hollow,' she said.

'The Hollow?' he repeated, his pale eyes narrowing in thought. Clearly, it wasn't the question he'd been expecting. 'That man's Hollow?'

'No, not his specifically.' She gestured vaguely. 'Just . . . the Hollow in general.'

'I already told you about it when I took you to that man's Hollow,' he said.

'Yes, yes,' Emilia replied. 'But surely there's more you haven't told me.'

'Like what?' he asked, releasing a theatrical sigh as though she were wasting his precious time.

'Anything.'

He gave her a long, unimpressed stare before answering.

'There really isn't much to tell. Like I've said before: it's a temporary place for the Living. A place for their souls to go when their bodies need rest.'

'Okay,' she said. 'So, their souls go to their respective Hollows when the Living sleep?'

'Well, yes, but not exactly.'

Emilia fixed him with a pointed stare, one that demanded he elaborate. The Nameless Spirit's reluctance was evident. He really didn't enjoy telling them more than they needed to know. But her unrelenting gaze, combined with the influence of the candy, seemed to win him over.

'The Hollow,' he began, 'is a kind of temporary dreamscape for the Living. Most souls go there when their bodies are resting, sleeping, if you will. And when they wake, the soul leaves the Hollow and returns to the body. Simple as that.'

He paused, his pale, featureless eyes flickering towards her, debating whether to continue. When Emilia didn't interrupt, he added, 'But there are cases where souls don't leave the Hollow . . . when their bodies remain in a state of extended rest.'

The meaning behind his words struck her, and she had to grip the counter for support.

'Comatose patients,' she said, the realization sinking in. 'Those who refuse to wake from their sleep.'

The Nameless Spirit gave a slow, deliberate nod.

'Yes.'

For a moment, neither of them spoke.

'I heard about your brother,' he said, his voice almost gentle, losing some of its sharpness. 'Is that what this is about?'

Emilia hadn't been certain before, but now she was. Sadie's words. The candy. The points. Sadie must have known. That was why she'd given Emilia the candy. Why she'd transferred her points. Not just as a gesture or a farewell gift, but as a deliberate nudge in this direction.

Sadie had wanted her to know there were options, possibilities beyond simply working for points and reincarnating. Options that included her brother.

'Is he stuck in his Hollow?' Emilia asked. 'My brother, I mean. Do you know if he's there?'

The Nameless Spirit gave her a solemn nod.

'Eldon, isn't it?'

'You know him?' she asked, startled.

'I know every spirit that passes through the Hollow. The ones who stay and the ones who do not,' he said, pausing before adding, almost casually, 'He was your subconscious in the Void.'

Emilia froze. She remembered the Void. It had been such a comfort to see her brother walking and talking again, even if it wasn't the real him.

The Nameless Spirit stared at her, his unblinking white eyes giving no indication of emotion as he waited for her to process his words. After a while, he spoke again.

'Do you want to see him?'

'I can do that?'

He shrugged as though it were the simplest thing in the world.

'I took you to that other man's Hollow, didn't I? Of course, I can take you to see your brother in his. If that's what you want.'

He studied her for a beat then said, 'That *is* what you want, right? I mean, this is why you came to see me today—to speak to him?'

Emilia was at a complete loss for words. But she recovered quickly and said, 'Yes. I want to see him.'

The Nameless Spirit didn't reply. He hopped off the counter with surprising grace and, without hesitation, swiped his hand through the air in front of him, tearing through the fabric of space as effortlessly as one might flip a page in a book. The gap he created revealed a familiar abyss of endless nothingness.

He glanced over his shoulder at her, a grin spreading across his face. This time, it was wider and more mischievous.

'Come on,' he said, extending his hand towards her. 'Let's go pay your brother a visit.'

47

Emilia stepped out of the dark passageway between the realms and into Eldon's Hollow. The first thing that struck her was the smell: ink, old paper, and, faintly, coffee, as though a fresh pot had just been brewed. It was a warm, nostalgic scent that reminded her of old libraries, so unlike the oppressive atmosphere of Marcel's Hollow.

Where the latter had been a surreal amalgamation of guilt and fragmented memories—dark and chaotic—Eldon's was bright, clean, and brimming with familiarity. It wasn't horrifying in the slightest. Instead, it was filled with the things he cherished most.

The space stretched endlessly, yet it was far from empty. Shelves lined the walls from floor to ceiling, crammed with books of all shapes and sizes. The spines were worn, their pages slightly yellowed with age. Disorder ruled here; newspapers lined every surface, journals were stacked haphazardly, and loose pages fluttered in the phantom breeze.

At the centre of the room stood a large, battered oak desk. Its surface was nearly buried beneath a mountain of scattered papers and open books. Pens and pencils lay strewn across it, some broken, others worn down to mere stubs. At one end of the desk, sat a vintage typewriter, its keys polished smooth from years of use.

The walls, though dominated by shelves, were peppered with clippings, sketches, and pinned photographs. Strings crisscrossed from pin to pin, forming intricate webs of connections that defied comprehension. Headlines screamed from newspaper clippings, capturing every notable moment of Eldon's investigative career. This wasn't just a workspace; it was a physical representation of his pursuit of truth.

Despite the overwhelming presence of information, the Hollow felt serene. It was a sanctuary for a restless mind, a cohesive reflection of Eldon's essence. Unlike Marcel's chaotic dreamscape, this space held clarity and purpose.

Towards the far end of the room, a smaller desk came into view. The chair behind it was turned away from her, but faint movements revealed the presence of someone seated there.

The Nameless Spirit nudged her gently, his voice hushed. 'Go. I'll wait here for you until you're ready to leave.'

His implication was clear. There was no need to rush; Eldon wasn't at risk of waking any time soon.

Emilia's heart raced as she approached the desk. The seated figure was hunched over, writing fervently. Her breath caught in her throat. He looked exactly as she remembered: his hair tousled, glasses slightly askew on his nose, and a determined furrow etched into his brow. He wore a white button-down shirt with the sleeves rolled up, and a pen was tucked behind his ear, despite the one already in his hand.

The sound of his pen scratching across the notebook filled the silence, his focus so intense that he didn't notice her. For a moment, Emilia hesitated, emotions swirling within her. Then, summoning her courage, she spoke.

'Eldon,' she said softly, her voice trembling as she stepped closer.

He froze, his pen halting mid-stroke. Slowly, he lifted his head, blinking as though rousing from deep concentration. His gaze landed on her, and his eyes widened in disbelief.

'Emilia . . .?' His voice was hoarse, filled with equal parts confusion and hope. 'Is that really you?'

Eldon's chair toppled backward as he stood too quickly. She crossed the distance between them, throwing her arms around him. His warmth was so familiar, so heartbreakingly real, that tears pricked her eyes. He hesitated, his arms hovering for a fraction of a second before wrapping around her, pulling her close. He held her tightly, as though letting go would make her disappear.

'How?' His voice cracked as he stepped back, his eyes scanning her from head to toe. 'How is this possible? You can't be real. You have to be a figment of my imagination.'

She shook her head, her lips curving into a soft smile.

'I'm real, Eldon.'

He studied her face as if trying to memorize every detail he could see.

'What are you doing here? This place . . . It doesn't make sense. I don't know where I am, but I can't seem to leave.'

Emilia's heart clenched. He didn't understand. He didn't realize he was trapped in the Hollow, caught between the Living World and the Void. He didn't know his body lay comatose, tethering his soul to this in-between space. As if sensing her hesitation, Eldon's expression shifted. His eyes grew sharper, his voice more urgent.

'But I have to get out of here. That company I was investigating—they're experimenting on people, developing some kind of neural implant. They're using them to control . . .' He trailed off, his hands gesturing wildly as he paced in front of her. His words spilled out with the same fervent intensity that had always driven him as a journalist. For a fleeting moment, she could almost believe they were back in her apartment, where he'd often ranted about his latest exposé over a late-night cup of coffee. But the truth snapped her back to the present. This wasn't their old life. She was dead, tied to the Spirit World, and he—

'Emilia?' Eldon's voice cut through her thoughts, tinged with concern. 'Are you listening to me?'

She blinked, startled out of her reverie.

'Yes. Yes, I'm listening. Sorry, I was just . . . thinking.'

She reached out, gently taking his arm and guiding him back to his fallen chair. With a quick motion, she righted it and gestured for him to sit. He followed her lead, though confusion flickered in his eyes.

'Eldon,' she began softly, lowering herself into the chair across from him. Her voice wavered as she spoke. 'There's something I need to tell you. A lot, actually.'

His gaze bore into hers, searching for answers she wasn't sure she could fully provide. She leaned forward, placing her hands over his. The gesture was meant to steady them both, though it did little to ease the tightening in her chest. Her thumbs brushed over his knuckles in a slow, rhythmic motion as she tried to gather her thoughts. How could she explain all of it? The Spirit World, the Hollow, his coma, her death? Where would she even begin?

Her mind flashed back to the Void, to the version of Eldon her subconscious had conjured to help her accept the truth of her death. It was her turn to play the part for him. She took a deep breath, steeling herself, as a bittersweet smile tugged at her lips.

'Eldon,' she began, her voice barely above a whisper. 'Do you know what happened to you? The reason you're here?'

'What do you mean? I—' he paused, struggling to find the words. His brow furrowed in confusion. Giving it some thought, he realized he hadn't truly considered it at all.

'No,' he said finally. 'No, not really. I just . . . I woke up here one day, and I've been stuck here ever since.'

Emilia tightened her grip on his hands, bracing herself for the difficult conversation ahead. She had to tell him the truth: about what had happened to him, about her death, about the Hollow.

'Emilia, what's wrong?' he asked, nervous laughter bubbling from his throat. 'Whatever it is, you can tell me.'

So she did. She told him everything. She explained what J.Tech had done, the incident that left him in a coma, and the nature of the Hollow they were currently in. Her words spilled in an unbroken stream. When she finished, silence descended between them.

Eldon stared at her, his mouth opening and closing, trying to form words but unable to. When he spoke, his voice sounded hesitant and unsure.

'I'm . . . in a coma?'

She nodded.

'And this is temporary, right?'

'Yes,' she said.

He let out a shaky breath.

'Okay, great. Good,' he said, relieved. 'So, I just wait it out. No big deal. I can do that.'

Then something shifted.

'But wait . . . if I'm in a coma and this is my Hollow, why are you here . . .?' His voice trailed off, the nervousness returning to his eyes.

'Emilia,' he said slowly, his voice tight with unease. 'What are you not telling me?'

She'd prepared herself for this moment, rehearsed it in her mind countless times, but now that it was here, the words felt impossible to say. She exhaled deeply.

'Eldon,' she said. 'The thing is . . . I'm—'

She faltered. Saying the words aloud was so much harder than she'd expected it to be.

'You're what, Emilia? What is it?'

She took another deep breath, forcing herself to meet his eyes.

'I'm dead, Eldon,' she said quietly.

For a moment, Eldon simply stared at her, the statement refusing to register. Then he shook his head, his denial immediate.

'No. No, you're not. That's . . . that's not possible.'

'Eldon—'

'No!' he snapped, standing abruptly. 'Don't say that! You're here. I can see you, I can touch you! How can you be dead if you're right here?'

'Eldon, please, just listen to me,' she said, standing with her hands raised in a calming gesture.

But he wouldn't hear it. He began pacing, his movements frantic.

'This is just some . . . some trick. It has to be. My mind is playing games with me because of the coma or—' He froze, his eyes darting back to her. 'You're lying. You have to be lying. You can't be dead.'

Her heart broke at the raw pain in his voice.

'I'm not lying,' she said gently. 'I wish I was, but it's the truth. I've been in the Spirit World for a while now. That's how I was able to come here to see you.'

He shook his head again, his hands tangling in his hair as he let out a choked laugh.

'No. No, this doesn't make sense. You're not—' he stopped, his shoulders sagging. Tears welled in his eyes as he looked at her, his voice breaking. 'Why didn't you tell me sooner?'

'I couldn't. I didn't even know I could see you until now.'

Eldon crumpled back into his chair, burying his face in his hands. Emilia knelt beside him, placing a hand on his arm.

'I'm so sorry,' she whispered.

For a long time, he didn't speak. Then, in a voice so small it was almost inaudible, he said, 'What am I going to do now?'

Emilia looked at the numbers inked onto her inner wrist.

'Eldon, there's something else you should know.'

She explained the points system—the strange, intangible currency of the Spirit World. She told him about her efforts at the Agency and the points she had accumulated.

'Why are you telling me this?' he asked.

She hesitated before answering, choosing her words carefully.

'I wanted to reincarnate at first. I thought it was unfair the way I died so suddenly, leaving you alone. I wanted to get back to you, to take care of you, like I always did. But I realized that even if I did come back, I wouldn't be me any more. I wouldn't be *Emilia*.

I'd be someone else with Emilia's memories and I . . . I don't want that. Not any more.'

Her voice softened as she continued.

'So, instead, I did everything I could to help from here. Everyone already knows the truth about J.Tech. All your research, the files, everything. They can't hurt anyone any more. It's over.'

'Why are you telling me this?' he repeated.

'Because I want you to know it's safe for you to leave the Hollow and return to your body. You don't have to be stuck here any more. Not unless you want to be.'

He stared at her.

'What about you?'

'I'm not going back, Eldon,' Emilia said softly, her smile tinged with bittersweet acceptance. 'I've come to terms with my death. I think it's time I let go of the life I had. But before I do that, I wanted to see you. To be with you, even if it's just for a little while.'

Eldon's face crumpled as the realization hit him.

'You came to say goodbye,' he said, his voice breaking.

She nodded, her expression filled with sorrow.

'Let me use my points for you,' she urged despite the ache in her heart. 'Please, Eldon. Go back. Live your life.'

He said nothing, his hands curling into tight fists, his shoulders trembling under the weight of his emotions. His gaze dropped to the floor as though searching for answers in the cracks and shadows. Finally, he let out a ragged breath, lifting his eyes to meet hers. They shimmered with unshed tears as he whispered, 'I can't . . . I can't just leave you. Not like this. Not when I just got you back.'

Emilia stepped closer, her voice a soothing balm despite the raw emotion threatening to overwhelm her.

'You're not leaving me, Eldon. I'll always be with you. But you have so much ahead of you, so many stories to write, lives to touch. Please, let me do this one last thing for you as your sister.'

The tears he had been holding back finally broke free as he pulled her into a fierce embrace, his arms wrapping around her to shield her from the inevitability of what was to come.

'I love you,' he choked out, his voice thick with emotion. 'I don't tell you that enough, but I do.'

Emilia's heart broke and healed all at once, her own tears staining her cheeks as she clung to him.

'I love you too, Eldon. Always.'

They stayed like that for what felt like an eternity, the quiet hum of the Hollow wrapping around them in a cocoon of warmth. It was as though the world itself had paused to give them this moment, this fleeting window of time to hold on to each other.

When they finally parted, Emilia smiled through her tears, her hand lingering on his cheek.

'You'll be okay,' she said. 'I know you will.'

And for the first time since her death, Emilia felt the faint stirrings of the closure she so desperately desired. She had done what she came to do. She had said goodbye. And that was enough.

48

The cemetery stretched across a gentle hillside; its serene expanse bathed in the waning light and muted hues of the evening. Shadows lengthened and deepened, cast by the golden glow of the setting sun. The air carried the mingled scents of damp earth, decaying leaves, and the faint perfume of fresh flowers left behind by visitors.

Rows of gravestones jutted from the ground like ancient teeth, their surfaces worn smooth by the passage of time. Simple slabs marked with faded names stood alongside elaborate monuments adorned with weeping angels or sculpted iron finials, each one a testament to the lives remembered there. The inscriptions on many had weathered into near illegibility, reduced to faint whispers of their former clarity.

A narrow gravel path meandered through the cemetery, crunching softly underfoot. It was bordered by patches of wild grass that grew unchecked, swaying gently in the evening breeze. Ivy climbed stubbornly up the bases of tombstones, curling like green tendrils seeking to embrace the stone. In the distance, mausoleums loomed, their iron gates rusted and moaning faintly as the wind stirred them.

The trees lining the graveyard's edge stood like sentinels, their bare branches stark against the darkening sky. As the sun slipped farther below the horizon, the trees' shadows grew bolder, creeping like fingers across the graves. The air chilled with the encroaching twilight, and the faint murmur of the wind carried the dry rustle of scattered leaves.

Above, the sky deepened into shades of purple and navy, a crescent moon rising low on the horizon. Its pale light spilled over the cemetery, casting a ghostly glow that blended with the first stars winking into existence. The lanterns mounted on posts along the pathway flickered to life, their warm, golden light pooling in small oases that contrasted sharply with the darkness.

The stillness of the cemetery was profound, broken only by the occasional hoot of an owl or the rustle of nocturnal creatures moving unseen through the underbrush. It was a quiet that felt alive, charged with an almost sacred energy, as though the dead themselves were listening.

Marcel's boots crunched against the gravel as he stepped through the gates, their sharp sound cutting through the cemetery's hush. The gates groaned faintly on their hinges before swinging shut behind him with a soft clang. He stood still, his breath visible in the cool air as he scanned the rows of gravestones that stretched out before him in uneven lines. His shoulders hunched slightly, and his steps betrayed a man who did not often tread these grounds.

He walked with a deliberate yet uncertain gait, reading the names etched into the stones. The flickering light of the lanterns caught on his face, illuminating a furrowed brow and the occasional tightening of his jaw. Now and then, he paused, squinting to decipher faded inscriptions, his frustration building with each fruitless stop. A low sigh escaped him, swallowed quickly by the vast silence surrounding him.

And then, he found it. His steps halted, his breath catching as his eyes settled on the gravestone before him.

The grave was modest but elegant, marked by a simple headstone of smooth grey granite. *Emilia Elliot* was etched deeply into its surface, the letters sharp and clean, freshly carved. Beneath it, in similar script, were the words: *Beloved sister and cherished friend. Her light remains in those she touched.*

Marcel crouched beside the grave, brushing fallen leaves off the cold stone. He placed the small arrangement of flowers he had brought with him at its base: white lilies and lavender. He didn't know what she would have liked, but the arrangement looked pretty.

A lump formed in his throat, and he swallowed hard.

'I didn't know if I should come,' he said. The stillness of the cemetery seemed to amplify his words, carrying them into the night. 'But you didn't come back after the first time, and I didn't know how else to speak to you. And, well, here I am. I don't know if this will work either, but I hope you can hear me.'

His words lingered in the air as he fell silent again. Above him, the distant shimmer of stars and the crescent moon cast a pale glow over the rows of headstones.

'All that stuff with J.Tech . . .' he started again, softer now. 'I found the evidence where you said it would be, and it held up well in court. The trial was taxing, but things went well.'

'I don't know what I'm doing here. I just . . . I felt like I needed to tell you that. To let you know that your efforts paid off.'

He sat there in the quiet for a little while longer, his gaze fixed on the headstone. The air around him grew cooler as the night deepened. He didn't speak again, but his hand lingered on the gravestone. Finally, he stood, brushing off the back of his pants, and gave the gravestone a gentle pat, as if to say goodbye.

Before he turned to leave, his gaze shifted to the grave beside hers, its headstone of darker, rougher granite, less adorned. Marcel studied it for a moment, his expression unreadable, before he reached into his coat and pulled out a small, dark bottle. He crouched down and placed it at the base of the grave. A bottle of Jack Daniel's whiskey. The amber liquid inside gleamed faintly under the moonlight as it settled into place.

'I know you don't approve of drinking, but,' he said, exhaling with a small smile, 'Humour me, all right? For old times' sake.'

He rested his hand on the gravestone. His head bowed slightly, though he said nothing this time. When he straightened and turned to walk away, his steps were measured, his shoulders relaxed. The silence of the cemetery smothered the sound of his footsteps as he disappeared through the gates.

The moonlight shifted just enough to illuminate the grave next to Emilia's: *Eldon Elliot. A seeker of truth, taken before his time. May he rest in peace.*

49

The persistent knocking had been going on for some time before Emilia finally noticed it. When it grew sharper and more insistent, she rushed to the door, pulling it open to reveal a young man who looked thoroughly dishevelled. His untucked shirt was wrinkled, his tie hung loosely around his neck, and his hair stuck up in all directions. Dark circles shadowed his eyes, giving him the haunted look of someone who had endured too many sleepless nights fuelled by coffee and stress. Except, of course, he was a spirit like her, and had no need for such earthly crutches. Exhaustion alone seemed to account for his appearance. A battered satchel hung over one shoulder, and in his hand, he carried a small bouquet of white lilies and lavender.

'Are you Emilia?' he asked. 'Emilia Elliot?'

'That's me,' she replied.

The man, whom she guessed was part of the Postal Service judging by the embroidered logo on his shirt, pulled an envelope from his satchel and handed it to her along with the bouquet. His movements had the mechanical efficiency of someone who had performed this task countless times before.

'Delivery for you,' he said flatly. His pale hands trembled slightly as he pressed the letter into hers, the faint shimmer of his energy flickering at the edges of his fingers.

'Are you all right?' Emilia asked, her brow creasing with concern.

He gave a tired shrug, his lips twitching in an attempt at a smile.

'You were kind of hard to track down,' he said. 'You weren't at your apartment, and you weren't at the Agency. It threw my whole route off. Had to run around looking for you.'

Emilia winced.

'Sorry about that,' she mumbled, her tone sheepish.

'I wasn't complaining,' he replied, exhaustion heavy in his gaze as it lingered on her in quiet assessment. Then he added, 'You don't get letters often.'

'No, I don't,' she admitted, her eyes drifted between the envelope and the bouquet with curiosity and suspicion. She wondered who had sent them.

'Enjoy your delivery.'

'Thank you,' Emilia said. He nodded before turning away, his haggard face impassive as he walked off.

Emilia watched him disappear into the distance. Then, curiosity got the better of her. She closed the door and set the flowers down on the nearest surface. Carefully, she unfolded the letter.

To her surprise, it was from Marcel. She smiled as she read his words. She hadn't visited him in his Hollow since their first meeting, assuming there was no real need to. But it was comforting to know that she still crossed his mind. The bouquet and letter felt like a gentle, unexpected connection in a world so often marked by its silence.

Placing the card aside, Emilia began searching for a spot to arrange the flowers when a sharp knock echoed through the room. Startled, she rose and opened the door to find the same haggard young man from the Postal Service standing there. His satchel hung low over his shoulder, and his exhausted expression remained unchanged.

'You're back,' she said, surprise evident in her voice.

This time, he handed her a bottle of whiskey and another sealed envelope.

'Delivery for Eldon Elliot,' he said in that same flat, monotonous tone. His eyes moved to the sign by the door, as if double-checking the address. 'Is he here?'

'He is,' she replied.

The young man nodded, a trace of relief smoothing his expression.

'I missed it the first time I came to give you your letter,' he explained. 'But please make sure he gets this.'

As if on cue, Eldon appeared behind her just as she was closing the door. His presence, still new in the Spirit World, brought an unexpectedly familiar comfort to her.

'Who is it? A client?' he asked.

'No,' she said, handing him the whiskey and the letter. 'For you, apparently. I didn't know you drank.'

'I don't,' Eldon said, tucking the bottle under his arm. With a curious glance at the envelope, he ripped it open and a small slip of paper fluttered to the floor. He caught it quickly, grinning as he read the two short lines scrawled there.

'Marcel?' Emilia asked.

'You too?'

She gestured towards the flowers on the table.

'He got me flowers.'

Eldon chuckled, shaking his head at his friend's antics. He set the bottle down and slid the note into his pocket, though not before reading it once more. Emilia watched him, registering the ease in his demeanour now compared to the first time she'd visited him in his Hollow.

She'd insisted he use her points to return to the Living World. Though he initially seemed agreeable, he soon grew adamant, refusing the idea, saying he needed time to consider. When Emilia came back some days later, Eldon had made his decision. He wanted to leave the Hollow and join her in the Spirit World rather than return to his life among the Living. His argument was simple: he refused to wake to a life without her. And now that the issue with J.Tech had concluded, he felt he had nothing to go back to.

'I'd rather be with you here,' he'd told her. 'The Living World isn't home without you in it. You've always been the best part of my life. The best sister anyone could've asked for.'

Although Emilia had been doubtful of Eldon's decision at first, watching him settle so easily into his new existence brought her a sense of reassurance. She knew he had made the choice that was best for him.

Thomas emerged from the backroom just then, his sleeves rolled up and a smudge of ink on his cheek. He looked at them expectantly and said, 'I heard a knock on the door. Was that a client?'

Emilia and Eldon looked at each other and broke into laughter. It was almost comical how Eldon had asked the same question just moments before. Thomas tilted his head in confusion.

'No,' Emilia finally managed to say. She gestured towards the flowers and the bottle of whiskey. 'It was the Postal Service. Marcel visited our graves and left us something.'

Thomas' expression shifted subtly, disappointment flashing across his face before he masked it with a shrug.

'Ah,' he said, tugging at the cuff of his sleeve. 'Maybe next time.'

Before they could dwell on it, another knock came at the door.

'That has to be a client!' Thomas said, perking up immediately as he rushed to open the door with enthusiasm.

But the sight that greeted him wasn't what he had expected. Standing in the doorway was Arthur, his coat draped over his arm, his expression betraying a hint of surprise at how quickly the door had swung open.

Thomas took him in, the fleeting lift of excitement giving way to reserve as he regarded Arthur's simultaneously familiar and distant presence. It had been a long time since any of them had seen him. After interfering in the affairs of the Living World, Arthur had gone away, and no one had heard from him for what felt like ages. His sudden reappearance was unexpected.

'You're back,' Thomas said plainly.

Arthur nodded.

'I am.'

Thomas studied him a moment longer before sighing and stepping aside. He was secretly glad to see him again, though he wouldn't admit it; at the same time, he couldn't deny the sting of dashed expectations.

'You're not a client, that's for sure,' he muttered half-jokingly before raising his voice, 'Emilia, someone's here to see you.'

'Who is it?' she asked.

She reached the doorway and stopped short. Arthur stood there, looking much the same as he always did. The moment he saw her, the tension in his posture eased as if some unspoken burden had finally been lifted.

'*Emilia*,' he said. 'I'm back.'

50

Emilia and Arthur were alone in the sitting room, the faint murmur of voices from beyond the backroom door only made the silence between them all the more pronounced. Seeing him again after all these years felt surreal. The initial shock of his return had overwhelmed her, but as the moments stretched on, awkwardness settled in. She didn't know where to begin, and from the way Arthur kept avoiding her gaze, neither did he.

Finally, Emilia said, 'Why didn't you say anything before you left?'

Her tone was calm, but there was an edge to her words that couldn't be ignored. Arthur looked at her then, his composure faltering for the briefest moment.

'I didn't think it was necessary,' he said. 'We'd already spoken in my office, and you seemed upset.'

Her jaw tightened at the memory. Years ago, after their heated confrontation in his office, Arthur had disappeared without a word. At the time, she'd told herself it didn't matter, that his absence didn't affect her. But the truth was, his silent departure had stung more than she cared to admit. She had expected at least a goodbye, but instead, he had left before anyone had even realized he was gone.

'Upset?' she repeated. 'Of course I was upset! But that doesn't mean you shouldn't have said something. You left without a word. Not to me, not to anyone.'

Arthur's gaze dropped to the floor again.

'I thought it would be easier that way. For everyone.'

'For you, you mean,' she shot back, her frustration spilling over. 'Because you didn't want to deal with it. Because it was inconvenient.'

His eyes met hers, and for a moment, it looked as though he wanted to argue. But instead, he said quietly, 'I didn't know what else to say to you. Not after the way we left things.'

'Do you have any idea how it felt, wondering if you were ever coming back?'

Arthur opened his mouth to respond, then closed it again. After a long pause, he admitted, 'You're right. I handled it poorly. I thought I was doing what was best, but . . . I should have said something.'

He shifted uncomfortably in the silence that followed, and Emilia's attention wandered to the flowers on the table.

'I'm sorry,' he said at last. 'For leaving like that. And for making you feel like you didn't matter enough to deserve a proper goodbye.'

'I just . . . I thought I meant *something* to you. Enough that you'd want to see me before you left. I didn't expect you to just disappear,' she said.

'I know. And I'm sorry.'

They sat with that for a moment, the tension between them easing slightly. Emilia couldn't fully understand the anger that burned inside her. It wasn't just that Arthur had left without saying a word. It was something deeper, an emotion she couldn't quite unravel.

Arthur could feel her anger pressing down on him. He had always prided himself on maintaining his composure, on keeping emotions from clouding his purpose. But now, sitting across from her, he felt as though he were standing on unsteady ground.

'I didn't mean to hurt you,' he said. 'I thought leaving the way I did was simpler. Cleaner.'

'Simpler for you, maybe,' she retorted, her tone sharp.

His hands were clasped tightly, knuckles white, as if restraining their urge to fidget.

'I didn't know how to face you. I didn't understand why it felt so difficult, why it felt so . . .' He trailed off, struggling to find the right words.

'So what?' she snapped, her irritation sharpening with each syllable.

Arthur's features tensed with conflict, a shadow of his inner struggle passing over his face before he softly said, 'So personal.'

He took a deep breath. 'I've spent so much time convincing myself that you were just a friend. Someone I could trust, yes, but nothing more than that. Grim Reapers aren't supposed to dwell on things like emotions, and I thought I was above all of that.

But somewhere along the line, that changed. I've never been good at understanding emotions, but I've come to realize that what I feel for you . . .' He paused. 'It's more than fondness. More than friendship.'

Emilia hadn't expected this. She had known he cared about her, but always as a friend. Never like this.

'I didn't recognize it for what it was until I left. And then, all I could think about was you. You were the first person I wanted to see when I came back. I don't know how else to explain it, Emilia, but I'm certain this feeling is real. It's . . . affection. For you.'

Neither of them spoke after that. Emilia's emotions churned, a tangle of disbelief, confusion, and something else she wasn't ready to name. She could see how hard it had been for him to say those words, how unfamiliar he was with the terrain of his own feelings.

'I . . .' she began, but faltered. 'I don't know what to say.'

A faint, self-deprecating smile ghosted across Arthur's lips.

'You don't have to say anything. I just thought it was something you should know.'

Part of her wanted to cling to her anger, to hold on to the hurt he had caused by leaving as suddenly as he did. But another part, the part that had missed him terribly, couldn't help but soften at his confession.

'I'm still mad at you,' she said finally, though her tone lacked the sharpness it had carried earlier.

Arthur's smile widened ever so slightly.

'That's fair.'

'But . . . thank you. For telling me,' she said. After a beat, she asked, 'You came here as soon as they let you go?'

'I went to the Agency first, but they told me you quit,' Arthur said, a note of anxiety in his voice. 'I was terrified. I thought you'd used your points to move on, and I'd missed the chance to see you one last time.'

'How did you find me, then?'

'I asked around. Some of the agents mentioned this place, so I came here right away.'

He gestured towards her wrist, where her points had dwindled to zero. The sight of it seemed to stir questions he had been holding back.

'Your points . . . You used them to bring Eldon here? I saw him when I entered earlier.'

'He decided not to return to the Living World,' Emilia explained. 'He didn't want to be there without me. So, I used my points to help him leave his Hollow and come here instead. He's much happier now, and that's all that matters.'

'And this place?' he asked, surveying the room for the first time. 'What exactly is this office of yours?'

A small grin tugged at her lips.

'You saw the sign outside when you came in.'

'Beyond Investigations?' he echoed, raising an eyebrow, clearly impressed.

'Eldon, Thomas, and I set this up. It was mostly Thomas' idea, but we jumped on it pretty quickly,' she said. 'We help spirits like us, those who can't move on because of unfinished business in the Living World.'

'So . . .' Arthur said. 'You're running your own Agency?'

'Not quite,' she replied with a small laugh. 'But something like that. And before you ask, we ran it by Sadie first. She drafted the guidelines we're meant to follow, so we're not doing anything we're not supposed to.'

Arthur visibly relaxed at her reassurance. He did not want a similar spectacle happening again. His gaze fell to the bracelet on her wrist, the one he had given her so long ago. The gem in the centre, once vibrant and swirling with his energy, was now dull and lifeless, its power drained since his departure.

'You still have it?' he asked in disbelief. 'It doesn't serve a purpose any more. Without my energy, it's just a piece of jewellery. You could have taken it off.'

Emilia's fingers grazed the cool metal as she glanced at the bracelet. Her thumb ran over its surface with a tenderness that made her hesitate before replying.

'Maybe it doesn't serve a practical purpose,' she admitted. 'But . . . it reminds me of you. It's like having a part of you with me. And since you've been gone, it's been a source of comfort to me.'

Arthur's mind blanked for a moment. His lips parted as if to speak, but no words came out. The stunned expression on his face was so uncharacteristic that she couldn't help but laugh.

'What's with the look?' she teased, a grin spreading across her face as the tension eased.

'I just . . .' he paused, shaking his head. 'I wasn't expecting that.'

Still smiling, he reached out and gently placed his hand over the bracelet. His touch was warm against her skin. Moments later, the gem in the centre of the bracelet shimmered to life, pulsing softly with a familiar thrumming of energy.

'There,' he said, his tone lighter than before. 'Now it's not useless any more.'

She raised an eyebrow.

'Did you just recharge it so I wouldn't take it off now that you're back?' she asked. 'You're ridiculous.'

'Maybe,' he admitted, his smile softening as he lowered his hand. 'But I missed you, and I'd really rather you didn't toss the bracelet aside. It's serving a practical purpose now.'

Her laughter faded, replaced by a warmth in her chest she hadn't quite expected.

'I missed you too,' she said quietly, her fingers brushing over the glowing gem, and she realized she truly meant it. A sudden thought struck her, and she tilted her head. 'But I thought you weren't allowed to share your energy with others. Didn't that get you in trouble the first time?'

He waved off her concerns.

'It's fine as long as you don't use it in the Living World. Sharing my energy wasn't the issue—it was someone else using it to mask their trace that caused problems.'

Whatever the specifics, she was glad to have his energy close to her again. The steady thrumming of the bracelet gave her a sense of comfort she hadn't realized she missed until this very moment.

They were interrupted just then by the creak of the office door opening. They turned in unison, just in time to see a nervous-looking woman stick her head cautiously into the room.

'Um, excuse me,' she said hesitantly, her eyes darting between the two of them. 'Is this . . . Beyond Investigations? I think I have the right place.'

Before Emilia could respond, a loud shout erupted from the backroom.

'*Finally*!' Thomas burst through the door, nearly tripping over himself in his excitement. 'A client! An *actual* client! My *first* client! I think I'm going to cry.'

Eldon followed at a slower pace, his expression betraying his barely concealed amusement.

'Don't scare her off,' he said.

Thomas ignored the comment, striding over to the woman with a wide, slightly overzealous grin.

'Welcome to Beyond Investigations!' he declared, throwing his arms out theatrically. 'You've come to the right place. We're here to solve all your supernatural problems, and we're the best in both worlds—living and dead!'

The woman blinked, startled but not entirely deterred. She took a hesitant step inside, clutching her purse tightly.

'I . . . um . . . need help,' she said.

Emilia rose from her seat, smiling reassuringly as she motioned for the woman to come further inside.

'You're in good hands,' she said.

Arthur stood as well, brushing off his coat as he moved aside. He glanced at Emilia, a small, fond smile softening his features.

'I guess business is officially open,' he said.

'It seems so,' she replied.

'I should let you get to it. You've got work to do.'

She turned to him sharply, panic rising in her chest.

'You're not going anywhere, are you?' she blurted.

He paused mid-step.

'Not if you need me here for some reason,' he said carefully.

'I need you,' she said, the words rushing out before she could stop them. Her chest felt lighter for having said it. 'I just got you back. You can't leave. I need you. Here. With me.'

Arthur stared at her. He nodded.

'I shall not leave then,' he said. 'I'll stay for as long as you need me.'

She exhaled, her shoulders sagging as her crippling anxiety drained away. Turning back to the others, she saw Thomas already guiding the woman to a chair, his enthusiasm practically radiating off him. Eldon leaned casually in the doorway, shaking his head but smiling nonetheless. He, too, seemed pleased to greet their first client.

Emilia lingered for a moment, taking it all in: the chatter, the movement, the strange, imperfect rhythm of this little group. Somehow, in the chaos and quiet alike, they had built something that mattered—

something that gave their afterlives purpose. It was messy, unconventional, yet perfect in its own way.

'Looks like you're going to be busy,' Arthur said.

'For a while, perhaps. But isn't that the point?'

As the client began explaining her case, Emilia's gaze drifted around the room once more. This office, this unusual collection of spirits—some dead, some not quite—gave her a gentle sense that, at last, everything was as it should be. A rare, steady calm settled in her chest, a feeling she hadn't known in years. The faint glow of the bracelet on her wrist caught her eye, and she couldn't help but smile.

It had been a long time ago now, but she remembered staring up at the sky as her life slipped away, wondering what awaited her beyond. She hadn't been ready then, clinging to life with a stubbornness born of fear. But now, everything felt different.

This was the start of a new chapter. Not just for her, but for all of them.

And this time, she was ready to face whatever lay ahead.

Acknowledgements

My heartfelt thanks to the wonderful team at Penguin SEA for believing in my writing and bringing this story to life with such care and thoughtfulness. Thank you for your patience, insight, and encouragement throughout this process, and for taking a chance on my work. Your trust in this story, and in me, has meant more than I can adequately express.

To my mother, Narinas, for her unwavering support and constant faith in me. Thank you for believing in this dream long before it felt tangible, for supporting a path you didn't always understand simply because it mattered to me, and for always being proud of me. You gave me the freedom to keep writing, and it's the reason I never stopped trying. This achievement is every bit yours, as it is mine.

To my cat, Yoda, who I still think of fondly, and whose presence remains part of this journey; and to my brother, Rayyan, who bought me a laptop and let me use his Microsoft account—this story exists in part because of your practical generosity.

To my best friends, Shannon and Nadiah, who have been with me every step of the way. You have known my love for writing from the very beginning and never once treated it as a passing phase or an impossible dream. Thank you for celebrating my every milestone, no matter how small, for your enthusiasm despite our busy lives, and for your genuine excitement even when the process was slow. Your belief and constancy mean a lot to me.

And thank you all for reading this story and allowing it to live beyond me. Once it left my hands, it became yours, and letting it go into the world has been both frightening and deeply meaningful.